FRIGATE

A Cold War Naval Thriller

John Wingate

FRIGATE

Published by Sapere Books.

20 Windermere Drive, Leeds, England, LS17 7UZ,
United Kingdom

saperebooks.com

ISBN: 978-1-80055-423-8

This book is dedicated to the biggest single factor in war: the man.

The Spirit of the Navy is too old, too varied and too subtle to be adequately interpreted by any outsider, no matter how keen his interest, how deep his affection...

Isn't it possible that the very thoroughness with which the Navy has protected the nation in the past may constitute a source of weakness both for the Navy and the nation? We have been safe for so long and during all these generations have been free to follow our own devices, that we tax-payers as a body today are utterly ignorant of the facts and the forces on which England depends for her existence... Some of us think that the Navy does not much matter one way or the other; some honestly regard it as a brutish and bloodthirsty anachronism which if it can't be openly abolished, ought to be secretly crippled as soon as possible. Such views are not shocking or surprising. After four generations of peace and party politics they are inevitable...

In peace the Navy exists under conditions which it takes years of training to understand; in war it will be subjected to mental and physical strain three days of which would make the mere sea-fight of Trafalgar a pleasant change. We have no data to guide us for the future, but in judging by our thousand-year-old past, we can believe and thank God for it, that whatever man may do, or neglect to do, the spirit of the Navy, which is manmade, but which no body of men can kill, will rise to meet and overcome every burden and every disability that may be imposed upon it — from without or within.

From *A Book of Words* by Rudyard Kipling (written six years before the outbreak of World War I).

ACKNOWLEDGEMENTS

My debt to the naval staff in the Ministry of Defence and to the officers and men of the Royal Navy and the Royal Marines is immense. Wherever I have travelled during my research, ashore and at sea, I have encountered nothing but forbearance, co-operation and kindness. I wish to thank everyone I met who unstintingly gave me their time, help and friendship.

My sincere gratitude is also due to those who gave much of their time and good advice in checking the manuscript. I should like to emphasise that if there remain errors of fact, judgement or opinion, they are entirely of my own making.

To Captain Godfrey French, CBE, Royal Navy, counsellor and friend, my thanks are due for his wisdom, guidance and enthusiasm.

Finally, this work could never have been undertaken without the support, encouragement and advice of Admiral of the Fleet, Sir Edward Ashmore, GCB, DSC. For his contribution in creating the superb ships of our modern Fleet, the nation and the Royal Navy owe much.

CHAPTER 1

The final ship to be berthed on that morning tide was *Arcturus Star*. Although the Soviet Union had joined the roll-on/roll-off league late in the day, they had more than a foothold on the European car market — and Rotterdam was now handling the majority of the Soviet's car exports into Europe.

Arcturus Star was the latest of Russia's 'ro-ro' ships and this was her fifth delivery to Rotterdam. Her master knew the ropes and was becoming known to the authorities — a difficult man who, until the last trip, had allowed his crew no shore leave. But now his crew were given leave until 2230, a privilege which amused the Rotterdam Docks and Customs Police.

Less than a month previously, the Dutch authorities had launched a new onslaught against the drug rings. In the van of the attack were the Rotterdam Docks and Customs Police, an efficient force, but confronted by a formidable challenge: Rotterdam was Europe's busiest port, handling ships from the remotest corners of the globe. On arrival at the port's outer limit, each ship was boarded and her master informed of the penalties he and his ship risked if drugs were found on board — and he was also informed that the police were empowered to conduct spot checks on any ship within port limits. This vigorous policy was taking effect: there was evidence that the international heroin operators were seeking other European ports for their trade.

That Saturday night, the Duty Senior Police Officer was Inspector Johann Hendriks. His radio had been busy but there was nothing unusual in the routine: his patrols were picking up returning drunks, more to protect the seamen from themselves than for any other reason. He lifted the telephone that was shrilling on his desk.

'Number Seven Gate, Sergeant Ramussen here, sir: I've got a tricky one for you — a Russian.'

'Political asylum?'

'Mixed up with dope, sir. Being a Russki, I thought you'd like to know.'

'Right, Sergeant. I'll come down.'

'Better hurry, sir.'

'What's the rush?'

'There's a mob of his shipmates outside. They're insisting on taking him back to his ship, *Arcturus Star*. She berthed this morning.'

'Hold him, Sergeant. I'm on my way.'

By the time Inspector Hendriks had reached Number Seven Gate, the bus-load of police reinforcements had arrived. Sergeant Ramussen saluted.

'*Arcturus Star*'s commissar saw we meant business, sir. He's taken his mob back to their ship.'

'Did they threaten violence?'

'Not to us. But I wouldn't bet much on their shipmate's chances.' He jerked his head towards the rear of the police gate. 'For his own safety, I've slapped him in cells. He speaks English, sir.'

'What's his game?'

'Drug rackets in the ship — says he's been threatened. They were chasing him down 38 Wharf. They'd almost got him when our duty car snatched him up. The patrolman locked the car doors on him when their commissar tried to bluster our lads into handing back the deserter.'

'Wheel the Russian in, Sergeant. I'll do the talking.'

The man who cautiously emerged from the cell seemed innocuous enough, but a fire flickered in his grey eyes — whether it was born of desperation or of fanaticism, Hendriks could not decide.

'Name?'

'Dmitri Vasilievich Sysoyov.'

'Who are you?'

'Lieutenant in the Soviet Merchant Marine.'

'Why were you running from your shipmates?'

Hendriks watched the young pallid-faced man, whose frightened eyes emphasised his sincerity as the words tumbled from his lips. He affirmed again and again his pacific ideals while he denounced Soviet militarism. He would take his own life, rather than return to the Soviet Union.

'So they're running drug rackets in your ship?' Hendriks prompted impatiently. 'But can you prove it?'

'If you search the ship…'

'One of the most difficult jobs there is, especially if the crew is alerted.'

'Sir, you *must* search the ship, even if you find nothing on the crew.' The man was pleading, gesticulating wildly with his arms.

'Where do I look?'

'Start on the fo'c'sle head.'

'Anything there?'

'No.'

'Why, then?'

'To remove suspicion; to make your search realistic.'

Hendriks nodded. 'Can't you be more specific, Sysoyov? We're short-handed — how do I know your story isn't a hoax?'

'Would I have risked my life if I wasn't genuine?'

'This seems very dramatic.'

'It is. Do as I ask, for God's sake. I know what I'm doing, sir…'

'Okay. I'll start for'd, but where do I concentrate?'

'In the safety lockers, right aft, by the car ramps. Search there…'

Hendriks remained silent, impressed by the man's intensity. Beads of sweat speckled Dmitri Sysoyov's forehead and his fingers clenched spasmodically.

'Take me seriously, sir,' Sysoyov whispered. 'Give me protection. They're waiting to kill me.'

Watching the master of *Arcturus Star,* Hendriks felt relieved. He had taken the precaution of contacting his chief before tackling the Russian; he had also doubled up his squad for the search and was covering the wharf with the remainder of his dutymen. Now that the new regulations were in force, he was fully equipped and armed with a search warrant.

'Thank you, Captain. I'll start forward. As this is a full search, I need someone with the ship's keys. I shall search each compartment.'

The Russian master had at last given up, though he had tried every trick in the book, even threatening to put to sea forthwith — but Hendriks had thrown the port regulations at him.

'Okay, Bruno,' he said, nodding at his deputy. 'Start in the forepeak. I'll stay on the gangway. Ring me there if you need me.'

Bruno met Hendriks's glance: they had been through this so often before and had learnt from their mistakes.

'I'm sorry, Captain,' Hendriks said, 'but this is my duty.'

'So Lieutenant Sysoyov's been talking?' The master flicked cigarette ash from the flap of his reefer jacket. 'An unreliable officer, Sysoyov.'

'Perhaps, Captain,' Hendriks said quietly. 'But we're trying to stamp out the drug rackets here.'

'You're wasting your time in my ship, Inspector. My crew can never get hold of the stuff.'

'I'm sure you're right, Captain. I'll let you know when we're finished.'

The master remained seated, smirking, as Hendriks let himself out. Bruno was an efficient Customs officer; the police sentries were unobtrusively placed at all the key points. Hendriks did not relish a lengthy wait in this cold, but the head of the gangway was the right place for him, despite the Russian officer and the two seamen sullenly manning it. Hendriks's burly sergeant of the patrol, steady and experienced at this game, was a reassurance at two o'clock on this morning, with his three constables strolling stolidly along the deck.

At 0218, earlier than Hendriks expected, Bruno appeared through the screen door, his search party close behind him. He spoke in Dutch.

'They're a cagey lot, sir. I've found nothing.'

'Have you searched right aft yet?'

'Up to the stern door, sir. Nothing there: the car deck is crammed with Ladas waiting to trundle down the ramp.'

Bruno stifled a yawn, his breath steaming beneath the deckhead lighting, a wisp of vapour in the freezing night. Could Sysoyov have hoaxed them?

'I'll take the sergeant and three men. I want another look at the unloading deck.' He caught the glance that flickered between Bruno and the sergeant. 'Wait here,' Hendriks ordered.

The Russian deck officer, and his bloodhound seaman with the keys, followed Hendriks down the three deck levels. The Dutchman, flanked by the sergeant and his three weary policemen, finally emerged through the car deck door. Vehicles, bumper to bumper, jammed the car deck from one side of the ship to the other. Hendriks stood there, daunted by the task facing him: heroin could be concealed in any of these hundreds of vehicles. But Sysoyov had said 'right aft'. The Russians knew that the cars could never be searched efficiently ...

Hendriks unconcernedly peered into a score of Ladas, then strolled aft until he was standing beneath the huge stern doors. The operating controls were sited in a cabinet perched on the port side, close to the unloading ramps.

'Hydraulic?' he asked, nodding towards the controls.

The Russian officer said nothing. He glanced impatiently towards the exit doors along the ship's side. 'I was on watch last night,' he said sullenly in passable, Americanised English. 'We had much bad weather. Hurry, please.'

Hendriks halted opposite a heavily constructed locker, the replica of another on the starboard side. Large red Russian lettering and the number 137 were stencilled on the door. The locker was built into the deck and a power hoist was sited alongside, plumbed above the hinged lid.

'What are these?' Hendriks asked. 'Life-saving equipment?' He noted the surprise in the Russian's eyes, sensing a cover-up as the officer replied too casually.

'Safety gear,' he said loudly. 'Usual stuff.' He began edging away, towards the exit doors.

'Open up, please,' Hendriks ordered.

The Russian and his bloodhound continued to walk away.

'Open these lockers, please,' Hendriks repeated, an edge to his voice. 'I wish to look inside.' He nodded to two of his men, who placed themselves between the exit doors and the Russians.

'I wish to speak to my captain.' The young Russian was getting flustered.

'Grab the keys, Sergeant,' Hendriks snapped in guttural Dutch.

The Russians were shocked at the speed and decisiveness. The sergeant, with the circlet of keys in his hand, firmly shoved the seaman towards the locker, while the other two held the officer.

'137, Sergeant,' Hendriks said. 'Open it, please,' he repeated, continuing to stare impersonally at the Soviet officer.

'It is forbidden!' the young man shouted. 'You have no right. You must allow me to telephone the captain.'

'Open the lockers,' Hendriks ordered in Dutch, glancing at his sergeant. 'Hold our friends by the door while I search.'

The sergeant extricated the correct key and inserted it in the lock. He prised open the heavy door, hooking the lid against the bulkhead beneath the control panel.

'Abandon ship gear, sir,' the sergeant said. 'Same type as ours, by the look of it.'

Hendriks peered perfunctorily inside. He was surprised to see that the locker floor was part of the ship's structure and went deep into the bilges.

'This inflatable equipment is almost international kit now, Sergeant. Lend me your torch.' Hendriks sensed his sergeant's impatience. 'Tell your men to escort the Russians up top,' he said. 'Give me the keys. I'll lock up.'

Hendriks waited until the exit doors had sprung shut. Alone on the echoing car deck, he took off his jacket. He leant into the locker, grasped the first life raft and yanked the circular container from the compartment. He cleared away a coil of rope. Beneath it, he was surprised to see a deep well where something glinted from the deck-head lighting.

He pushed clear another raft-container, propping it into his right arm. Using his left hand he shone his torch into the hollow void beneath. He whistled softly, slipping out his miniature camera. Seconds later, the flash blinded him.

Hendriks replaced the gear, then lowered and snapped shut the lock on Number 137. Threading his way swiftly through the cars he was back at the gangway in less than two minutes. He spoke in English.

'That's all, Sergeant: the search is finished.' He handed the keys to the Russian officer. 'Please thank your captain for his co-operation.' Hendriks returned the man's salute and walked briskly down the gangway to the quayside below.

Three days after this incident, *Arcturus Star* moved to the 'ro-ro' terminal for discharge. In spite of intense pressure from the Soviet Consul, Holland's Foreign Minister accorded political asylum to Lieutenant Sysoyov, the deserter from the Russian ship.

Sysoyov was escorted from the docks area and handed over to the immigration department.

Eight days later, a weekend fisherman was securing his launch when he found the bloated corpse of a man wedged between the fenders of the two inboard boats. Despite decomposition and the ravages of fish, Police Inspector Johann Hendriks found no difficulty in identification.

CHAPTER 2

Whitehall, 30 November.

The Second Sea Lord, Vice-Admiral Peter Hawke, was thankful to reach the warmth of his office; he was finding it difficult to feel cheerful on this dreary afternoon. After the clinical efficiency of Northwood, it was pleasant to return to the familiar friendliness of this ageing building. This backwater was the brain cell of the services, and he — like most senior officers — had long ago learnt its mysteries, become accustomed to its musty corridors with their fading aura of the pre-war days.

His PA Wren officer rose from her desk, as he peeled off his greatcoat. 'Captain Trevellion is due here at four o'clock, sir.'

Hawke strode into his office. Spacious and decorated traditionally, with sombre dignity, mahogany furniture and dark blue leather chairs, it was a room he appreciated when he needed serenity. He slumped into his chair and stretched his legs before him, exhausted by the abortive Northwood meeting.

The First Sea Lord himself, in the presence of the NATO 'top brass', had stressed the importance of the report which the Director General of Intelligence had presented so succinctly. The Soviet merchant vessel, *Arcturus Star,* had been detected carrying the most modern of mines; she could have laid them when and where she wanted in Rotterdam's approaches, and thereby have closed Europe's northern port. *Arcturus Star* need not be the sole Russian ship to be so equipped ... but the weight of the top military men could not budge Europe's politicians. The Staff's demand to search any Soviet ships using NATO ports was peremptorily refused — on no account must the Russians be irritated from *detente*. In Hawke's opinion, this policy of appeasement was a fundamental error when dealing with the Soviets. If he had his way he would annoy them to the utmost, on every possible occasion, to display to the world and to their own people the falsity and hypocrisy of their system. He would bung agents into Russia from every conceivable quarter, to stir up the malcontents in their own disintegrating empire. The USSR was no Union, nor had ever been; it was certainly not socialist, and to call itself a republic was an insult to that honourable system.

The Second Sea Lord sighed, rising slowly from his chair to stand, hands behind his back; the question of leadership was another problem which was exercising many minds at this moment. And because Vice-Admiral Peter Hawke was also Chief of Naval Personnel, his main responsibility concerned the selection, training and appointment of officers — not an easy job in these tempestuous days of social change. The eighties were very different from the thirties and forties, when Hawke's generation had been trained; moulded in naval tradition and forged in the crucible of war, they had learnt the real meaning of service under the leadership of men whose quality was almost tangible. Nowadays it had become fashionable to talk of 'management', but too often the jargon was a soft option to pander to the anti-elitism brigade, both in industry and in the services. It was not surprising that some of today's young officers did not know where they were going, confused by both the insidious influence of a welfare state and disillusioned by insufficient firm guidance from their own senior officers — senior officers who were also influenced by the pressures of contemporary opinion. After these disquieting reports from his personnel team, Hawke had decided to send for Pascoe Trevellion, an impressive member of that committee.

His PA was tapping softly on the door. 'Captain Trevellion is here, sir.'

Hawke was not going to rush this meeting. He encouraged Trevellion to relax in the armchair in front of his desk.

'Well, Trevellion, what d'you make of your new appointment? *Icarus* will be a challenge after two years sitting on your backside at MoD.'

'Your Personnel Liaison Team prevented much harm to that part of my anatomy, sir.'

'It's a long time since you were my commander.'

'Seven years, sir. I'm looking forward to a small ship.'

'Tell me,' — and Hawke pressed together the tips of his outspread fingers — 'how are you going to run your frigate? I've read your recent report, but I'd be interested in hearing your personal views on today's discipline.'

Peter Hawke settled himself back in his armchair as Trevellion spoke, the better to assess this unusual officer. Since those early days during his first carrier command he had watched Pascoe Trevellion; later, with the Personnel Liaison Team, the man had been deceptively quiet and self-contained, needing to project no image — perhaps it was the tragedy of his private life which gave him inner strength. He had talked unfashionable common sense on the subject of discipline; although often in the minority, he never balked at risking offence to his seniors if he was convinced that he was right.

'Did you know your predecessor, Roger Nicolson?' he asked, breaking into Trevellion's views on discipline.

'He was a year senior, sir — I never really knew him.'

'He's been overworking, so I've had to listen to the doctors. You're in luck to be taking over from him — right place, right time.'

'Glad to be getting to sea again, sir.'

The Second Sea Lord prided himself on his ability to judge character: he was pretty certain he had selected the right man here, and could confidently commend him to the First Sea Lord. He met Trevellion's gaze, liking what he saw in those steady grey eyes sunk deep in their sockets. His large nose was hooked and his face was lean and gaunt. His ears stuck out from the great head, the brown hair of which was beginning to thin across the top.

Pascoe Trevellion was a man you could trust, thought Hawke — as straight a chap as he had ever met. Perhaps it was his strict self-discipline that made him the man he was? He neither smoked nor drank, which made him different to the others. He had been an outstanding athlete, playing for the Navy in most games.

Trevellion was a big man in both senses of the word: over six feet two, with long arms and huge hands, he moved like an amiable bear. He walked with a long, springing stride; and when talking to you, he kept his hands behind his back as he leant forwards to hear better. Hawke could not remember which was Trevellion's bad ear, but he could certainly recall the battle he had fought on the officer's behalf to avoid an adverse medical decision on his future.

Yes, an unusual man and, at forty-two, still in the zone for the rarefied strata of promotion. He was a thinker, a quality which had mixed blessings. He was passionately fond of history, and had written an outspoken paper to Their Lordships on their decision to discontinue the teaching of naval history at Greenwich. Trevellion's view was similar to the Second Sea Lord's: this decision cut at the roots of the Navy.

Trevellion's face was lighting up with that genial grin of his.

'What's amusing you, Trevellion?'

'I was remembering the day you hit the lock gate in Antwerp, sir.'

'Best forgotten, I think.' Hawke chuckled. He had become incensed with their Belgian pilot that day, but his second-in-command had remained silent, evidently containing his mirth.

'Trevellion, you've done nearly two years in my Personal Liaison Team, so you know what I'm looking for when I talk of morale and discipline.'

'One's complementary to the other.'

'Who told you that?'

'You did, sir.'

The Second Sea Lord smiled as he leant forward.

'You know, don't you, that Roger Nicolson has had a nervous breakdown? Strange, because he seemed relaxed — if anything, *too* casual…' He hesitated, then again glanced at Trevellion. 'I like a taut ship. See what you can do about it. I've not relieved her first lieutenant; he's holding the weight until he hands over to you.'

'Bermuda, sir?'

'Yes. I'm afraid you'll have no time to become used to the ship. Things are hotting up politically and there will be NATO exercises in the Atlantic almost as soon as you arrive. How quickly can you be ready to fly?'

'I've got to go home to collect my gear, sir.'

'I've booked your RAF flight for Tuesday.' Hawke paused, then asked casually, 'Your wife… is she happy about your appointment?'

'She's a normal woman, sir.' Trevellion was regarding him squarely. 'I expect you remember, sir, we've got Benjamin.'

'Oh yes.' The Second Sea Lord rose briskly. 'Give my regards to your wife.' He glanced at his watch. 'You'd better hurry, if you want to catch your weekend.'

CHAPTER 3

Cornwall, 3 December.

'How long have you been awake?'

'A little while.' It was no use deceiving Rowena. After eighteen years of marriage and all that they had suffered together, they knew each other too well.

Her arms were encircling him. 'What time is it?' she asked softly.

'Just after five. You're going to be all right, Ro?' He asked the question, knowing it to be foolish. Rowena had always coped, even after the accident — and, as always, the stab of remorse pierced Pascoe as the nightmare of those few terrible seconds flashed again across his mind.

His five days' leave had, for once, coincided with Benjamin's and Rebecca's holidays; the weather had been perfect. Time might eventually heal the bitterness — though, God, he had tried not to feel sorry for himself. It was the intimate interludes which always threw him — some phrase, some slight cast of her head, when the scar across her face was at its worst. On some days, however hard she tried to conceal it, the livid weal would stand out, an angry slash across her forehead, above her eyes and the bridge of her nose. Despite the skill of the plastic surgeons, the parchment mask that was now her face remained a constant condemnation of his rashness when he had overtaken that juggernaut.

So Becky was dead, hurled through the car door, which had flown open on impact. Ben's temporary blindness; his irreparable brain damage; his paralysed legs … in Pascoe's bad moments he had cursed God for allowing Ben to survive. He and Rowena could have started again, slowly rebuilding their lives — she was still young enough to start another family — but she had Ben to care for now, for the remainder of the boy's natural life.

Ro had been rock-like: that disfigurement would have broken many women. Dear God, he loved her, possibly more now than ever.

'You'll be all right, Ro?' He repeated his question in the darkness. 'I'll be at home more often this time: *Icarus* is a Plymouth ship.'

'I'm not getting any younger, Pascoe,' she murmured, rubbing the stubble on his chin. He had never heard her complain before. 'And we can't always rely on the Butlers to take Ben when you've got a few days' leave.' Her arms tightened about him as she picked her words. 'I'll think about Ben's future,' she murmured. 'I promise.'

He pulled her to him and felt her snuggling close. They had no need to talk. The Butlers had suggested acclimatising Ben to the idea of spending periods away in one of the new establishments for the disabled, if one could be found. That way, if either — or both — of the parents suddenly died, Ben would have become used to living without them. Pascoe and Rowena had already visited such a place, not far from Truro and within weekend visiting.

'There'll be a place for him soon,' he said gently. 'With help, we can just afford it.'

She clung to him fiercely, trying to hold on to time.

'It's only just five,' he said.

'Tonight's been so perfect,' she whispered. 'Let's keep the memory.'

So they dressed in the dawn, and he packed the car while she threw the breakfast together. Ben was at his most loving, and pathetically trying to help.

'You'll take care of Mum for me?' Pascoe asked him. The boy hovered in the background, grunting and laughing in his chair.

And so, in the cold of a December morning, Rowena at the wheel, they drove to Plymouth. The wind was whistling through the platform.

'Write a lot,' she said, gazing down the tracks to the west.

'You too,' he said. He could not continue: the partings grew worse as the years passed.

Pascoe put his arms around his son, tried to meet the eager smile. He felt Ro's hand on his sleeve as he turned from her and boarded the train, fumbling about with his baggage in the carriage until the jolt of departure. He could not speak, but he went into the corridor to wave at the diminishing figures on the platform. Ro was fluttering her scarf. Ben sat in his chair, holding her hand, his head jerking from side to side as each carriage clattered past.

CHAPTER 4

Bermuda, 6 December.

Three days later Captain Trevellion landed on schedule at Bermuda. Waiting in the Customs lounge was a short, sturdy officer in blues.

'Lieutenant Lochead, sir,' he said, saluting. 'Compliments of the first lieutenant, welcome to Bermuda. The Land Rover's outside.' He led the way out into the bright sunlight.

'Thank you. Where's *Icarus*?'

'She's in Malabar. The dockyard's closed down, but there's berthing room for STANAVFORLANT. It's pleasant there, away from the big ships.' Lochead smiled hesitantly as he held open the vehicle door. He looked flabby and pale, so presumably had not been out here long. His shoes needed cleaning and his 'sirs' were a bit sparse. The driver, a Leading Radio Operator wearing the *Icarus* cap ribbon, was saluting by the side of the Land Rover. He climbed into the driver's seat.

'What's your name?' Captain Trevellion asked.

'Leading Radio Operator Osgood, sir. Thursday is the duty day for the Land Rover, sir.'

'How does an L/RO get the job?'

'Volunteered, sir — gets me out of the office.'

Trevellion sat in the front with the driver. The Land Rover bumped along the narrow road leading to the north-eastern tip of Ireland Island where the dockyard lay, the ex-stone frigate, HMS *Malabar,* with its ghosts of the pre-war American and West Indies Squadron.

Captain Trevellion watched the turquoise blue of the Hamilton approaches sliding behind the pink oleander hedges. The glare of the white, low-pitched roofs dazzled him in the sunlight; hibiscus rambled in profusion across gateways and walls, while bougainvillaea draped its purple togas over every available space. Ignoring all speed limits the Land Rover thrashed onwards, shaving the walls of the poorer cottages which bounded the narrow road.

'Somerset Bridge,' Lochead was shouting above the din of the engine. 'The road narrows here, sir — and that's the old American base *Glorious* is using.'

Between the gaps in the hedges, Trevellion glimpsed the aircraft carrier swinging to her anchor in the sheltered waters of the coral bay. It was good to see her, the white ensign fluttering proudly from the round-down of her flight deck. She and *Furious* were the last of Britain's carriers, two ancient hulls filling the gap while the Navy waited for the through-deck carriers that were being built so agonisingly slowly. But these splendid old ships, serving in their stopgap role as combined commando and anti-submarine aircraft carriers, were playing a vital part at the moment, not least because they were a continuation of the carrier expertise which had been learnt at such cost over the past fifty years.

Submarine hunting was their primary role now, for which *Glorious* bore a full squadron of Sea King helicopters. Trevellion felt a twinge of pride: his *raison d'être* as captain of HMS *Icarus* was to become part of STANAVFORLANT (Standing Naval Force, Atlantic), the team whose function was to track Russian submarines in peacetime, hunt them during periods of tension, and destroy them in wartime. The Sea Kings that he could glimpse ranged on *Glorious*'s flight deck were the cutting edge of the weapon which the Royal Navy wielded in exercising sea power through NATO.

'There's the dockyard, sir.'

Lieutenant Lochead was pointing through the windscreen: the mastheads and upperworks of the ships comprising STANAVFORLANT were ranged alongside the dockyard walls, the outer mole and across the outer arm. *Glorious* swung at anchor, a toy carrier floating on this sparkling turquoise sea that could only belong to Bermuda.

L/RO Osgood drove slowly past the Bermudian policeman at the gates, then swung the Land Rover in a half-circle across the white gravel of the dockyard. A superbly proportioned, two-storied building of mellow light-grey stone brooded over the bustle which, during this week, had resurrected the defunct dockyard. Many years had elapsed since the rusting hands on those black dials had chimed the passing of the hours from the twin square clock towers. The fact that STANAVFORLANT's squadron was once more using *Malabar* was a sign of the times, and of the mounting tension which Russian naval might was provoking.

'*Icarus* is the outboard ship in the trot,' Lochead was saying. 'The first lieutenant thought you might like to sail earlier than the others tomorrow — to get the feel of her, sir.'

Trevellion nodded. He could see the sidesmen of the German frigate, *Goeben,* mustering smartly at the gangway. Her officer of the watch was discreetly signalling to the ship on *Goeben*'s outboard side. Trevellion jumped from the Land Rover and nodded to L/RO Osgood, who was extricating his gear. He smoothed the jacket of his lightweight grey suit and placed his felt hat squarely on his head. Then he strode towards the brow leading on to *Goeben*'s upper deck. Raising his hat to the officer's salute, he walked briskly across the ship's quarterdeck.

Icarus's gangway staff were at attention, the officer of the watch facing the brow. Trevellion heard the side party being called to attention; he noted the lieutenant commander scurrying to take his place alongside the officer of the watch, fastening the top button of his reefer as he saluted. He must be Jewkes, the first lieutenant, who had been holding the weight since Roger Nicolson had departed three days ago.

Captain Pascoe Trevellion, Royal Navy, stepped on to the quarterdeck of his new command. He stood at attention, raising his hat first to the officer of the watch, then to those manning the gangway; finally he turned towards the stern again, doffing his hat to the white ensign which was fouled around the ensign staff. Then he turned to meet the first of his officers.

'Lieutenant Commander Jewkes, sir,' the first lieutenant said, introducing himself. Trevellion took the man's podgy hand, noting the caution in his brown eyes. He was stockily built, about five foot nine. His hair was on the long side and his sandy sideburns were well down his cheeks. His bushy eyebrows emphasised the 'yo-ho' image he seemed to project.

Jewkes then introduced the officer of the watch. 'Lieutenant Gubbay, sir — our Senior Watchkeeper.' Gubbay, a solid-looking man — probably 'Special Duties' — saluted smartly and looked his captain squarely in the eye.

'And the Master-at-Arms, sir,' Jewkes continued, 'Fleet Chief Campbell.'

Trevellion liked the look of *Icarus*'s senior rating. The Master-at-Arms was lean, with no spare fat on him, and his face was gaunt and lined, with the amused sky-blue eyes of the Highlander.

'Where d'you come from, Master?'

'Wester Ross, sir. Ullapool.'

Trevellion turned to his first lieutenant. 'I haven't much time before sailing to meet the ship's company, so I'll do rounds of the ship tomorrow afternoon at 1430. Presumably you'll be giving Saturday afternoon leave on Saturday, Number One ... till midnight?'

'Yes, sir?'

'Good. I'll see heads of departments in my cabin tomorrow morning.'

'Ship will be under sailing orders, sir?' the Master-at-Arms asked.

Trevellion nodded. "I'll be slipping at 0600 on Sunday. I'll be carrying out ship-handling manoeuvres in the Sound before the force sails. Thank you, gentlemen.'

'I'll lead the way, sir.' The first lieutenant trekked for'd through the screen door, along the main passage — the Burma Road, the troops called it — up one ladder to the officers' quarters — and then another to the captain's cabin beneath the bridge.

'The bo'sun's mate is bringing your gear, sir.' Jewkes drew back the curtain in the cabin doorway. He nodded towards the white-jacketed figure standing motionless in the pantry. 'Leading Steward Rowlans,' Jewkes continued. 'Your steward, sir.'

The slight, neatly turned-out rating smiled nervously, his face glistening in the artificial lighting. 'Welcome to *Icarus,* sir.' Trevellion felt he was in luck with Rowlans.

'Would you care to come down to the wardroom, sir?' the first lieutenant asked. 'The officers are there to meet you.'

Trevellion did not answer immediately. Then he faced Jewkes and said quietly, 'I'm used to the captain meeting his officers for the first time on the quarterdeck, Number One.' He stared into Jewkes's cautious eyes. 'Be so good as to assemble them aft at once.'

The first lieutenant hesitated, then turned for the door. 'I'll report, sir, as soon as they're mustered.'

'Ten minutes,' Trevellion snapped. He turned to his steward. 'My uniform, please, Rowlans — number one suit.'

Captain Trevellion was experiencing that numbed mental and physical state produced by jet lag. He found it difficult to grasp that forty-eight hours had elapsed since he had taken over command on Thursday: it was now 1345 on Saturday afternoon, 8 December. He had interviewed all his heads of department during this Saturday morning, and now he felt he must lunch alone in his cabin. Rowlans had sensed his captain's exhaustion and had unobtrusively turned down the bunk in the inner cabin.

'You're right, Rowlans,' Trevellion smiled. 'Give me a shake during the first dog. I'll see the navigating officer before dinner.'

'Aye, aye, sir.'

Pascoe stripped to his pants and climbed between the sheets. It was warm despite the air conditioning, and sleep eluded him. His thoughts were in a turmoil after these crowded hours. The impending problems seemed out of proportion — because of his jet lag, no doubt. But Pascoe could not dispel the disquieting niggle at the back of his mind; again he felt that unease he had experienced during his rounds of the ship yesterday afternoon.

He had deliberately not hurried his tour of the ship. He wanted to meet as many of *Icarus*'s company as he could, so he concentrated on the messes. He began in the chief's mess, the

Master-at-Arms introducing the men upon whom the Navy most depended. *Icarus*'s chief petty officers seemed a good lot, friendly and relaxed; most were in overalls, straight from their various jobs.

'Our Fleet Chief Marine Engineering Artificer, sir,' the MEO (Marine Engineer Officer) introduced. 'He's leaving us when we get back to Devonport.'

Trevellion regarded the lightly built Fleet Chief in the white overalls.

'And where are you off to?'

'I don't know yet, sir.'

Then the MEO, Lieutenant Sparger, explained quietly, 'He's been promoted to Fleet Chief, sir. I was hoping his relief might have joined in Bermuda — there won't be much time for a turnover.'

Trevellion sensed the appraisal of the men grouped around him. He knew that they were assessing him as closely as he was trying to judge them: steady men, skilled technicians every one of them, without whom the ship would be only a floating steel hulk. Highly intelligent, these senior ratings were truly the Navy's backbone. They had given longer service than most; they had watched the Navy's evolution during these difficult years of change. They had brought up the youngsters, kept the complex machinery and electronics functioning, provided the firm rock upon which young and unsure young officers could lean. Trevellion felt satisfied as he left their mess.

The first lieutenant had opened the door of the adjoining compartment, the petty officers' mess. Much younger, some only twenty-two years of age, the petty officers were typical of this age group in today's Britain. After talking to them, he sensed that several had joined with one eye on the world outside — he would have to get to know these men better.

They had decorated their mess in an effort to transform the rectangular steel box into a facsimile of a London pub, but instead of the royal portraits and the restrained prints of pastoral England adorning the chiefs' mess, the bulkheads in the petty officers' mess were garishly decorated with nudes from girlie magazines. Continuing his rounds, he visited the junior rates' mess decks — in one of which he recognised L/RO Osgood — then the galleys; the combined recreation room and dining rooms. In the sleeping accommodation — where each man had his own fore-and-aft bunk — the junior rates were packed in close, the senior rates being marginally better off.

'The petty officers' quarters, sir.'

The first lieutenant stood with his back against the door. The communications yeoman, one of the senior petty officers, was standing by the bunks, which were adorned by pin-ups of ladies wearing nothing but toothsome smiles. Here was another key man on whom Trevellion would greatly depend. He was broad-shouldered and squat, with the dark skin and steady eyes of a Cornishman.

'Where are you from, Yeoman?'

'Sennen Cove, sir.'

The music in the name struck a chord in Trevellion's memory. He and Rowena had often driven out to the cove during the winter months to watch the Atlantic seas smashing against the rocks and rolling up the beach.

'You're the only other Cornishman, sir,' the yeoman grinned. 'The ship'll be all right now, sir.'

Trevellion smiled: the relationship between yeoman and captain was special.

He edged out from the cabin. Jewkes backed away from the door, and Trevellion saw that it bore a huge, rampant phallic symbol, complete with genitalia.

Pascoe glanced at it, then at the petty officer, then finally at Jewkes, who turned away in embarrassment, uttering something which the captain ignored. Trevellion walked on in silence to visit the next cabin, before inspecting the sonar compartment deep in the bowels of the ship, then into the diesel generator compartment and the engine room. Finally he visited the Weapons Engineer Officer's department: the radio rooms, the electronic warfare offices and the switchboards.

Last night, during the hours when sleep had eluded him, his sense of unease about this ship had been impossible to dispel. Now, as exhaustion propelled him to sleep, he realised that he must bide his time, an exercise at which he knew he was inept. The things he had heard and seen during his rounds yesterday afternoon were only first impressions, and probably superficial. As he lapsed into sleep, his thoughts were of Rowena, to whom he had not yet had a chance to write.

'Four-thirty, sir.'

Trevellion heard Rowlans's words, but he was disorientated, unable at once to grasp where he was. Then he saw the steward's friendly face, the proffered cup of tea. 'The navigator is ready to see you, sir.'

Pascoe hauled himself from his bunk, downed the strong tea and pulled himself together. He felt refreshed, and he could at least now think straight. He could see the outline of the navigator outside the curtained doorway, charts and books in his hands.

'Come in, Pilot.'

Trevellion knew he could lay on an easy manner when he wished, but today he would remain remote — and particularly with his navigating officer, Lieutenant Brian Neame.

'Draw up a chair, Pilot. Spread the chart on the table: more comfortable here than up in the charthouse.'

According to the Appointer, Neame had collected a bad report. But as he discussed the passage plans with him, Trevellion began to suspect that Neame's supercilious facade masked a lack of confidence.

'You're under report,' Trevellion said, facing Neame squarely. 'Let's forget that. Do your job to the best of your ability, that's all I ask of you. Now, how are we going to get *Icarus* out of Bermuda and through the Narrows?'

Neame was an 'ex-Dart', heavily built and beefy, with a red face and small pouting mouth. He began to relax as he presented his passage plan, but Trevellion could not help sensing the considerable chip on Neame's shoulder. He seemed to have little time for anyone, and his sarcasm irritated Trevellion — a pity, because the navigating officer could take much of the weight from a captain's shoulders — even if, as in Neame's case, he had not excelled in his navigating course.

The first lieutenant was tapping on the doorway. He peered through the curtain.

'I forgot to ask you, sir ... you'll join us for sherry before dinner?'

'Certainly, Number One. Thanks.'

Neame was rolling up the charts; Rowlans was laying out Trevellion's mess undress for dinner. Pascoe Trevellion looked forward with mixed feelings to meeting his officers unofficially.

CHAPTER 5

Bermuda, 8 December.

'Coming ashore, Oz?' L/RO Osgood heard his oppo shouting through the hatchway.

'How long have I got?' he yelled back.

'Seven minutes to libertymen.'

It was rare for Niv Fane and he to share a run ashore: Niv, a Leading Marine Engineering Mechanic, worked a different watch-keeping rota when the engine room was hard pressed.

It took Niv and Oz over an hour to reach Hamilton. Loaded with British, Americans, Dutch and Germans from the STANAVFORLANT force, the craft wallowed past Hogfish Beacon and up the Big Ship Channel to Two Rock Passage. It was hard to believe that Bermuda had always been the base for the Royal Navy's American and West Indies Squadron.

Then they were ashore, idly wandering through Hamilton's bustling main street, one side flanked by its green, pink and chocolate-coloured shop fronts. Gharries, drawn by flea-bitten nags, threaded through the crowd of American tourists. The tang of cedarwood smelt sweet and the varnished woodwork of the shop facades gleamed in the sunlight — evidence of the days when Bermuda was clothed by its cedar trees, before disease had killed them.

Niv and Oz bought their presents, their last chance before returning to Plymouth. 'What've you got Merle?' Niv asked.

Osgood held up the print he'd chosen, an airy watercolour of delicate blues, white walls and hot grey dust. 'Bit different from the usual,' he said. 'Don't suppose we'll be back again, and it'll be something to remember.'

Niv was fingering a pink coral bracelet. 'My old woman'll like this.'

Back in the glare of the sunlight, Osgood took a photograph of the harbour to show Merle. He felt at ease with Niv: though he was two years older he had turned into a good friend. They walked on, swapping yarns about their families, sharing the confidences of their private lives. Niv was a good mess-mate, patient when listening to Oz's anecdotes about Merle, his 22-year-old wife, and Debbie, their year-old daughter. During those first difficult months when Oz was rated up to leading hand, Niv had backed him up.

'C'mon, Oz,' Niv said, elbowing him through the jostling herd on the street. 'Let's get out of here. This place stinks of money.'

Cut-away powder boats with towering top hampers careered across the bays, bow waves splashing in the sparkling blue. Underdressed and overweight matrons in Bermuda shorts monopolised the pavements with their clacking mouths and clicking cameras.

'Let's get out to the coast, up to Gibb's Hill,' Osgood suggested. 'The old shopkeeper told me you can see the whole island from the lighthouse.'

They carried on a desultory conversation, but failed to avoid the subject of the ship and her new captain.

'You saw him yesterday, Oz … what's he like?'

Osgood did not answer at once. He stopped to watch a group of Bermudian children tossing white pebbles into a circle scratched in the dust. Hens clucked and scrambled, while the sound of singing drifted from inside the whitewashed cottage.

'He's different from Nicolson,' he said. 'Difficult to tell yet.'

'Nicolson was okay if he liked you,' Niv said. 'Too much of a Popularity Jack for my liking. I never really felt he was man enough for the job. He made rods for his own back by trying to be one of the boys.'

'I liked him,' Oz said. 'Sorry he's gone.'

Niv had slowed his pace. 'Our new Chief MEA saw Trevellion on the platform at Plymouth,' he said. 'He was saying goodbye to his missus.' Niv paused, looking up at a cardinal bird fluttering in the oleanders. 'She was terribly scarred about the face, apparently, and she was pushing a wheelchair with a kid in it – their son, the Chief thought. He was crippled, and he couldn't talk properly.'

'Maybe that's why this bloke's different,' Osgood said.

Niv lowered his voice. 'Ease off to the left, Oz. Dodge behind that house.'

Then Osgood spotted the hazard: Mick Foulgis was sitting at one of the red tables that stood in the shade of the pink-walled hovel boasting the name of The Coronation Hotel. A girl sat on either side of him, and even from this distance Oz could hear their strident laughter.

'Hey, Fane ... hi, Osgood! C'mon, join me for a jar.'

Niv was about to ignore the invitation when Oz stopped him. 'I'm bloody thirsty, Niv. He's got the lolly.'

'He hasn't got a wife, that's why,' Niv said.

'No bird would put up with him.' Foulgis was known as Mick the Moaner in the mess deck.

'He seems to be doing all right,' Niv said as reluctantly he led the way to the hotel. Mick yelled over his shoulder and a surly Bermudian slapped the beer down on the red tabletop.

'Shirley,' Mick introduced. 'And this is Ruth.'

'Hi, boys!' said the taller one, the dark-eyed Ruth, who was lying across Mick with her hand inside his shirt.

'We're getting acquainted,' Mick said, winking at Osgood.

After downing their beers, Osgood began fumbling for his ten-dollar bill.

'Put that away, mate. This is my day ... I got only one run ashore last time.'

He knows we're skint, Oz thought, *and that we're married.*

They sank two more beers, chiakked with the girls and felt better. As the evening cooled, the girls led the way inside the house to a large room, dimly lit and musty. Mick ordered whisky and was soon on his usual argumentative form. Niv stuck to beer, but Oz downed the spirit, feeling the kick of the alcohol.

From upstairs came the sound of a band. 'There's dancing upstairs, boys,' Shirley said. 'Five dollars.'

She took Niv's and Oz's hands and led them to an upper room where couples were swaying to the rhythm of a worn disc by a West Indian steel band.

'Five dollars...' Shirley said standing before them, a hand outstretched. 'The manageress says all clients are to pay first: this is a club, see?'

Ruth giggled as she dragged Mick on to the floor. A tall blonde Danish girl came over, red lips pouting at Oz; he grinned stupidly, seeing her nakedness beneath her silk shirt.

'I like English sailors,' she whispered. Her laugh was low, like syrup, cloying and sticky. She took his hand and gently pulled him to the floor, beckoning to the barman as she did so.

Oz saw Niv shaking his head at Shirley, watched him push back the fresh glass while he remained seated at the table. Oz turned his back on him and began to dance. Before him swayed the delicious girl, tits jigging beneath the silk. His body responded as she moulded herself into him ... through the beat of the rhythm he heard her murmuring softly.

'The dollars are for Mrs Hobbs ... I won't take anything from you.' She pressed close as she steered him towards the gloom of the passageway down which Shirley and Mick had already disappeared. Over the girl's shoulder Oz saw Niv picking up the camera and pushing back the table.

The whisky was raw and cheap, and Oz knew it was taking effect. He firmly unlocked the girl's arms from him, then crossed the floor to Niv's table. 'Let's go.' He grabbed his camera and hurried from the sleazy room. 'Thanks, Niv.'

As they walked on, the streets became busier. Oz's monologue was suddenly interrupted by Niv. They were standing outside a pseudo-English pub.

Niv pushed his face close to the pane of glass. 'There's only five of 'em,' he murmured softly. 'Weedy-looking blokes.'

'What's up, Niv?'

Fane's conspiratorial whispering was out of character. He jerked his head towards a notice in bold red lettering above the door: DOGS AND BRITISH SAILORS NOT ADMITTED.

Osgood felt the rage mounting inside him. 'You lost your old dad out here, didn't you, Niv?'

Fane nodded.

Osgood methodically peeled off his cardigan. He folded it neatly, patting it in place upon the windowsill, then pushed open the door, Niv following at his heels.

'You the landlord?' Osgood asked softly, staring at the smooth-faced publican across the bar.

'What's it to you?'

'I'm a British sailor ... and so's my mate.'

The anteroom was at the far end of the long and narrow compartment which served as the wardroom: functional, perhaps, because this shape provided less danger to stability from free-flood water, but as a home for the officers it was an awkward place.

The more senior members were standing around the seats lining the tiny anteroom; the others were squeezed against the bar. Firebrace, the lanky fair-haired sub-lieutenant, was hunched outside, his naive open face peering around the corner stanchion at the after end of the bar Jewkes had scrounged during the last Devonport refit.

'Sherry, sir?'

The MEO, Lieutenant Joe Sparger, a tall, angular man, made room for Trevellion to sit in the centre of the U-shaped settee. He was a Special Duties officer, an ex-Chief ERA, as steady as a rock, judging by the level gaze of his blue-grey eyes. His confidential report certainly confirmed Trevellion's judgement of this reliable-looking man. Three years older than his captain, his hair was greying and he had that preoccupied look of most chiefs. The 'trickle-drafting' system and the continuous supervision of junior rates straight from training class gave Joe Sparger a uniquely difficult job. He tried to keep his engine room department running at top efficiency, but, once again, so much depended on his senior ratings.

'Cheers, Chief.'

'Cheers.'

Conversation was soon flowing naturally as various officers broke off to sign for their drinks. The supply officer, Lieutenant Bernard Towke, was dispensing behind the crescent-shaped bar. Trevellion felt that the tension was easing and that he was no longer a stranger among them. They moved into the narrow wardroom, where a Formica-topped table ran down the centre of the serving hatch. Before taking his place, Trevellion walked towards the servery. The PO Steward, a humorous character by the look of him, introduced his two stewards, in white short-sleeved shirts and blue serge trousers, who were standing awkwardly at attention.

The first lieutenant, as president of the wardroom mess, sat in the centre of the table, his back to the door. Trevellion sat down on Jewkes's right as the chairs scuffed backwards and the officers took their places.

Jewkes rapped his gavel and intoned, 'For what we are about to receive, thank God.' The stewards then served the soup, which the PO Steward was ladling through the hatchway.

After a second glass of South African sherry, the conversation gradually became general. Trevellion flipped his napkin and began talking to the neighbour on his right. Lieutenant Commander Ivor Caradoc Jones wore black-rimmed, thick-lensed spectacles, behind which his intelligent eyes appeared to accept the vagaries of life with benign tolerance. He was comfortably plump and of average height, dark, with a permanent shadow about his jowls.

As the soup plates were whisked away, Jones called across to the supply officer, ' I bet you're giving us "herrings-in" on this auspicious occasion, eh, Bernie? Mustn't go wild during these difficult days, eh?'

'Take no notice of the Philistines, sir,' the patient Towke replied, resignation on his face as he smiled at Trevellion. He was a tall, thin man with black face fungus. 'They're jealous of us pussers.'

The conversation warmed and Trevellion was soon able to observe his officers discreetly. Jones was an unflappable technician, highly qualified and immensely proud of his large weapons department. In a small ship, it was a truism that each man depended on his opposite number, each one watching upon the other; and each department upon the other departments: there was no room for skivers. The WEO (Weapons Engineer Officer) shared with the MEO the responsibility of keeping the technical running of the ship efficient.

Lieutenant Commander Jones had cause to look weary: he was responsible directly to his captain for the three electrical categories of his branch, Radio, Control, and Ordnance. 'Trickle drafting' played the same havoc with his department. Jones's concentration was divided as he listened with his other ear to the discussion opposite, between the cadaverous, gaunt-faced Principal War Officer (Underwater), Lieutenant Commander Julian Farge, and the helicopter pilot's observer, Lieutenant Rollo Daglish. Both had finished the snapper and were leaning across the table — Towke had provoked the argument.

'They'll *have* to honour the promises they made. There are too many men in the ship slapping in their notices.'

'But Jack will never catch up at this rate.' The speaker was a pleasant-faced, fair-haired lieutenant sitting at the far end of the table. This was Alastair McKown, a university entrant and the PWO (Air). He had sharp eyes and a sardonic twist to his mouth. 'I can never understand why we don't just have a national government. The two-party system is self-destructive if its tolerance is abused and manipulated by the wreckers.'

'No one thought our new national government would honour the Pay Code, though, did they?' The Senior Watchkeeper, Sam Gubbay, peered across from the far side of the table.

Jewkes banged the table with his gavel. 'Gentlemen, we've had enough of this conversation. When I first came to sea, discussion of pay was taboo. You can add it to our other three *verboten* topics, gentlemen,' he continued, rapping the table again. 'Politics, religion and women.'

'Nothing worth talking about, then,' the helicopter pilot murmured. There was laughter from that end of the table.

'What's his name again?' Trevellion asked Jewkes quietly.

'Gamble, sir.' He called across to the Lynx pilot. 'How d'you get your name, Hob?'

Gamble glanced across at Jewkes, face deadpan.

'Had an argument during flying training, with a double-decker bus, sir.' He turned towards his captain as he fiddled with the spoon in front of him. 'At my court-martial, the prosecution's main witness was a bus driver, a Pakistani. He insisted on addressing his pride and joy as his "hobnibus".'

Trevellion chuckled. It was obvious that Hob Gamble was liked in the mess: he and his observer, Lieutenant Rollo Daglish, were the only officers who regularly risked their lives. Gamble was one of the Navy's best chopper pilots, having come top of the air-sea rescue stakes at Culdrose last year. *Icarus*'s new Lynx helicopter was the first of the modified Mark VIIs, and Hob had been selected to carry out trials on her.

'Hob'll never find a Russian, not if Rollo's navigating.'

The chat began to rattle across the table. These men were used to each other; they had learnt tolerance over the months, making allowances for each other's foibles. Trevellion, no longer scrutinised, was able to listen to the chat around him. And then came the inevitable topic, the reason for *Icarus*'s existence; it continued down the table, and even the sub-lieutenant — the tall, rangy Firebrace — was shyly taking part.

The Russians' magnificent fleet, its aggressiveness and its harassment of the NATO navies produced a different reaction in the Royal Navy than in the breasts of politicians. Most sailors were all for annoying the Russians on every possible occasion, instead of weakly playing their game of one-sided *detente*. The new men in the Kremlin had never been bloodied in battle; they didn't remember the Great Patriotic War. Now that there was subversion inside the Soviet Union — sometimes induced from outside her frontiers — the untried and unknown Kremlin masters might be compelled to divert the discontent of the masses. What easier solution than the traditional appeal to the patriotism of the Russian? The temptation to strike while she could still win might be irresistible to the younger team in Moscow. There could be doves amongst the hawks, even in the Kremlin; the idea might be growing that a trial of strength in the remote wastes of the Atlantic using conventional weapons, would be preferable to the devastation of nuclear annihilation.

'They're winning without even firing a shot,' said Farge. 'Why would they need to fight when they can use inflation as a weapon? The Arab oilmen have given them that for free. The Russian leaders keep on telling us they aim to destroy us and our system, so why shouldn't we believe them?'

'Yes,' Jewkes said. 'By building up their military might, they're forcing the West to spend money it doesn't have. That makes us live beyond our means. The Russians don't need to provoke a hot war: they're wrecking our economies by subversion, and by forcing us into a game of one-upmanship with the armaments.'

'If the Soviets cut our oil route round the Cape, that means war, whatever our collaborators may say,' Jewkes said. 'The

Yanks aren't so diplomatic now they've got China on their side. And NATO,' he added as an afterthought.

Neame said, 'That's all too remote: they'll try much nearer home.'

'Iceland?' Farge murmured.

'The Yanks will never allow it,' Ivor Jones said. 'Even if the Icelanders invite the Russians, the island is still vital to NATO. Don't forget, the West's early warning chain depends entirely upon Iceland's radar.'

McKown, the honours degree man, chipped in again. 'The Faeroes and northern Norway — that's where they'll probe — North Cape is now America's eastern frontier.'

Trevellion had remained silent, listening to his officers. The stewards were discreetly waiting to clear the table. Jewkes passed the port and then banged the hammer. 'Mr Vice: the Queen.'

Sam Gubbay, acting as vice-president at the after-end of the table, raised his glass:

'Gentlemen: the Queen.'

The glasses were raised, the toast drunk. Trevellion noted the supercilious smirk on Brian Neame's face. For an instant their eyes met, and from then on Trevellion knew from which quarter he could expect trouble. The cynical, contemptuous navigator had caught the malady of the times: patriotism, for him, was archaic. In Trevellion's opinion, doctrine such as this would bring Britain to the brink.

'Please excuse the Officer of the Day, sir,' Jewkes said quietly into Trevellion's ear. 'He's wanted by the Master-at-Arms.'

The Officer of the Day slipped out through the door and Trevellion caught a glimpse of the Master-at-Arms, Fleet Chief Campbell, waiting outside in the flat, clipboard in hand. He was an upright, impressive figure.

The rest of them adjourned to the anteroom, where Ivor Jones poured the coffee. Before they had finished the telephone buzzed. Gubbay answered it, then turned to the first lieutenant.

'For you, Number One,' he said, handing him the instrument. 'The Hamilton police.'

CHAPTER 6

Western Atlantic, 9 December.

'Singled up and ready for sea, sir. All hands on board,' the first lieutenant reported, standing in the doorway of the captain's cabin.

In the chill of the early morning breeze that whistled across the wheelhouse roof, Captain Trevellion took his new command to sea for the first time. It was bleak on the exposed deck: the sun was a cold yellow disc only a few degrees above the horizon, and white horses were churning up the sound. *Icarus* was turning up nicely into the wind, as long as he kept a touch of headway on her. The frigate was swinging swiftly now, lining up to the gap between the breakwaters.

'Finished with the tug. Thank her, Yeoman,' ordered Trevellion. 'I'm going below.' But before he swung himself down the ladder he saw that *Icarus* was too close to the south-west arm of the breakwaters.

Lieutenant Joe Sparger, who had come up on to the wings of the bridge for a breather, could see Trevellion striding from side to side of the bridge in an effort to see the screwflagman on the roof of the helicopter hangar. The manoeuvre was being watched by the hands on *Goeben,* standing smartly to attention while waiting for *Icarus* to clear the dockyard; Sparger could well understand Trevellion's annoyance at this conspicuous display of clumsy ship-handling. Seconds later, he felt the deck trembling beneath his feet: *Icarus* was steadying after the lurch caused by the correction of her swing. The yellow stonework of the arm, at one point precariously close, slipped behind. Sparger glimpsed *Glorious*'s outline where she was still at anchor off Somerset Island. A light was winking from her bridge island, and the yeoman moved out to his signalling projector.

Until the yeoman reported that the next ship in the seniority stakes, *Jesse L. Brown,* was leaving harbour, Trevellion exercised his ship's company and himself. *Icarus* handled well, even in the stiff breeze: she was one of the last of the broad-beamed Leanders and was reputed to be a good seaboat. Trevellion did not reproach the first lieutenant over the series of minor mishap — due almost entirely to inefficiency — which occurred during the exercises, but his air of apparent unconcern cost him some effort to maintain when a signal arrived from COMSTANAVFORLANT.

TO ICARUS INFO ATHABASKAN, GOEBEN, JESSE L. BROWN. MANOEUVRES BADLY EXECUTED. REPORT REASONS WHY TWO RATINGS WERE NOT IN RIG OF THE DAY WHILE LEAVING HARBOUR.

Trevellion frowned. 'Show it to the first lieutenant.' He then turned to Firebrace, who was conning the ship with a nervous expression on his face. 'Stop together.'

As *Icarus* lost way, he eased her into the wind to wait for the senior officer. *Jesse L. Brown* was creaming up astern, while *Goeben* was clearing the harbour entrance. The Canadian destroyer, *Athabaskan,* swept by, her blue NATO flag fluttering stiffly in the wind, the commodore's pendant flying proudly.

Trevellion, waiting for *Goeben* to take station on *Athabaskan,* saw *Jesse L. Brown*'s wake frothing as she moved up on *Goeben*. Leaving Five Fathom Hole to port, the ships adopted their cruising stations in order of seniority: they were dispersed over three miles apart, where they zigzagged independently to follow a mean line of advance of 082 degrees towards the Azores. Trevellion moved out to the wings for a last look at the low-lying islands as disappearing in the murk below the horizon.

Glorious and her group of replenishment ships would soon be threading their way out through the channel: the carrier was invisible, but her group would be exercising tomorrow while they caught up with STANAVFORLANT.

The Senior Officer of STANAVFORLANT, the American Commodore Harry McKenzie, with whom Trevellion had spent a rushed half-hour on Saturday, was devoting today to drilling his new commanding officer. Communication exercises and action manoeuvring would take place all day. At ten-thirty, the clouds to the westward began to lift and patches of blue began to show. The wind moderated and the pounding of the ship improved to an easy motion as she rose and dipped to the Atlantic swell.

Trevellion felt the soft breeze as he watched the heaving, dark blue mass of the ocean. It was a long passage that lay before them. He looked up as he saw the lookout pointing towards a helicopter coming up from the westward: one of *Glorious*'s Sea Kings. Sparger moved into the bridge.

'*Glorious*'s mail-run, sir,' Neame said to Trevellion. 'I've warned the Flight Deck Officer.'

The captain brought his ship round, thirty degrees off the wind. The dark-blue helicopter hovered above the quarterdeck, lowering the wire from which dangled the mailbag. Then she was away, swooping to port as she made for *Athabaskan,* whose upperworks were visible above the south-eastern horizon.

The first lieutenant was waiting patiently by the command chair.

'Yes, Number One?'

'When will you see defaulters, sir? I'm afraid I've got a difficult one.'

The captain hesitated, then replied, 'It's Sunday, First Lieutenant.'

'Tomorrow, then, sir?'

'Yes — before the RAS, when we'll be topping up with fuel. There'll be plenty of time, seeing as I'm last in the queue.' He turned to regard his first lieutenant. 'What's the trouble?'

'Leading Stoker Fane and Leading Radio Operator Osgood, sir. Run in by the patrol last night.'

'Serious?'

'Could be, sir, though Osgood hasn't been in trouble for some time. He used to skylark a bit before he was rated up.'

The yeoman was trying to catch the captain's eye, and Towke was also hovering in the background, a pile of 'bumph' in his hands.

'Executive signal for the communications exercise, sir,' the yeoman broke in.

'A letter from the Admiral, sir…' said Towke at the same time. He resembled a penguin in his orange waistcoat and the blue anorak of his flight deck gear.

'What's it about?'

'Fane and Osgood, sir. Complaint from the shore authorities: a police report to the Admiral.'

Trevellion submerged his annoyance. He had quite enough on his plate.

'See me when this exercise is finished, and bring the Master-at-Arms with you. I'll not have my ship brought into disrepute.'

He turned to the navigator and took over the ship himself. The whisper of the breeze outside the bridge screen was the only sound at that moment.

Back in his cabin, Joe Sparger sighed as he pulled the chair up to his desk. He was beginning to feel his age. Theoretically the modern maintenance procedures were splendid; in reality, initiative in the younger ERAS and MEOS was being stifled. He disliked being a puppet, and wondered how long the Fleet's complex machinery could be kept going in wartime when communications broke down.

As always, before settling down to the paperwork, he glanced at the framed photograph above his desk: Julie and the kids. They were all smiling at him, but the photograph had been taken so long ago. Frank was at university now, and Colin might soon be following; fools, like their dad, they both wanted to become mechanical engineers. Whether he could recommend an MEO's career for his sons would take a lot of thought ... but in the meantime, how the hell was he to keep the ship functioning safely if *Centurion* could not draft him replacements? His role seemed to be more about training junior rates than operating dangerous machinery. 'Haven't got anybody,' was *Centurion*'s invariable reply to Sparger's protestations — but he still had to take the can when disaster struck. An enormous responsibility was falling on his senior men, and he wondered for how long their loyalty could continue to be relied upon. His best senior rating was leaving the service, and Sparger knew that it was not only lack of money that was disillusioning these fine men. He sensed that they felt cheated, somehow — that they were searching for something more satisfying than money, for a motivation which their leaders, without the stress of war, seemed unable to provide.

Pride in their service, that was what people sought. In a small ship like *Icarus* there was no slack to take up if there was a man short, or if a man was relieved by someone with less training. Ships were doing so much sea-time that it was difficult to keep things going. The diesel generators were a typical example. Sparger disliked the Manxan diesel, and Leading MEM Fane, who was reassembling No. 1 generator after having stripped it in Halifax, shared Sparger's opinion. A good hand, Fane — he never complained about the eighteen hours a day he put into maintaining his diesels — but why had Fane run amok yesterday? Was his sudden lapse a result of overwork? Fane had four children and was leaving the service to join a container ship where pay was much higher. It was a bloody shame to lose a man of his calibre: he was a specialist on Manxan diesels now, after spending so much time on them.

The MEO reached for his rule to underline the essential repairs for his defect list: *1. Complete overhaul or replacement of the two diesel generators.*

When the diesels were running continually, a fuel spill pipe sheared at least once a week, sometimes twice — and there was no warning. Fuel sprayed out at high pressure to shoot across the hot exhaust pipes: it was miraculous there had been no major fires yet. Whenever Fane juggled at sea to replace the fuel spill pipes, Sparger adopted full fire precautions while the other engine continued running. Although automatic CO_2 drenching was provided, he always rigged fire hoses. It was irritating having to take Fane off his work at this critical moment to attend Captain's Defaulters. The stand-by diesel had to be available for RAS (Replenishment at Sea) as a precaution against electrical and hydraulic failure.

Joe Sparger glanced up as the Master-at-Arms tapped on the frame of his cabin door. 'Captain's table in ten minutes, sir.'

'Right, Master. You've told the Fleet Chief?'

'He's relieving Fane now, sir. They've stopped work on the diesel.'

The WEO, Lieutenant Commander Jones, never relished defaulters, even at Officer of the Day level. Captain's Defaulters he hated, and L/RO Osgood was one of his best leading hands. What *had* come over him? The WEO had interviewed Osgood privately, but Osgood's lapse failed to live up to the touch of genius for which 'Oz' was renowned.

The last time the WEO had defended the L/RO was after an MoD complaint: Osgood had been among a party of sailors stranded at an RAF airbase. To pass the time, they had built a mammoth snowman near the guard house on the edge of the airfield. A sergeant of the RAF, infuriated by this naval levity on RAF property, had ordered the demolition of the offending snowman. The sailors, believing this to be an inter-service challenge, refused. The RAF sergeant, incensed, jumped into the police Land Rover and drove it at full speed into the snowman, which collapsed in a flurry of snow.

Later in the afternoon, the sergeant was once again carrying out his perimeter rounds. To his fury, there on the edge of the airfield stood a super-snowman, a colossus with an inviting smile on its snowy face. A hundred yards off stood Osgood and his friends, watching with anticipatory grins on their faces, a fact which should have alerted the sergeant. But he wound up the Land Rover to full revs, lined it up carefully on his target, then charged full tilt into the gigantic snowman. The sergeant suffered a broken jaw and concussion, and the vehicle was a total write-off: the second snowman had been built around a very solid concrete post.

But Osgood's recent escapade, though smacking of the same panache, had not the same innocence.

The ritual had begun, and the Master-at-Arms was reading the charge: '…at about 2100 on Saturday, 8 December, did bring discredit upon their ship HMS *Icarus* when ashore as libertymen; and did cause an affray resulting in their arrest by the local police. Also, did cause bodily harm to the landlord of the Bunch of Grapes, Belmont, and damage to his property.' The Master had not drawn breath.

The WEO was watching his new captain. This, Jones sensed, was an important moment for the ship. Osgood and Fane were popular on the lower deck: loyal, trustworthy leading hands. The mess decks were watching, assessing their new captain on how he would deal with what, after all, seemed a British sailor's proper duty. They knew that the previous captain would have awarded a warning and a day's pay stopped — and probably a metaphorical wink and commendation.

'Why did you take it upon yourselves to avenge the insult?' Captain Trevellion asked the two men. He was standing back from the table, arms behind his back, head and hulking shoulders hunched forwards as he fixed Fane, then the shorter Osgood, with his sharp grey eyes. 'You could have returned to the ship and told the Master-at-Arms about it; you could have requested to see me.'

Fane shuffled his feet. He opened his mouth, but Osgood — impetuous idiot that he was — spoke up in his soft Devon burr for them both.

'There were only a couple of hours to go, sir. And once the ship had sailed…' Osgood faced his captain, looking upwards at him like a bulldog who would not let go. 'Would have been no good, sir. Nothing would have happened. Too late...'

Jones was struck by Trevellion's control. This tall man, bent forwards to avoid the deckhead, said nothing, but his brain must be working fast. All the frustrations of the rule-fettered junior ratings; the logical constraints which made for sensible conduct among civilised folk; the formal complaints through the proper service channels, complaints which slowly lost momentum as they ground to a halt. Jones had to suppress a smile as he listened to the closing stages of Osgood's case.

'After all, sir, it wasn't just me and Fane: the pub was insulting ... all of us — the whole Navy, sir.'

Oz's plea might have brought tears to the eyes of lesser men, but Captain Trevellion's mouth was a thin line, his facial muscles taut. Only his eyes betrayed his sense of the ridiculous. He turned to Bernie Towke.

'How much is the publican claiming for damages, Supply Officer?'

'Two and a half thousand dollars, sir — about a thousand pounds. The assessor reports that it's a fair estimate.'

'You'd do it again, would you?'

Osgood's under-hung jaw jutted forward, his eyes half-closed, as he spoke again for them both.

''Course we would, sir. He was asking for it. But it was my fault, all of it, sir. Something just came over me —' he half-turned to Fane — 'and Niv, sorry sir, L/MEM Fane, he just backed me up, sir.'

A nostalgic look briefly crossed Osgood's face. According to the official report which Towke had shown Ivor Jones, Fane and Osgood had torn the pub apart.

Jones was watching Trevellion. This was the moment for which the ship was waiting. Trevellion could have been excused some histrionics, some Pilate-decision: *I would have done the same, lads, but* ... Everyone would have understood what he was implying.

The stern face, with its wrinkled forehead, was staring directly at Jones. 'You're RO Osgood's Divisional Officer?'

'Yes, sir.'

'What's your opinion of Osgood?'

'A good leading radio operator, sir: reliable and hard-working.'

'Has he ever given you any disciplinary trouble? Does he give a good example to his subordinates?'

'Never any trouble in this ship, sir. He's a good leading hand.'

The captain turned to the L/MEM. 'What have you to say, L/MEM Fane?'

'Nothing to add, sir; we were in it together.'

Trevellion glanced at the MEO.

'One of my best men, sir,' Sparger said. 'He never complains, even though he works twelve hours a day in the DG room.'

'That might explain his lapse,' Trevellion murmured. 'Is Osgood overworking, Lieutenant Commander Jones?"

'The teleprinter machines are very worn, sir. Osgood doesn't get much let-up.'

Trevellion drew back from the table to consider the two men in front of him. Fane shifted his feet, clenching his cap. Osgood, a stocky barrel of a man from Devon, was forged of different stuff. He had drawn himself to his full height, resembling a man in the condemned cell, staunchly awaiting execution. His jaw was set and he was staring his captain in the eye.

'I've heard what your divisional officers think of you both, and I can sympathise with your outraged feelings. But you've brought' — Trevellion hesitated, carefully selecting his words — 'discredit upon our ship. The Bermudians will remember *Icarus* for a long time, and I don't expect the Admiral in *Glorious* will forget this fall from grace. Have you anything to add?'

'No, sir,' Fane said. 'I'm sorry, sir.'

'No, sir. Nothing.' Osgood remained defiant.

Captain Trevellion turned to the Master-at-Arms.

'Seven days' leave stopped for both ratings. They are to pay for the damage they caused, regular allotments being remitted from their pay by the supply officer.'

The first lieutenant saluted the captain as the defaulters were dispersing. 'Officer of the Watch's compliments, sir. He's increasing speed to take up position for the RAS.'

Ivor Jones saluted too, then watched the gaunt figure of Trevellion as he hauled himself up the ladder towards the bridge. There was no compromise about this man: was this the message he intended to convey to his ship?

The chief had stopped by his cabin door and was waiting for Jones.

'Bloody shame,' Sparger said. 'But the Old Man's right.'

'The ship's company will get the message,' Jones replied.

'Things won't be the same again.'

Jones nodded. 'Maybe that's not such a bad thing.'

The chief nodded towards the ladder leading down to the Burma Road on the deck below. 'See what I mean, Ivor? Fane's already back on the job in the DG room.'

CHAPTER 7

Hob Gamble replaced his coffee cup on the bar in the wardroom anteroom as the first-comers entered for stand-easy. He squinted into the glass of the framed watercolour depicting the wartime *Icarus* and tried to smooth down his shock of fair hair. Though it would never sit down properly, he was trying to get away from the scruffy image beloved by some. He had long ago decided to set his own standards, going it alone if necessary.

His twenty-four-year-old face was freckled from the bridge of his nose upwards; his eyebrows were somewhat darker than his fair hair — a peculiarity that he thought was grotesque — and his deep-sunk eyes were blue-green and restless. He supposed that ugly dial must reflect his character. He knew he was ambitious, and could be ruthless if his flying was threatened, but he looked deceptively amiable, with his quizzical, faintly genial expression.

He slapped on his cap and left the wardroom. The sub., George Firebrace, was on watch on the bridge. He stood at the pelorus, binoculars around his neck. A gangling youth, fair-haired and shy, he seemed unsure of himself. His claim to fame in the wardroom was being brother to a curvaceous sister who visited the ship too rarely.

The Master-at-Arms was easing himself into the helmsman's seat at the quartermaster's console as he took over the ship's steering preparatory to the RAS. Hob got on well with

Campbell; he was a good Master-at-Arms who did not compromise, and a steady coxswain on the wheel. The set of Campbell's gaunt head on that lean frame, even from the back, exuded confidence among those around him.

Hob Gamble enjoyed coming up here: the bridge, to him, seemed so leisurely after his mini-cockpit in *Perdix*.

'What brings you up into this rarefied atmosphere, Hob?' Neame was extracting himself from the chart table, which was centrally placed at the back of the bridge. Next to it, to port, was his navigational radar, screened by a black hood for night use.

'Perdix has her off days too,' Hob said. 'When's the captain expected?'

'Any moment, I hope. Defaulters ought to be finished soon ... *Jesse*'s been fuelling for over half an hour.' Neame nodded towards the American frigate, who was still hitched by her umbilical oil hose to the Dutch Fast Combat Support Ship, *Oileus*.

The officer of the watch replaced the engine-room phone. 'That's the Chief,' the sub reported to Neame. 'The engine room's at RAS Special Sea Dutymen.'

To the northward Hob picked out the remainder of the force: the Commodore in *Athabaskan* was in the act of altering to her new zigzag. It was a sparkling day, and the ocean was the deep, leaden blue of the Atlantic. The forecast was reasonable for the next twenty-four hours.

Hob glanced at his watch: 1022, and a lamp was winking from the *Jesse L. Brown*'s square bridge. He enjoyed these quiet moments when he could watch things. He was beginning to appreciate how the 260 officers and men worked their ship — often for the sole purpose of giving *Perdix* a platform from which to fly off to hunt submarines and surface ships below the horizon.

He had never regretted joining *Icarus,* when he had brought the new Mark VII Lynx with him. Neither had he regretted making the Royal Navy his life, to the chagrin of his father. The result of Mr Gamble's views on disarmament and lack of patriotism could have been predicted for any youngster of guts: Hob adopted a reciprocal course. He would fight for the things in which he believed. He knew he was something of an odd man out in these cynical days, but, being top pilot for last year's Search and Rescue stakes from Culdrose, his *Icarus* mess-mates had quickly learnt to respect him — and to give him a wide berth if argument touched him on the raw.

'Take cover!'

Hob heard the first lieutenant's whistle blast even from a distance, and saw the hole in the buffer's face as he repeated the warning. The RAS crew huddled behind the Exocets, hunched, their arms protecting their heads. These French surface missiles in their corrugated containers were a stopgap before the arrival of NATO's ASSM, and provided cover from the breaking seas for the foc's'le party.

The coston-gun line whistled overhead, and he watched the hands jumping to dash for the line sent over from *Oileus.* He'd been daydreaming, and had not noticed that Trevellion was now conning *Icarus* alongside. Hob nipped back into the bridge. This was *Icarus*'s thirty-fifth RAS since leaving Plymouth last June.

Captain Trevellion sat, relaxed and cross-legged, in the command chair. A charred pipe jutted from his mouth, its stench percolating through the enclosed bridge. Occasionally he would extract it from his mouth and turn to the coxswain to pass a wheel order. He never raised his voice, and seemed to expect the same sangfroid from others; he had ticked off the Royal Marine quartermaster and the sub, who had been nattering in the port corner.

Trevellion's head was slanted, as if he was instinctively feeling for the wind, one eye on *Oileus*'s massive grey side smashing through the seas only a cricket pitch's distance away. The distance line was being secured on *Icarus*'s for'd guard-rail, and from the starboard wing Number One was yelling at the hands who were hauling in the telephone cable, hand over hand.

'I'll ease back now, Cox'n. Steady on zero-zero-five.'

'Aye, aye, sir. Course zero-zero-five.'

The refuelling at sea continued, a routine for *Icarus*'s company, but a fresh experience for her new captain. *Oileus*, a purpose-built tanker of nineteen thousand tons complete with helicopter pads and hangar space for five machines, forged ahead at eighteen knots, conned by her master and a couple of officers who were gazing down from her port wings. No fuss, no shouting ... an officer by the fuelling derricks holding up the oiling procedure boards, that was all.

The jackstay was sent over, then run away by the *Icarus*'s RAS party. It was snap-shackled to the RAS anchor-point, abaft the starboard Exocet, while the fuelling derricks towered above the frigate, the bights of oil hose dangling and swinging above the threshing seas as *Oileus* surged ahead.

The captain nodded and the hose came sliding down the wire jackstay, the male connecting probe slamming home into the female cone at *Icarus*'s RAS-point.

'Start pumping.'

Hob glanced at the clock: 1039. The first lieutenant returned to the bridge and stood by the captain's chair. 'The Chief says about twenty minutes, sir, just a top-up.'

Hob saw the rubber pipe swell as the oil began pulsating through the hose which dangled from the stirrup slung from *Oileus*'s derrick heads.

At 1050 the RAS communication number shouted up to the first lieutenant, who was back again in the starboard wing.

'Ten minutes to go, sir.'

Number One nodded to the buffer, who was listening in on his walkie-talkie.

'Stand clear of the guard rails ... Stand by to slip the hose,' the buffer hollered.

Two seamen were bowlined to a safety line: then they crawled on hands and knees beneath the hose, to squeeze themselves between the casing of the Exocet and the exposed ship's side. The seas snarled against the ship's side as they prepared to knock off the slips.

Hob watched the buffer, his face red with anger beneath his beard, yelling at the awkward youngsters. The heaving line, which they were using as a lanyard for taking the weight while they undid the bottle-screws, had fouled round the guardrails. The first lieutenant was breathing down the buffer's neck from the starboard wing. Hob glanced at the bridge clock: 1052. The fuel tanks would be full at any minute.

'Three minutes to go for the next zig, sir,' Neame announced.

'Thirty degrees to port at 1055.'

The distance line was sagging between the ships — either *Icarus* or *Oileus* had taken a sheer.

'Watch your steering, Cox'n,' the captain commanded. 'Nothing to port.'

Hob watched the two ships crashing through the seas. He heard a shout. He swung round to see Firebrace's face turned towards the captain with a look of total disbelief. Speechless, he pointed to the flashing red light in front of him.

L/MEM Fane worked for an hour, heaving and shoving, trying to reassemble the bits and pieces into No. 2 diesel generator. He felt better, wringing the resentment from his system after the captain's punishment. The Old Man had certainly weighed off Ozzie and him. The seven days' leave did not matter so much, as they would be worked out before they got home — but a *thousand* quid, five hundred each, to pay that bugger in the Bunch of Grapes…

He had not had a chance to talk to Oz, but they would meet at supper. The Old Man obviously ran by the book, so the lads had better adjust their sights bloody quickly.

Fane wiped the back of his neck with the cloth he kept in his hip pocket. He had dispatched the MEM for his cuppa when 'stand easy' was piped. He'd be returning soon with a Coke, for Niv was too weary to traipse up a deck to the NAAFI. Instead, he slumped down on the upturned bucket in the corner and lit a cigarette — against orders down here, but what did it matter, given the risks he'd been running for so long?

His head jerked up as he heard the sharp hiss and the drop in revs from No. 1 diesel. He felt the thundering vibration, smelt the escaping fuel as the compartment was suddenly sprayed by the evil-smelling stuff — another shearing of the spill pipe. Jumping to his feet, he was blinded by a sheet of flame.

The searing heat hit Fane in the face as he leapt for the emergency stop button. There was an explosion — a white-hot blistering flash. He fell backwards as his existence disintegrated into a sheet of crimson flame and agonising pain.

Icarus's junior MEM had been down to the engine room only

once, when he had first joined the ship. He had spent two months watch-keeping in the boiler room, so was chuffed when the Chief MEM had told him to report to the engine room. That had been two days ago, but his new surroundings still awed him.

The boiler room, with its darting flames and the blazing furnace, was impressive enough. The superheated steam harnessed in those writhing steam pipes always made him think, and after listening to the Chief's description of a superheated steam blow-out, the sprog MEM remained apprehensive.

But he was more nervous of the engine room, because it was all so new — the gleaming machinery, the spotless footplates and the ladders running down to them; the shining paintwork and the stain of oil swilling in the white-painted bilges; the throttle valves which admitted superheated steam from the boiler rooms to the ahead turbines in their massive, snail-shell casings; the diminutive stern turbines and then the great cubes of the main gearing units. He was beginning to recognise it all, but it was difficult to believe that *he* was really here, on watch and entrusted to looking after this machinery…

He kept the log book, watching the pressures and temperatures, and entering up the readings every hour. His main duty was watch-keeping on the auxiliaries and the turbo generators, the high-revving, steam-driven turbines which supplied the ship's electricity. The high-pitched scream of the machines had unnerved him during his first watches, and even today he did not relish being too close to the turbo generators

He felt a tap on his shoulder as the leading hand of the watch beckoned him to come over and operate the main engine throttles. Those huge bulkhead stop-valves; the gleaming throttle wheels and the battery of gauges — the junior MEM breathed again when he was sent back to the turbos. He crossed to the starboard side, took the temperatures, watched the flickering needles on the pressure gauges. He dodged back to No. 2 on the port side, and stopped in front of the machine. Pressures? ... okay. Temperatures? He squinted again, feeling his heart jump ... what was happening? Did the reading usually shoot up like this?

He could see the column rising well into the red now. He turned, his face white. But his yell for help was drowned by a mounting scream as No. 2 turbo ran wild.

Even Hob Gamble had to admit that sometimes things moved fast on the bridge. It was 1053 when Neame shouted, 'Monitor's showing fire in the DG room, sir.'

Keeping his eyes firmly on the ship's head, Captain Trevellion rose from his chair. 'Take over from the Officer of the Watch, Pilot,' he ordered. 'Sub., go down and find out what's happening.'

The second hand on the bridge clock was ticking to 1054 when Neame said, 'One minute to go for the zig to port, sir.'

'Ten-degree steps?'

'Yes, sir. On the siren.'

'What's the delay in slipping the hose?' This was the first time Hob had heard the Old Man raise his voice. 'Buck up, and report when you're ready,' he snapped through the intercom at the first lieutenant. Hob watched Neame concentrating on the ship's heading of 005 degrees while he set the zigzag clock.

'Ten fifty-five, sir. Alter thirty degrees to port.'

Oileus's hooter boomed from somewhere above them.

'Port ten, Cox'n,' Trevellion ordered. 'Steer three-five-five.' He glanced at Neame. 'Pilot, reduce speed to fifteen knots.'

Hob felt the tension. This was hardly a propitious start for Trevellion's induction — being on the inside of the turn, *Icarus* must also knock down her speed or she would leap ahead and ram the oiler amidships.

From the wing, Number One was shouting down to the RAS party. Hob watched the ship's jackstaff sweeping gently across the horizon, steady up, then settle.

'Course, sir,' Campbell reported calmly from the wheel, 'three-five-five.'

Hob glanced at the grey slab side of the tanker towering above them. She was very, very close.

'Watch your steering, Cox'n,' the captain said quietly. 'Nothing to starboard.'

'Nothing to starboard, sir.'

Hob heard the crashing of the seas outside. He glanced at the clock. 1057 — the next zig was in thirteen minutes. He jumped when an alarm began ringing behind him.

'Steering breakdown, sir!' Neame yelled.

'What wheel have you on, Cox'n?'

'Five of starboard, sir!'

'Break away!' Pascoe Trevellion said crisply into the intercom. 'Stop port engine…'

'Wheel locked with five degrees of starboard on, sir,' Campbell reported tersely.

As *Icarus* lost way, she began to lose her relative bearing on *Oileus*.

'Break away!' The buffer was leaping for the RAS slip, where the man stood with the hammer; the oil hose was tautening, beginning to drag forward.

'Knock off the flaming thing!' the first lieutenant yelled through his loudhailer. The buffer snatched the hammer and clouted at the slip himself.

Hob felt the shiver as the wire jackstay, complete with probe, hose and roller jockey, flicked clear. *Icarus* was relentlessly swinging to starboard, her stern now abreast *Oileus*'s funnel and the towering superstructure of her after island.

'Full astern port engine.'

Trevellion's command cracked like a pistol shot. Hob held his breath as the quartermaster's fingers tore at the telegraphs. The two ships were separated by only a few yards ... in his imagination, Hob could hear the scream of tortured steel.

The telegraph repeat indicators flickered their response; the ship trembled, and when Hob looked up again he glimpsed the faces of Dutch seamen, peering down from the *Oileus*'s guard rails from her flight deck high above. The huge curve of her transom was rolling on top of *Icarus*'s jackstaff — and then the frigate was shuddering and pounding to the colossal astern power. The seas boiled white as *Icarus* was heeled over by the tanker's threshing wake.

Sparger felt the shock wave. Even from where he was sitting at his desk in his cabin, he knew instinctively whence the explosion originated: his cabin was two decks above the DO room. For months, day and night, he had been dreading it. As he reached for his cap, the fire alarm brayed through the ship.

He could smell the reeking fumes even before he reached the Burma Road — and then the stench of fire as he dropped down the second ladder. The hands were already unreeling the hose and wrenching at extinguishers.

The Chief Stoker was taking charge. While the firefighters were scrambling into their 'fearnought' gear, others were prising out the axes and reaching for the breathing sets. One of the ship's standing fire party had already 'crash-stopped' the ventilation.

'Fane's down there!' the sprog MEM screamed at the frenzied hands, his face white.

The Chief Stoker crouched over the CO_2 drenching valve to the DG room. He glanced at his MEO, the agonising question in his eyes.

'Hold on,' Sparger shouted. 'You ready, fire party?'

A white heat fanned from the DG hatchway; tongues of crimson flame darted through, while gobs of brown fumes billowed outwards. Sparger sprang backwards as the sheet of fire flayed his skin. The roaring conflagration drowned his orders as he watched the scene helplessly. A grotesque figure in a fire-fighting suit stumbled past, the nozzle hose in his gloved hands. Sparger felt the bulkhead doors thudding shut above him, heard the hatches slamming down.

The fire-fighter staggered backwards, his arm across his face. He shook his head, choking as the flames leapt higher, curling along the deckhead and the passageway. No man could have survived the inferno below, and the whole ship was now at risk.

'Open the drenching valve,' Sparger shouted, grabbing the fire-fighter's arm and pointing to the hatch still clipped back on its Samson post.

'Shut the hatch!'

The man lumbered forward; his ponderous gloves fumbled with the lock. He dragged at the hatch, lurched backwards and watched it crash on to its coaming.

Crouched over the open valve, the chief stoker stared up at Sparger. Glimpsing the momentary signal of understanding in the man's tormented eyes, Sparger stumbled aft, choking from the fumes and smoke. Someone caught him as he fell and bundled him over on his back. As they smothered the flames flickering across his clothing, Sparger passed out.

It was 1154 when he finally saw the temperatures dropping in the thermometer which was stuck on the outside of the hatch. The CO_2 drenching had been total. Even if the gas had not drowned the conflagration, the flames must have long been extinguished: the ventilation was still shut off, the hatch clipped down...

L/RO Osgood had been trying to reach the scene of the fire. They let him through, silently elbowing him towards the front of the fire-fighters as the ship wallowed, stationary, in the Atlantic.

'Chief Stoker!' Osgood shouted.

The sweating chief turned. 'Okay, Osgood. Put on a suit.'

The fire party took him down with them.

The silence was what unnerved Osgood most as he clambered down the ladder, the stillness in the compartment through which the air was blowing. When he reached the plates, still hot beneath his feet, a fire-fighter in a fearnought suit pushed him gently towards the port after corner of the DO room. Something lay on the deck on the far side of No. 2 generator, behind the ladder.

'Oh, Christ,' he whispered, his eyes focussing on what had once been Niv Fane. Oz bent down and pulled the gold ring from the remains of Niv's finger. It came away easily. He knelt down and felt the shrivelled flesh again, glancing over his shoulder as the leading medical assistant began slipping the Neil-Robinson stretcher beneath the remains. Oz covered the corpse with the blanket the LMA gave him, then they began the trek up the ladder and aft to the sick bay.

'C'mon, Osgood.'

It was the Master-at-Arms who took him by the shoulder and firmly pushed him from the green-painted compartment.

71

He led him back down the Burma Road to the Regulating Office.

'You'll be needing a tot,' was all Campbell said, closing the half-doors behind them.

It was 1730 when flying stations were piped. The ship had cleared *Oileus*'s counter by only a few feet and was under way again. She was steaming at twenty-five knots to catch up with STANAVFORLANT, the MEO having diagnosed the problem in the recalcitrant turbo: a matter of a faulty governor. Osgood had the first dog watch, but the chief radio supervisor had relieved him when the pipe — 'Hands lay aft for funeral service' — came through the general broadcast.

The cold breeze cutting across the quarterdeck jerked Osgood from his shocked state. He shook his head, sniffing the air, as he pulled the collar of his anorak about his ears. On the grid was the Lynx, the ship's flight party fussing about it while the pilot inspected the machine, peering beneath the fuselage, checking, always checking. The 'tell-tale' ribbons were fluttering in the breeze; dropping through the angry line-squall, the sun was already dipping towards the endless rows of white horses spilling along the horizon.

Silent officers and men fell in by divisions across the quarterdeck. A pathetic bundle, swathed in its white ensign, lay on the deck amidships, a few yards ahead of the Lynx's nose. Everyone not on watch seemed to be there. When Osgood reached the quarterdeck, the ranks shivered where room was made for him.

Oz could not absorb the reality of the moment. A few hours ago, he had been beating it up, ashore with Niv. When Oz had awkwardly tried to thank him for his support in the brothel, Niv had sworn at him and changed the subject.

And not even Merle would ever know now of the run ashore. Oz raised his head, half-turning towards *Icarus*'s port quarter where the sun's rays were piercing the dark clouds piling up to the westward. He closed his eyes, to blot out the images. Somehow, Niv's marriage with Gwen had appeared to reach deeper than Merle's and Oz's. Was it because the Fanes had four kids?

A shaft of sunlight shot through the orange-tipped cloud, the six men in the funeral party silhouetted against its light. They were in 'blues', the Master-at-Arms at attention in front of them, where they surrounded the shrouded body. Campbell had been drilling them the whole afternoon for this moment, and Fane would not have derided their efforts. Though the ceremonial of the next few minutes might compare abysmally with the professionalism of Whale Island, the simplicity was rendering the moment unbearably moving.

'Ship's company ... *'shun!*'

The first lieutenant was now standing by the hangar doors, and Oz watched him saluting as Captain Trevellion ranged down the starboard side, his tall frame swaying to the ship's roll. At the quarterdeck he halted; his hand came to the salute and remained there a full five seconds. The guard came to attention; the rifle butts thumped on the deck; the captain marched to the centre of the hollow square and faced Fane's shroud.

'Stand at ease,' he ordered the first lieutenant. He withdrew a scrap of paper from his pocket. 'The Commodore has sent us this signal,' he said. Then, raising his voice above the buffeting of the wind, he read the message.

TO ICARUS FROM SO. COM STANAVFORLANT. INFO ATHABASKAN, GOEBEN, JESSE L. BROWN. THE

FORCE SENDS ALL IN ICARUS ITS DEEP SYMPATHY
FOR THE FATAL ACCIDENT SUFFERED BY MARINE
ENGINEERING MECHANIC FANE. WE JOIN WITH
YOU THIS EVENING IN PRAYING TO ALMIGHTY
GOD THAT FANE'S SOUL MAY REST IN PEACE, AND
THAT HIS NEXT OF KIN MAY BE SUSTAINED AND
COMFORTED.

Trevellion folded the paper and replaced it in his pocket. His eyes rested on the crumpled ensign, then turned, deliberately meeting the gaze of all those gathered there with him.

'I have requested a full inquiry to be held,' he announced. 'I have asked the Marine Engineer Officer for a full report on the diesel generators and also for a record of his previous complaints on the state of the machines. He tells me that you will keep the DGS running until they are replaced or modified. I think you'll agree that this would be what Fane would have wanted.' The captain half-turned towards the overalled men who made up the engine-room department. 'Lieutenant Sparger tells me that Fane would never let up: he insisted on working upon the generators although he, more than anyone, knew what risks he was taking.'

He paused, then gazed upon the lonely bier. 'While there are men like Fane in the Navy, doing his duty as he felt it ought to be done, there can never be misgivings about the service. He will be taken over to *Glorious* who is eighty miles to the north-west. His family may wish to have his body flown home, but should they prefer it, L/MEM Fane will be buried at sea by *Glorious*'s chaplain with full naval honours.' Trevellion looked around again at the faces before him.

Oz's thoughts were back in Plymouth: if Gwen wanted Niv buried in Roborough, at least she would have Merle to comfort her.

'I never knew him as you did,' the captain said quietly. His words were easily heard above the wind, for he spoke clearly and without artificiality. 'I met him only once, as you know, at my table. I summed him up as a fine man then. We're having our own service for L/MEM Fane; I've taken the form from the naval prayer book. If anyone would like to leave for his own reasons, this is the moment to do so.'

Oz heard only the waves sluicing against the ship's side, the frapping of the wind against the superstructure. Somewhere there, below the lowering horizon, the carrier and her group were steaming for the Azores, where Fane's body would be flown by one of *Glorious*'s Sea Kings.

'Off caps.'

Behind the Master-at-Arms, Oz caught sight of the observer and the pilot struggling to remove their 'bone dome' helmets. Niv would have liked that bit; he had always savoured the ludicrous, though he always respected other people's feelings. He was no sneerer like Mick Foulgis. Oz caught the Irishman's eyes calmly appraising the scene; so Mick the Moaner had decided to come after all.

Oz had never been a religious man. He'd never been forced to think about it: life was too full. Courage was needed these days to stand up and be counted. But on this evening, at sea in the open Atlantic, with the ensign spread across the deck, the ancient formula stirred his emotions. The words which the captain was reading could not be ignored; these awesome phrases from the burial service jolted Osgood into understanding these solemn words for the first time. His eyes riveted upon Niv's mortal remains, Oz assimilated every word.

He turned to the westward, where the faint outline of *Jesse L. Brown* was dipping into the swell, sheets of spume flying across her bridge as she plunged out of phase with the swell. The starkness of death had a remarkable effect on his concentration, he thought: for the first time, he was beginning to have an inkling as to why he was out here in the Atlantic, far off the shipping lanes, with thousands of other seamen, burning up their lives to guard against a nightmare which civilians hoped would go away.

Niv's funeral service ended quietly with the muttered *Amen*s of the ship's company.

'On caps. Face aft.'

The rotor blades of Hob's helicopter swirled, gathering speed as the jet engines warmed up. The high-pitched scream became overwhelming ... and then *Perdix* was ready, the pilot visible in his cockpit, the observer at his side, engrossed in his pre-flight checks. The funeral party bent down, then carefully handled the ensign-covered stretcher through the helicopter's open door.

The flight deck officer was watching the captain. Trevellion's mouth opened, he nodded his head, and then Lieutenant Towke was talking into his mike. The Master-at-Arms was bawling at his six-man guard, drawn up in line across the stern.

The rotors swirled, the air pounded, the jets screamed. Hob Gamble suddenly lifted her off. Oz glimpsed, through the open door, the flash of crimson and white on the ensign. The helicopter steadied, then dipped her nose in salute as the side door closed. She canted to port, then swooped away, climbing, disappearing into the twilight for her rendezvous with *Glorious*.

Though the weather improved as *Perdix* flew northwards, the last of the evening twilight was fading before Rollo Daglish,

Hob's observer, caught sight of *Glorious*. He saw first the slick of her wake, then her awkward shape ahead, eight hundred feet below.

They had talked little during their flight: it was difficult to realise that in the cab a few feet behind them lay the remains of one of their shipmates. Rollo never talked much, even on the ground. Hob liked him, a buttoned-up individual, except for his rare outbursts. He was a General List officer, an ex-Dart, who had made flying his vocation. He was a keen but self-effacing observer — and never, though eight months senior and two years older, pulled his seniority on Hob, who was a Supplementary List officer holding a Type B commission for helicopter flying duties…

'Okay, Hob,' he said into the mike strapped about his throat. 'Spot seven — you can go in now.'

'She's showing up like a house, even with her night deck-lighting.'

He put down *Perdix*'s nose and let her drop from the sky. He'd show these Sea King boys a thing or two — half their pilots were only recently 'frontline' and had been in the Navy only two and a half years. He knew that they'd be on the quarterdeck, or in Flyco, the flight commander's bridge which protruded above the flight deck, on the port side of the island. They would be watching the approach of this Mark VII, the new Lynx, a machine they ached to fly.

At a hundred feet, he pulled her out and lined up on the centre line. 'They've got a reception committee,' Rollo said. 'Both sides.'

'Not for us.' Hob was concentrating now, watching the eerie violet lights sliding up to meet him. There was the batsman, his luminous truncheons flickering weirdly. *Perdix* was over the round-down and Hob felt the draught snatch at her, as he went into the hover ... *gently does it ... there ... smack on spot seven.*

He listened to the deck procedures from Flyco, saw the handlers dodging beneath the cab, received the okay to run down. He cut the engines and, as always thankful to be down, he waited for the rotor to lose momentum...

'Okay, Rollo.'

'I'll open the door.'

Hob could see through his window the motionless silhouettes of the guard. At least twenty-four file, the officer of the guard out in front, the commander, the carrier's executive officer, to one side. Even after sunset they were paying Fane their respect.

If there had been no 'Clear Lane' exercise, and if the Lynx's visit to the carrier had not been such a solemn occasion, Hob and Rollo would have been dined that night by the squadron. But the refuelling of *Perdix* gave them a chance to meet their Culdrose cronies — it did everyone good to swap experiences during these NATO exercises. As soon as *Perdix* had landed, *Glorious* increased to maximum cruising speed to close the Azores. The MoD had signalled that, at the request of the next of kin, Fane's body was to be flown home. The Navy's welfare organisation, Hob acknowledged, was first rate. A carrier was being diverted at speed for some four hundred miles.

'Beer, Hob?'

'Squash, please.'

They were sitting in the aircrew mess. It was good relaxing here in their flying gear, yarning of Culdrose and catching up with the latest gossip. Before coming out to *Glorious*, one of the pilots had bumped into Allie, Hob's wife.

'She's not missing you, Hob.' The man was grinning.

'Sure…?'

'She's okay.'

Hob wasn't listening as he stared at the garish prints of Scotland stuck on the bulkhead. He could see her, his Allie, tall and slender, with the laughter in those restless dark eyes. She was on night duty during the heavy flying spell.

'…and I took her out to dinner.' The pilot glanced at Hob from the corner of his eye. They laughed: a 'frontline' pilot's girl was sacrosanct.

'And how d'you like your Mark VII Lynx?' someone asked.

'Scruffy little thing.'

Inevitably they talked shop: if you spent your working life in the air, the stress produced a remarkable interest in the machine you were flying. Hob knew every nut and bolt, every peculiarity that was *Perdix*. 'They've given her enough power this time, which was what we all worried about,' he said.

And then they talked of the Mark VII's role, the new generation of Lynx which frigates now carried. This helicopter was part of the ship's weapons system, but the Lynx's prime roles were to detect and attack submarines at long-ranges before the Russian nuclear boat could launch her attack on the parent frigate, and to destroy with its four Sea Skua missiles enemy surface ships at ranges below the horizon.

And so they went on. The Mark VII Lynx, having been dispatched to destroy the enemy submarine whose approximate position had already been relayed from the RAF's LRMP (Long Range Maritime Patrol), would first localise the contact. An automatic system was provided for accurately pinpointing the target's and the helicopter's positions relative to the frigate.

The Mark VII Lynx was fitted with the latest ASW weapon to be produced by the boffins: the 196 'Active' Short-Range

Sonar Buoy ASRB. Dropped in the vicinity of the suspected contact, the buoy automatically 'pinged', transmitting its readings back to the mini-computer for analysis in the Lynx. Tied to the sonar plot, the active short-range sonobuoy greatly enhanced the Lynx's role in hunting and attacking submarines. Although still fitted with MAD (Magnetic Anomaly Detector) the Active short-range sonobuoy was vastly increasing range detection and thereby providing real killer capability to the Mark VII. Data-linked to the ship, which could be forty miles away below the horizon, the ship-borne Lynx-helicopter system was carrying ASW warfare deep into the enemy's back yard.

'What fish are you using now?' someone asked.

'The Mark 46. Bloody good Yank torpedo,' Hob said.

'And if you've a surface target?'

Hob explained that the Mark VII was fitted with Sea Skuas, a surface-skimmer missile integrated with the Lynx's electronic support measures and Sea Spray radar. The system was an automatic air-to-surface weapon which needed no aimer — and was difficult for the enemy to counter.

'She's a good bit of kit, without a doubt,' said one of the pilots. 'Coffee, Rollo ... Hob?'

They were due to take off at 2130, the briefing being in half an hour's time. The coffee did its stuff; Hob relaxed and was enjoying being with the squadron again.

'Your Lynx will never replace a Sea King, though,' commented an older pilot, 'however versatile this new Mark VII may be.'

'Okay, okay,' Hob said, grinning. 'It's all right for you and your lumbering mastodons. At worst, you work in pairs, seldom alone, out ahead. We're on our tod, bloody miles out.

If I have an enemy nuke under me, even if I'm on MAD, I'm never absolutely certain that he doesn't know I'm there.'

'He'll never know if you're passive. You'd get him on Sea Spray if he used his stick,' the tall pilot said.

'That's what we all say,' Hob replied. 'My point is, we assume they play to our rules. I bet they don't.'

'Our submariners don't feel happy when there's a chopper around, and I don't suppose the Russians do either. They'd knock us out of the sky if they could.'

'It's unlikely they've got anything,' Hob said. 'We gave up SLAM, remember?' He was talking about the converted army "Blowpipe" weapon which had had six missiles grouped circularly on one of the submarine's masts and a TV camera on the other.

'She disclosed her presence the moment she fired — that was the official line for why they abandoned the project. But, of course, the real reason was money.'

'The Russians haven't got it,' Rollo added. 'That's what we were told.'

'My point,' Hob said, 'is that when a new weapon shows up, the Russians immediately counter it.' He downed his coffee. 'Come on. Let's go.'

Hob and Rollo collected their bone domes and made their way out of the aircrew mess. 'Thanks, you guys,' said Hob. 'Things are hotting up, if what they tell us is the truth,' he added.

CHAPTER 8

HMS Icarus, 14 December.

Corporal Roderick Burns, Royal Marines, wished now that he had told Mick Foulgis to get stuffed. Foulgis, though a highly competent aircraft handler, was a disrated Leading Airman (for what reason, Burns had never been able to discover); he was also a persistent scrounger. He had invited himself into the Royals' mess for this Friday night — and then arranged for his cronies to come. The mess was crammed, but the watchkeepers were not yet ready to turn in: most were enjoying their pre-supper can. Foulgis had turned up with a load of cans, probably scrounged off the newly-joined innocents.

Burns knew that his mess — a deck lower down, snug and out of the way — was popular. *Icarus*'s detachment of nine Royal Marines were a happy lot. Burns was in a good billet: his CO, Captain Richard Stoddart, was absent for another three weeks, lent temporarily to HMS *Gloucester,* the latest of the Type 42 destroyers. Stoddart was a good boss; younger than Burns, he was intelligent enough to realise that his corporal thrived on using his own initiative. Happily leaving Burns in charge of the detachment, Stoddart was attempting, in three weeks, to set *Gloucester*'s Royals on the right lines.

'Evening all...'

The visitors scrambled down the ladder. Behind them was Charlie Owen, the Lynx's SMR (Senior Maintenance Rating), who was borne on *Icarus*'s books when the flight was carried. Charlie and Burns shared common interests, both with responsibilities above the ordinary; both were 'outsiders' in *Icarus*'s ship's company.

'Oz here yet?' Foulgis was asking. 'Where's he been since *Perdix* got back from *Glorious*?' He accepted the can held out to him and wrenched the tag open.

Rod Burns listened to the hum of conversation, but he longed for a bit of peace, as he had done ever since that sad Monday. Oz had taken Fane's death badly, keeping his lone vigil in the chill of the night, sheltering in the lee of the hangar, waiting for the Lynx's return. They had left him to himself. Not until he was convinced that *Perdix* was empty did he go below — and then he went straight to his middle watch on the teleprinters.

Oz's mess-mates had blamed shock and lack of sleep for his withdrawal into himself. Niv had been killed, Mick was insinuating, for doing more than was expected of him. 'It's murder, I say.' The Irishman, in the centre of the shocked circle, had relished the silence — until Oz had told him to shut his gob.

The next day, Wednesday, the government pay announcement was on the notice boards; an hour later, the captain made his broadcast; then Lieutenant Commander Farge gave his sitrep on the initial proposals announced by the government, the details being announced by MoD later in the week. The first impression was much better than hoped for; the new government did at least realise the priorities. Then yesterday — Thursday — the Foxer had been lost.

Someone had slipped up in the Foxer drill: a relay had inadvertently not been switched off and the expensive decoy had cut itself adrift, to plunge to the bottom of the Atlantic. There had been an inquiry, but no one had come forward to accept the blame. It was lucky that a prowling Russian AGI had not got the buzz: NATO's countermeasures against their homing torpedoes would have been compromised in one fell swoop.

Burns swigged at his beer. This cat-and-mouse intelligence war seemed to have no end. The next war would be won by the side that knew most about the enemy's weapons, and then acted quickly on that knowledge — hence the presence of the AGIS whenever NATO concentrated its forces — and also the tightening of NATO's own security measures. Rod Burns shook his head: it had been a bad week so far for *Icarus* and her new captain.

Burns was keeping an open mind about the Old Man. Captain Trevellion was a close one as yet — he seemed to be biding his time. A different sort to his predecessor, he seemed buttoned up, watching things, never needled, however bad the mistakes — and he had had every excuse to lose his cool this week as the force had zigzagged across the Atlantic towards Gibraltar.

'Cheers, Oz — here's your can.'

The L/RO had joined them, unnoticed and morose. He unpeeled his can and took a long swig. He belched.

'Better, Oz?' Mick grinned. 'Plenty more.'

And so the evening began. The loud-mouthed steward, a wretched whining runt, held the stage, bellyaching as usual. He was going outside — the Navy would be well rid of him, though he himself thought he was indispensable. Mick lapped up the gems that the stewards relayed from the wardroom, but most men treated the gossip with sardonic amusement. And now, inevitably, they were beefing about the pay deal ... Foulgis, as usual, provided all the answers, stirring it over the recent pay announcement. Burns noted with distaste that

Foulgis was continually topping up the young steward with beer and stoking the fires of discontent.

At last Oz spoke. 'It's not *just* pay; we count for nothing in civvy street.'

Foulgis looked up. 'What they pay us, Oz, is what they think of us.'

'It goes deeper than that,' Oz said. 'They don't seem to care no more. We're always being told we're the same as everyone else.' Oz thumped the mess table angrily. 'But the Navy *is* bloody different.'

'We'll be special enough when the Russians come,' Burns said. 'But by then it'll be too late.'

'It's the smug way they talk about things that gets on my wick,' Oz said. 'I told you, the Navy's different to the other services; *we* know that. We live at sea for months on end; our way of life's different, so how can they compare us? But look at the poor bloody RAF — *seven* squadrons to defend the whole of Britain ... Seven squadrons. It'll be the same as '39.' He laughed bitterly. 'Pathetic.'

'You can't blame the politicians for everything,' Burns said. 'They haven't the guts to tell us the truth.'

'Like this ship,' Mick Foulgis said. 'We're like mushrooms: we're kept in the dark and we're fed on shit.'

'Come off it, Mick,' Charlie Owen interrupted. 'What about the sitreps? They try to tell us what's going on.'

Mick was pouring the steward another beer. 'It's not my fault I'm uneducated,' he said scornfully. 'I'm fighting a losing battle with my postal City & Guilds. The stuff's too technical, they just leave you to get on with it.'

'Where does it go wrong, then, Mick?' Oz asked unemotionally. 'You beef a hell of a lot, but how d'you put things right?'

Then Charlie chipped in. 'No *real* communication is encouraged, Oz, between junior rates and the officers.' He looked across at Foulgis. 'At least not in this ship.'

'Course it bloody ain't. The Navy's still run on class distinction.'

'Rubbish…' Oz held out his hand for another can. 'Bloody rubbish, Mick, and you know it.'

'Yeah? What about when we get into Lisbon? The wardroom'll be quite happy to let us fester down here, while they're having their cock-and-arse parties on the flight deck.'

The young steward was weaving unsteadily on his feet. 'Yush — you're quite right, Mick — if you ask me—' He lurched suddenly, looking green about the gills.

'Bucket!' Burns shouted.

He was too late: the wretched steward had doubled up and was spewing across Foulgis's shoes. The stench was revolting.

'Mop it up,' Burns growled. 'It's your fault, Foulgis.'

Mick was grinning. 'He's only a lad. Not like you, Bootie, trained to be men … we're just kids, us matelots.'

'What you getting at, Mick?' Burns felt his anger getting the better of him. He stood up, carefully set down his beer. Foulgis was opening yet another can and was leering up out of the corner of his eyes.

'The Officer of the Day came into the mess during our last night in Bermuda,' Mick said. 'Pulled out the television aerial; ordered us to turn in because it was 2300. "We're at sea tomorrow, lads," he told us. "And you'll be up all night".' Foulgis laughed bitterly. 'We're treated like children.' He spat out the words. 'Petty rules … that's why I'm going outside.'

'Bloody good thing,' Oz added. 'You're always pissed; you keep us awake half the night.'

'And some of you scabbed to the divisional officer,' Foulgis shouted. 'I know — you asked him to run me in—' He was yelling, his piggy eyes ugly. 'The DO hasn't the guts, you'll see!'

'You're pissed now,' Oz said.

'You bloody creeper ...'spose you'll pay Niv's part of the damages, won't you?' He flung the words at Oz. 'I'd tell 'em to stuff it up their arse!'

'Shut up and mop up the puke,' Burns said. 'Then get to hell out of our mess.'

'Do it yerself...' and Foulgis began lurching towards the ladder. Burns thumped him hard across the jaw. As Foulgis slithered and fell, Burns heard footsteps on the ladder behind him.

''Ere,' rasped a familiar voice. 'What's going on?'

Burns swung round, wiping bits of skin from his knuckles. The Fleet Master-at-Arms stood before him. His clear blue eyes were pitiless, steady and very, very daunting.

CHAPTER 9

HMS Icarus, 15 December.

Pascoe Trevellion sat in his command chair and stared towards the horizon, where the silhouette of the American frigate merged with the rain squalls. For the first time since joining *Icarus* nine days ago he was beginning to feel part of her: not merely her official 'driver' as he had felt when conning *Icarus* out of Bermuda dockyard for the first time, but her captain. His ship's company had been assessing him for over nine days and had certainly not deprived him of incidents upon which they could base their shrewd judgement. 'Command' must be one of the loneliest jobs in the world.

This Saturday morning he had taken a decision which could not please everyone. Things would have been different if he could have more confidence in his first lieutenant. Jewkes was too affable, and too frequently Trevellion sensed he was resented.

Watching the force steaming across the horizon, Trevellion mulled over the events of the past week. Jewkes clearly did not rate with the Chief, the WEO or most of the other two-and-a-halves. He had lost no time in hinting how much Trevellion's predecessor had been liked, how the chap had entered into things, looked the other way more often than not, and made sure that his blind eye did not go unremarked. Trevellion found it hard to dismiss from his mind his doubts on Jewkes's total loyalty, ever since the first day.

'Two minutes to the zig, sir. Thirty degrees to port.' Lieutenant Samuel Gubbay was Officer of the Watch; he was also the Senior Watchkeeper, so Trevellion could rely on him — Gubbay was a fine officer, brought up the hard way, an ex-GI with Whale Island behind him. These men, a dying breed, stood out from the rest these days and confirmed Trevellion's definite views on discipline — just as the perpetual balls-ups during these last days underlined that *Icarus*, at the moment, was anything but the sort of frigate for which the Second Sea Lord yearned. Trevellion was sure of one thing: if a loafer was allowed to get away with it, the resulting cancer destroyed a ship's morale more swiftly than any other disease. *Icarus*'s better characters seemed to be landing in trouble, which was worrying though not surprising: there was a limit to forbearance and frustration.

Osgood had been indirectly involved with the fracas in the Royal Marines' mess, but there was no charge against him. He had appeared at the defaulters' table only as a witness to last night's stupidity, resulting in Corporal Burns being charged with striking a junior rating. It could not have come at a more awkward moment, so soon after Fane's death.

The Hamilton police were unlikely to allow that case to lapse. Trevellion had known that something was in the wind when Number One and the Master-at-Arms had come to him discreetly on Wednesday: would it be within the rules if the ship had a whip-round? And could the canteen funds be used to help out Osgood, who now had to pay the total bill? The obvious hint had been dropped that the two men had reacted as anyone worth his salt would have done. The status of the Royal Navy was a sensitive matter at this moment.

'New course, sir, zero-five-five,' Gubbay reported. 'Next alteration to starboard in seventeen minutes.'

'Very good.'

The pay announcement had left the Navy unmoved. Under previous governments the forces had been led to believe that efforts would be made to achieve parity with civilians. But only the nurses, the sailors, soldiers and airmen, because of their innate loyalty and the restraint imposed by the Services' Acts, could be safely ignored by the politicians. To volunteer for being shot in the back in Ulster, disintegrating in a fireball at Mach 1.5, or being overwhelmed by an implosion at depth in a submarine, requires a fundamental appeal to a young man's spirit — not his pocket. The ideal of patriotism, not necessarily only for one's own country, was as true and essential today as ever it was — perhaps more so, to combat the sinister evils now arrayed against mankind; and the natural urge of belonging to an elite band of comrades, so proudly demonstrated by the genuine coalminer, was a basic instinct of man.

To be proud of himself, and of the service in which he was giving his life, man needed a positive sense of status. For most British citizens, 'status' nowadays meant money. To evince public esteem, the sailor, soldier and airman had to be slotted high in the snakes-and-ladders status game — on which, as defenders of the realm and its people, they deserved to be.

Trevellion, during his two years at MoD, had seen how the Navy's bosses spent most of their time waging war against the bureaucrats instead of the potential enemy. He had seen the Defence Chief, an Admiral of the Fleet, grey with anxiety and fatigue after a heavy week battling for funds and for the research technology without which the Royal Navy must deteriorate into a coastal force, unable even to defend the British Isles from landings from the sea. 'Over-stretch' (the current jargon for working with too few men under wartime conditions, but without the shooting) eventually sapped a man's determination to stay in. Trevellion was convinced that the serviceman felt he was regarded as a sucker to be working such hours for so little cash; that he belonged to a forgotten service; that he was meat for the sacrifice when the shooting started...

Trevellion pulled himself together, slid from his chair and checked the position on the chart. Number One would be up at any minute to take him down to the wardroom where the chiefs and petty officers would be gathering. It was the loss of the Foxer on Wednesday, 12 December which had finally crystallised Trevellion's thoughts. The WEO's inquiry had been entirely negative. So many incidents, both trifling and serious, had happened in the short time since he had taken command. No one, not even a senior rating, had come forward with an explanation for the loss of the decoy, and Trevellion had spent a sleepless night analysing each incident and every lapse. He knew he was blessed with intelligence, and Rowena had often told him she was shocked by his ruthlessness when he wanted to achieve a goal he knew to be right.

His conclusions, at the end of the long night, had not been pleasant. He had recorded his opinions — and his intended remedies — in writing and locked the record in his safe. Very soon, after talking frankly with his senior men, he would know whether they diagnosed the same ills, and afterwards he would talk to his officers. He had decided not to share his thoughts with Number One but to have him present, in his capacity as second-in-command, at the chief's meeting.

He sensed Jewkes standing behind him. 'The chief and petty officers are mustered in the wardroom, sir.'

Trevellion returned the salute and walked briskly from his bridge.

They stood up when Captain Trevellion entered. He took the chair at the head of the table and, in silence, allowed his glance to pass round the gathering, meeting each of his senior men squarely in the eye.

'Please sit down, gentlemen.'

The meeting was soon relaxed, the petty officers fully aware of their captain's request that, for the benefit of *Icarus* and the Navy, the views for which he was asking must be frank. As Trevellion had asked, the Master-at-Arms had obtained the views of the senior leading hands. Their opinions would have been carefully considered: their recommendations would be for the good of the service. Trevellion was prepared to be hurt, if the process he had instigated was to be of any value.

The Master led off, listing the leading hands with whom he had talked. The others followed, in formal seniority, each summarising his views on what was wrong in the Navy. There was little interruption and much of the criticism was repetition, though couched in different terms.

Only a quarter of an hour had elapsed when Trevellion opened the proceedings for general discussion. He sat back, determined to listen, to offer no excuses, make no defence.

It was a shock to listen to these men talking so passionately about the Service they had served for much of their lives. If they criticised, it was not to destroy, but to remedy and to improve — and they evidently realised what enormous difficulties their leaders had surmounted to build today's fleet. Trevellion felt a prick of pride at having been selected to lead men such as these sitting at the table around him. They were the cream, the backbone of Britain; and the Navy had fashioned them, the finest professional sailors in the world. But, if his instinct was right, why were they so unsure for its future? Why were they leaving in such disturbing numbers?

'We've moaned for a long time, sir,' the Master-at-Arms said, 'and I don't want you to think that there's too much wrong with the Navy. There's still a lot right, good things like comradeship and runs ashore…'

'When you're not under the glare of the missus,' said the chief stoker, and they all chuckled.

In the silence that followed, Trevellion rose to his feet. 'I've listened to you, gentlemen,' he said. 'As it happens, I agree with most of what you've said. You've confirmed my personal opinions and I intend to do something about it. I shall be speaking to my —' he corrected himself — 'our officers tonight.'

'Excuse me, sir,' the Master said. 'D'you mean to change things?' His sandy eyebrows were arched, a couple of half-moons above his steely eyes.

'With your general approval,' the captain said. 'After all, we're still a democracy.' He smiled as he looked up, first at Number One and then at each member at the table.

'That's what we'd like, sir,' the Master-at-Arms said quietly.

'That's what we're looking for and we'll back you and your officers all the way, sir.' He pushed back his chair. 'We'll show 'em, sir, who's the crack ship in the fleet.'

'I'll have prayers on the flight deck tomorrow,' the captain said. 'I'll speak to everyone there — and over the broadcast system to those on watch.'

They stood back for him as he made for the door. For the first time since taking command of *Icarus,* he felt the warmth of loyalty, of comradeship, as they held open the door for him.

CHAPTER 10

HMS Icarus, 17 December.

Captain Pascoe Trevellion had snatched an early breakfast because the 'Clear Lane' war simulation exercise was due to become hot at 1000. He realised that he would be on his feet for most of the time over the next ten days.

Since clearing the Narrows in Bermuda, the force was enjoying what was euphemistically termed a 'period of tension' when diplomatic relations between the enemy and NATO were assumed to be strained. At long last even the politicians had ceased to dress up the identification: in the exercise orders, the enemy was Russia, and it did everybody good to know that the hypocrisy was over.

For the 'Clear Lane' exercise STANAVFORLANT had remained on White Alert for the last few days, but had come to Blue this morning at dawn: the radar contacts had been picked up during the night. As the visibility improved, the identification of two ships acting as Russian destroyers was confirmed by *Jesse*'s LAMPS helicopter, which had been sent up to shadow. First light proved the report right, though the exercise orders described the destroyers as different classes: *Gloucester,* one of the latest Type 42s, represented a Kashin who was shadowing on the other side of the force: and *Phoebe,* representing a Krivak, was tailing *Icarus* at half a mile.

I suppose it could *happen like this,* Trevellion thought, *but it seems too unreal.* The MoD and NATO staffs had a difficult task planning these exercises years in advance.

He strolled out to the wings to sniff the air before the curtain went up. The sea sparkled where the sunlight touched the breaking waves. Spume drifted upwards from *Icarus*'s dipping bows, floated in rainbow arcs against the horizon, dissipated, then flung high again in ceaseless succession. The waves curled, breaking into white horses at the crests. It was a perfect day for a submarine at periscope depth: impossible to sight her sticks in this sea state, but the wind was not kicking up the sea too hard to prevent periscopes being picked up on radar. To the northward Trevellion sighted the dim shape of *Gloucester* — the Krivak — who had been modified to carry two of the Mark III Sea Harriers.

Trevellion sucked in a draught of the sweet air, a welcome change to the potted stuff inside *Icarus*'s citadel. His watch showed 0820 as he kept an eye on the Krivak following in *Icarus*'s wake. But in reality, what a contrast to a Krivak was *Phoebe,* that splendid frigate, neatly scything through the seas as she shadowed at four hundred yards. Her Exocets, with a range of twenty miles, did not compete with a Krivak's striking power, but were devastating against surface ships within range.

Phoebe was the crack ship of the force: she had put in more steaming time out here in the Atlantic than most. Hamish Carnegie had forged a good ship's company into a first-rate fighting team: in *Phoebe,* his officers rolled up their sleeves and mucked in whenever the occasion demanded. Yet she was run with a firm discipline; Hamish, with his humour and light touch, had managed to strike a happy balance. She was a taut ship. Trevellion felt he could not go far wrong if he emulated Hamish Carnegie's example.

'No more Christian names,' Trevellion had told his officers on the Sunday. 'Address ratings and officers by their rates and ranks; caps are to be worn on the upper deck at all times in harbour; have as few rules as possible, but enforce them rigidly; never turn a blind eye to drunkenness on board, which is a serious offence; uphold a high personal standard of behaviour and language; never admonish a senior rating in front of a junior; never discuss officers in front of ratings, nor among yourselves; and all officers are to set a dignified example of dress when ashore.'

To the surprise of *Icarus*'s officers, the majority of ratings wished to go ashore in uniform. One of them had told the Master-at-Arms, 'Once we've left the service, most of us want to be identified with the Navy; we wear lapel badges or even naval ties. So why can't we show it while we're still in? And the birds like the uniforms.'

The wardroom had been amazed, but had accepted the innovation cheerfully. It would be interesting to see how many other ships would follow suit. Trevellion decided to give this fresh disciplinary approach a three-month trial.

Trevellion had been too long out here in the wings — *Phoebe*'s bow was scything through the water, less than two cables off the port quarter. With her mythical potential, she was only too lethal for the less powerful *Icarus,* though not at this range — but Hamish Carnegie would never throw away a trick, so what was he up to?

Trevellion glanced at his watch: 0845. *Phoebe* was heeling as she turned away and increased to full speed, her wash threshing white in the deep indigo of the ocean. Hamish was opening the range, as a real Krivak would do...

Trevellion had noticed that the men seemed reluctant to disclose their reactions to the decisions he had announced, after the short Sunday service which he had conducted yesterday. He had been determined to hold the church service despite the imminence of 'war'. He wanted, first, to show what he believed in and the spiritual values for which the free world was prepared to fight. Even Trevellion was surprised by the response, particularly from the younger element. He had glimpsed Osgood there, tucked away at the back against the hangar door, but he had not caught sight of Burns, the Royal Marine corporal.

Trevellion had considered very carefully what to do about the corporal. He had 'stood over' Burns's case; he needed time to consider the evidence. He had to uphold discipline without hurting the splendid soldier. So Captain Trevellion had not removed his stripe, though he punished him with the maximum allowed — a colossal fine and stoppage of leave. Corporal Burns had not appreciated the relatively harmless punishment, which was probably why no Royal Marine attended the Sunday service. Why was it, Trevellion asked himself bitterly, that it was so often the good men who took the can in a slack ship? Osgood was in the same mould as Burns.

It was regrettable that no one in the Royals' mess had pinned anything on Foulgis, the troublemaker. Being the lower deck sea-lawyer, no one had wanted to pin on him the only charge possible: the hoarding of beer. How else could that steward have become sloshed on the official two cans a day? Burns had refused to cast insinuations, but the Master had sized up the situation accurately enough ... and why did *Icarus*'s officers not know what was going on?

He had gathered his wardroom officers into his cabin and, with brutal frankness, listed incident after incident. He described in meticulous detail where he judged his officers to have fallen below the standards he expected. He had referred to none of them by name. At the conclusion the senior types were anxious to show their loyalty, refusing to gainsay his ruthless summing-up.

Then Jewkes cleared his throat. 'We're a bit shocked, sir,' he had said. 'With respect,' (how Trevellion detested this euphemism!) 'with respect, sir, you're being a bit unkind. This is how we did things before, with your predecessor.'

'Well, you won't from now on, First Lieutenant. I expect complete loyalty from you all. And I look to every one of you to give what the ship's company seeks but hasn't been getting: firm and impartial leadership.'

Perhaps he had been unfair? In the loneliness of his bridge, Trevellion experienced a fleeting moment of regret: perhaps he had been too hard on them.

Pascoe saw the navigating officer standing in the screen door, a signal in his hand. 'From the Senior Officer, sir — Blue Alert. Assume State Two.'

Trevellion returned to the bridge: things were hotting up. He could meet aggression with aggression ... he smiled to himself as he watched the 'Krivak' creaming into the distant horizon. Hamish had done his homework: the exercise was due to start at ten, and a Krivak with her SSN 14s could out-range *Icarus* from far below the horizon. *Okay, Hamish* ... Trevellion smiled as he picked up the telephone to the flight deck officer.

'FDO — bridge.'

'Captain here. Is *Perdix* ready?'

'Ready to take off, sir.'

'Take off. I'm turning into wind.' He nodded to the officer of the watch. 'Bring her round, Gubbay.'

Jewkes was on the bridge, binoculars jammed beneath his ginger eyebrows. 'She's steaming, sir.'

'Go to action stations, Number One.'

Jewkes moved to the port console and picked up the broadcast mike.

Osgood was fed up with the bickering in the Greenies' mess. He had come in for a soothing smoke before returning to the office to finish repairing the latest teleprinter to go on the blink. He had never known the mess, normally a happy one, to be so divided into cliques. In running the mess he had counted Foulgis as an oppo, but now he was certainly living up to his name as Mick the Moaner. Mick appeared to revel in stirring it among the junior ratings — and Oz had had enough.

Mick had been at them ever since the captain's homily at 'church' on the flight deck yesterday. Ridiculing the new order, Mick was presenting the case for firmer discipline as high-handed autocracy for which Captain Trevellion had neither the power nor the mandate. Something flared inside Oz.

'For Christ's sake, Mick, turn it in. Our mess is becoming worse than Speakers' Corner.'

There was a hush in the small compartment, the pounding of the screws the only background noise. Then Foulgis guffawed — a scornful, unpleasant sound.

'So you've fallen for it too, Oz?' Mick glanced round the sea of faces. Osgood watched the nervous grins of the uncommitted. 'L/RO Osgood: our good, loyal leading hand of the mess,' Mick jeered. 'Creeper to the pigs.' He blew a jet of tobacco smoke in Oz's direction.

'I reckon the skipper's right,' Osgood said calmly. 'Most of us want discipline. You shouldn't have joined if you don't like it, Mick.'

'Captain Bligh's not within his rights,' Foulgis said. 'He's forcing things on us — things outside the regulations.'

'Mick's right,' one of the visiting stewards said. 'He's going to write to his MP.' Osgood saw the satisfied smirk on the youngster's face.

'So what?' Oz said. He looked at Foulgis in disgust. 'Why don't you just slap in a transfer to the glorious Red Fleet?'

They were both standing, measuring up. Osgood hated Mick's guts at that moment, but for the first time in the mess he felt on his own.

'Ever since they killed Niv,' Foulgis added, 'you've been a bloody blackleg. How you goin' to pay his share of the punishment now, eh?' He shoved his leering face straight into Oz's. 'Go on, hit me.'

Someone was grabbing Oz's arms from behind.

'Go on...' Mick taunted. 'They'll take your hook off yer — that'd be good news.'

'Don't be needled,' the leading chef called across to Osgood. 'He's not worth it, Oz.'

Osgood stomped from the mess, the jeers of Foulgis's cronies behind him. He nipped up to the upper deck, feeling the morning breeze against his face, savouring the warm sun. Over to starboard was *Athabaskan,* covering *Oileus* and *Guardian,* the two replenishment ships upon whom the whole force depended — and, presumably, the prime target for the enemy. Tailing them and easily keeping station, the Russian AGI trawler was smashing through the seas two miles astern, the spray flying high above her bridge. Oz took a deep breath, his cool returning.

He couldn't go on like this. Bastards such as Foulgis were everywhere... it was so bloody easy to criticise, to cause ill-feeling. But the evil was difficult to combat by argument if you couldn't express yourself adequately. Well, he was going to do something about it. He'd slap in his notice to quit the Navy —

and if his request was turned down, he'd put in for transfer to the Fleet Air Arm. He'd have a man's job to do there, in the helos, hunting subs — and the money was good. He smirked grimly: that should keep Merle happy.

He'd go up to the EW room to make his request, where there was peace and quiet. It was 0932 by his watch: just time before the panic began. He entered the citadel and set off towards the EW office.

Minutes later, the 'action stations' alarms shattered the peace of the office. He'd have to draft his request during the dogs if he didn't get his head down…

There was a roar from aft, and the Lynx reared off the deck, turned on her tail, then flew towards the blur that was *Phoebe* dropping below the horizon. Her four Sea Skua missiles stood out, two on each side of her cab, gleaming lethal and ready to drop if the 'Krivak' meant business. Suddenly there was silence, save for the buffeting of the wind against the glass windows of the bridge. To the north, *Gloucester,* representing the Kashin, had doubled back and was opening her range on *Goeben.*

'That riser must have been the threat, sir.' Alastair McKown, the PWO (Air), was talking through the loop, his speech crackling through the bridge speaker. 'Out to the north to draw us off. *Athabaskan*'s lost the contact.'

'Roger,' Trevellion acknowledged. There was a Dutch submarine in the area: they were good and pressed home their attacks.

It was 0959 and *Phoebe*'s mast was just visible above the horizon — outside Exocet range now, but inside *Perdix*'s Sea Skua missiles. For some reason, *Gloucester* was still within range of *Icarus*'s Exocets, though she might be outside *Jesse*'s and

Goeben's capabilities. *Athabaskan* was on the other side, off to the south-eastward, covering *Oileus* and *Guardian,* the Canadian replenishment ship, with her Sea Sparrow surface-to-air point defence system.

The PWO (Underwater), Julian Farge, was talking in the background. Then McKown cut in briskly: 'There's a report coming in, sir.'

Trevellion, feeling the tension of his first moment in command of an action, stared through his binoculars at the blur that was *Phoebe,* now on the north-western horizon. Then he glimpsed the flickering beam of her signalling projector. The hands of the bridge clock showed forty seconds past the hour.

'*Phoebe*'s opening fire on us,' he called into the loop system. 'Tell the Lynx to engage her with Sea Skua.' He snapped down at the yeoman: 'Make an enemy report.'

Things were moving now. His training over the past months was paying off, he hardly had to think, so automatically did the sequence come.

'Range of *Gloucester*?' someone called.

'Eighteen miles, sir,' from the PWO.

'Stand by to open fire with Exocet on *Gloucester*,' he ordered. 'Steer 345 degrees, Officer of the Watch.' He called down to the ops room: 'Have you got her?'

'Yes, sir. We've got her.'

'Come hard left, Gubbay. Full ahead both engines.'

'Aye, aye, sir. Port thirty...' The senior watchkeeper kept his eye on Campbell, who was fighting with the steering. The ship began to heel, then the repeat bells from the engine room telegraph tinged in the background. Pascoe felt a sudden elation; this was what he had been trained for all these long years. *This is what it's all about!* And he felt the bite of reality —

a Krivak's missiles would be striking into *Icarus*'s upperworks at just about this instant ... the ship was weaving to her new course now, her deck trembling beneath his feet as she responded to the full power being delivered by her twin steam turbines. But *Gloucester* was twisting like a tropical sea snake, slithering away out of range, boosted by her extra 20,000 HP from her twin Olympus gas turbines. The Krivaks had an edge of eight knots on NATO's Type 42s, presumably because of their additional tonnage of some seven hundred tons.

'Course, sir. Three-three-o, sir,' Campbell called.

'Open fire with Exocets on *Gloucester*,' Trevellion ordered as soon as her light projector began blinking. 'She's opened fire on us,' he yelled down to the ops room. 'PWO — Captain. Have you got the flash report out yet?'

'It's going out now, sir,' McKown said.

'Come hard left, Officer of the Watch,' Trevellion ordered, his mind racing. 'Steady on *Gloucester*. Stand by to engage her again with Exocet.' He heard Gubbay meeting the swing, his orders calm and reassuring: the Kashin's missiles were in the air, on their way... 'Midships, Cox'n. Starboard twenty.'

'Flash report passed, sir,' from the PWO.

'Roger,' Trevellion snapped. 'Open fire with Exocet.'

'We are at war, sir,' the PWO reported nonchalantly.

A chuckle of amusement rippled about the bridge. 'Roger,' Trevellion acknowledged. 'Pass to the Commodore: Have engaged *Gloucester*.' He smiled to himself: so it was Red Alert, State Three, and every man for himself — a relief after all the waiting.

'Roger, sir,' McKown acknowledged. '*Perdix* has engaged *Phoebe* with Sea Skua. She's standing off and shadowing.'

'Have you told her to rejoin?'

'Yes, sir, I've told her. She's not acknowledged yet.'

Poor devils, Pascoe thought: it would be a hot spectator's seat for Hob and Rollo out there, amidst the shooting.

The PWO was talking again, immediacy in his voice. 'Air Raid Warning Red, sir.'

'Roger. Stand by Sea Cats.'

Phoebe and *Gloucester* were racing below the horizon, their tasks completed for the moment. How would the real Krivaks and Kashins have fared — and how many British sailors would now be either mangled corpses or struggling in the filth of an oil-fouled ocean? It was difficult not to feel, as he watched *Goeben* vanishing behind curtains of flying spume while she tore after the receding enemy, that the whole thing was unreal — but how else could the NATO fleet keep up to scratch, year after year, decade after decade?

'We're now swimming, I suspect,' Trevellion said in an aside to Neame, who was standing at the chart table. Then he called down to the ops room: 'Reload Exocet.'

'Captain — PWO.'

'Yes?'

'From the Commodore, sir: scrum down ... twenty-five.'

'Roger.' So they were switching to the first alternative on the AWC (Air Warfare Co-ordination) net — the air cover frequencies were being swapped.

'From SO, sir: assume air defence screen to the eastward ... Air Raid Warning Red — all ships.'

'Roger. Stand by Sea Cats.' So the Yanks were sending in their fighter bombers from USS *Nimitz*, somewhere east of Gibraltar.

Trevellion turned to Gubbay. 'She's all yours, Officer of the Watch. Don't hit anyone.' He glanced at the clock — 1035 already — then he swung past the chart table and clambered swiftly down to the ops room. Could NATO depend upon the

Russians playing the game to their rules? Would confrontation be like this?

As he swung down the ladder to the ops room, he bumped into the chief radio supervisor, who was knocking on the wardroom door. 'Top secret signal, sir,' he amplified. 'I'm looking for the crypto officer.'

'He's not on the bridge, Chief,' Trevellion said. 'I'll be in the ops room when you've got it deciphered.'

The morning's classified signal had been an anti-climax, merely warning all commanding officers that a further classified message was in the pipeline. STANAVFORLANT was still awaiting the second signal — which, presumably, would be extraneous to 'Clear Lane'.

Dusk was drawing in when the force approached the Tagus estuary. Cape St Vincent lay out of sight to the south, where the coastline merged into the grey horizon. Captain Trevellion could see the flat, low-lying cliffs, black and uninviting, on the northern side of the Tagus estuary. Against this background NATO minesweepers were sweeping the channel ahead of STANAVFORLANT.

Glorious's Sea Kings fluttered, apparently stationary, above the white horses that slashed the dark brown waters of Lisbon's main artery. The night sky was dark and menacing; only a few streaks of milky grey could be seen above the cliffs.

The standard dusk air raid had been artificially injected into the exercise by the PWO. Missiles at a speed of over Mach 1 were on their way, so Trevellion had brought the ship round to port to a reciprocal course, to open 'A' arcs in order to cover the force. The missiles were still seventy miles distant and were being tracked from the ops room. The PWO (Air) had fired his chaff to seduce the incoming missiles' attack.

'*Jesse*'s raking them with Sea Sparrow,' the PWO reported briskly. 'Here they come, sir ... I've got 'em on 993. You should have no trouble.'

The drill continued, as it had all day, ever since the 'war' had started this morning. Trevellion was beginning to feel fatigue creeping through him. He would witness the final stages of the minesweeping, and then, after the force turned south again for Gibraltar, he would get his head down for an hour.

Exercise 'Clear Lane', though less than twelve hours old, was going well. Submarine attacks from the Dutch and Portuguese boats during the morning; aircraft attacks from *Nimitz*'s planes, complete with jamming exercises during the afternoon; and now the approach of the force to the Tagus, for the 'safe and timely arrival of the convoy'.

Portugal, a grey smudge to the north-east, was a NATO partner. One of her submarines had carried out an audacious attack during the afternoon; her Exocet frigate, *Oliviero E. Carmo,* was breaking away, her lamp flickering in the fading light as she made her farewell to *Athabaskan.*

Here, off the Tagus, Trevellion counted twenty-one ships from six nations, all determined to fight for their common way of life. The complexities of naval warfare had been mastered by NATO's fifteen nations, now operating together as a formidable naval force. NATO's shield had provided peace for a world that was beginning to forget what the reality of war meant — the horror of blood and guts and tears, the misery of death, the anguish of separation. As Trevellion watched the mine countermeasures squadron turning up towards the Tagus he remembered that the Russians, by tradition, had always favoured the mine. A weapon often ignored by seafaring nations during peacetime, it was easy to forget that German magnetic mines, more than any weapon, had almost brought the Allies to their knees during the winter of 1939-40. The mine had to be beaten, the deadly machine that lay silently in wait for months on end. The devilry of modern technology had devised such complex mechanisms that it was a continuing battle to devise countermeasures. A mine could be moored; it could be acoustic, magnetic or — most difficult of all to combat — a pressure mine. NATO's three standard types of minesweeper and minehunters were operating efficiently at sea, but there were not nearly enough of them.

Trevellion loathed the mine: not only did it cause appalling casualties but its effects, relative to the minelaying effort and the cheap cost of the weapon, were highly damaging to an enemy's war effort. Declared minefields — whether mines were laid or not — diverted forces into areas where their fleet could be assaulted by other weapons. The Norwegians had, for years, declared the minefields they had laid in peacetime to protect their 'leads' between their islands and fjords.

He watched the departing MCMs merging into the estuary: the elderly Portuguese minesweepers *Lagoa* and *Rosario,* two Hunts from the RN; three of the Tripartite MCMs (two Dutch, one Belgian) from the standard French-Dutch-Belgian programme; and one of the German Troika MCMs. Except for the two obsolete Portuguese ships, the squadron was as up to date as any in the world, and working with brisk efficiency, in both hunter and sweeper roles. Mercifully, NATO had woken up to the threat of the mine.

'Excuse me, sir.' Pascoe turned to find the sub-lieutenant at his elbow. 'Top Secret classification, sir,' he said, saluting. Security was vital these days, because the side that knew most about the enemy held all the cards. The policy of knowing only what you needed to know was a good one, which was why certain areas in the ship — such as the EW rooms — were out of bounds to all, even officers, except those working therein.

'Thank you, Sub.' Trevellion turned to the officer of the watch. 'She's all yours, Lieutenant Lochead. Switch on navigation lights. I'll be in my cabin for half an hour.' He could leave the ship in Lochead's hands now that *Icarus* was well out on the south-west side of the screen and steering for Gib. Even the unreliable Lochead would have difficulty in finding someone with whom to collide out here.

Trevellion went below to the privacy of his cabin. 'Come in, Sub.'

Firebrace looked serious as he passed the signal to his captain.

CLASSIFICATION TOP SECRET
TO COMSTANAVFORLANT FROM SACLANT
EVIDENCE OF UNUSUAL RUSSIAN TROOP MOVEMENTS TOWARDS BORDERS ON CENTRAL FRONT. DUE TO BREAKDOWN ON SALT SUMMIT MEETING, NATO AND US FORCES ORDERED ALERT STATE ONE. ALL SHIPS ADOPT RULE OF ENGAGEMENT FOURTEEN, REPEAT, FOURTEEN. EXERCISE 'CLEAR LANE' TO CONTINUE. ACKNOWLEDGE.

The sub was staring at him, waiting to be dismissed.

'All right, Sub. Keep this news to yourself. This doesn't alter anything.'

'It hasn't upgraded the rules of engagement, sir. We must still be sunk first.' He smiled ruefully as he left the cabin.

Pascoe longed for sleep, but this signal demanded warlike measures. He would send for Jewkes and the two PWOs, then gather all his officers together before the expected submarine attacks began, probably off Cape St Vincent. There were five ships listed in the exercise orders — two Royal Navy, two Dutch and one American — and they could cause havoc when forming an 'Iron Ring' across the cape. The new Commodore, commanding STANAVFORLANT for the first time, would certainly be topping up all his ships with fuel, and the next few hours could be interesting — particularly if 'Clear Lane' was curtailed.

CHAPTER 11

HMS Icarus, 18 December.

The PWO (Air), Lieutenant Alastair McKown, was beginning to feel flaked at 0235 on this Tuesday morning. He had been coping with a succession of concerted air battles during the past three and a half hours, contests between the Blue Force (STANAVFORLANT) and the Orange Force which was in the Mediterranean, east of Gibraltar, trying to deny Blue Force's passage through the Straits. Fighter bombers from *Nimitz* had been carrying out continuous air attacks, the last having only recently finished. *Goeben* had engaged the final sortie and had fired her birds, but the umpires in *Athabaskan* had declared *Goeben* damaged.

The five Russian Backfires (represented by *Nimitz's* Phantoms) had approached to within twenty miles before *Athabaskan* and *Jesse* fired their birds, but in reality the enemy would have loosed their missiles while still four hundred and fifty miles away. There seemed to be a lull in the air battles, and *Icarus* was settling into her station on the starboard bow and south-western flank of the force.

McKown put down his chinagraph pencil and straightened himself in his chair, which faced his air warfare display. He had spent so much time in the ops room lately that he knew every nook, every nut, every bolt: one of the largest compartments in the ship, it was sited in the centre of the main deck level. The displays glowed in the semi-darkness; there was no talk, save for the operators who spoke quietly into the Rice systems. One

ear for the internal loop in the ops room; one for the bridge —
but another ear was required to listen to the external loop
linking the force. Even now, McKown was unused to needing
three ears.

There were two batteries of arrays: his, where he controlled
the air warfare; the command display alongside him, where
Captain Trevellion was sitting watching the total battle picture;
and, at the end of this row, the ASW display, with Julian Farge,
tense and silent, waiting for the next submarine attack. There
had been three attacks so far, on the other side of the force
and close to Cape St Vincent.

McKown had been impressed with his new captain's rapid
grasp of his new surroundings. He had remained unflappable,
patient, but decisive. This morning, for the first time, he had
not concealed his irritation over the last submarine battle,
when *Athabaskan* had made a nonsense of the counter-attack ...
the Commodore had reacted too slowly, and the submarine
had got right in among the force before the STWS torpedoes
were fired.

Trevellion must be over-tired, for he had been at it non-stop
for almost twenty-four hours — the snap judgements and
decisions were always exhausting. He sat at his command
display, his large frame hooped like a fish-hook over the
glowing PPI, where the orange light was reflecting on his lined,
grey face.

McKown stiffened as *Oileus* came up loud and clear on the
loop connecting all ships in the force. 'The sub was quite
brazen. Did you get a sniff of her?'

Jesse then chipped in, saying that she had held and confirmed
the contact.

'Sonar contact 125 degrees,' the sonar supervisor rapped out
suddenly. 'Twelve thousand yards from us.'

McKown saw the backs stiffening at the displays, noted the Anti-Submarine Warfare Director (the buffer) pinpointing the contact on the display for the benefit of the PWO (Underwater).

'Tell *Perdix* to stand by,' Trevellion ordered. 'We may be needing her.'

This submarine contact was on an unexpected bearing — it might even be a Russian deliberately making her presence known. No one knew why they did this, but the deliberate disclosure of their position was not uncommon.

'Turn towards,' the captain ordered. 'Stand-by STWS.' So the Old Man was going to launch his ship-borne torpedoes. Julian Farge had time to think about this contact, because the submarine was much nearer *Jesse,* and was not an immediate threat to the force. One of *Athabaskan*'s Sea Kings was dipping on that bearing, five miles to the eastward — she might be going active at any moment.

'Another contact,' the sonar supervisor was reporting. 'Cutting right ... possible ...' Seconds later: 'Contact compares with doppler. Good visual, moving left.'

'Give us your cut, then,' the buffer goaded impatiently from the ASW display.

'Tracker One cutting through ... she's moving out.'

Alastair felt the tension mounting, as it always did when the quarry was confirmed. In the reality of war, either the submarine or *Icarus* would survive, depending upon who was fastest on the draw.

'Original bearing 105 degrees. Original range 8,500.'

McKown glanced over his right shoulder to the STWS control panel and its switches, where the buffer was waiting.

'Good visual, good audio, PPI and doppler.'

'Good cut, PPI zero-nine-eight ... eight-five. Doppler change two high...'

The drill continued until the buffer chipped in. 'What d'you reckon his course? Bearing's steady, isn't it?'

'Drawing slowly right — no cut, no paint... both displays.' McKown heard the sonar operator swearing. 'Aah ... now no cut, no paint, PPI no echoes. Wish she'd stop mucking about.'

'PPI investigating doppler,' the supervisor reported.

'We'll have a closer look,' the captain said quietly to Julian Farge. 'There's a fishing vessel between us and the submarine — could be its nets.'

'That's no bloody fisherman's nets,' McKown overheard the sonar supervisor muttering to himself as his eyes flickered between the sonar displays.

'HE contact one-nine-zero...' the hydrophone effect operator drawled. 'Classified surface ship.'

The supervisor raised his eyebrows and grinned.

'The fishing boat's about there,' the captain said. 'I'll go along with you. Check those co-ordinates.'

The officer of the watch, who was always listening in on the loop, called down from the bridge: 'HE contact one-zero-zero. Classified surface ship, sir.'

There was a short silence, then laughter. This was not the first time that the shadowing Russian AGI (spy ship) had been mistaken for a contact, although she had been tailing them for over two days.

Icarus was well out on the south-easterly flank of STANAVFORLANT, which was widely dispersed against air and submarine attacks as it forged on towards Gibraltar. The ships would soon be clear of Cape St Vincent; at this speed, even though *Goeben* was declared damaged by the umpires, it would be some time before the lurking submarines could gain enough bearing to carry out further attacks before reaching the Straits.

'There's a report coming in,' Julian Farge told the captain, who had left his chair to stretch his legs. '*Jesse*'s LAMPS has picked up a firm contact ten miles ahead of us, but well to the southward. *Athabaskan*'s asking us to cover, sir. The LAMPS has a problem and is returning to mother.'

'Roger. Tell Boss we're replacing,' Trevellion ordered as he replaced his earphones and mike. 'Fly *Perdix* off as quickly as you can, as soon as she's reloaded with torpedoes.'

'She's ready now, sir. Hob's just been in again. He and Rollo got some zeds in.'

Captain Trevellion nodded. He was listening to the reports coming in, and by his expression McKown knew something was up.

The American LAMPS pilot cut in brusquely with *Athabaskan:* 'No doubt, sir. No doubt at all. Signature gives a nuke. Steaming fast, sir.' A position followed, timed 0347, with course and speed of the contact.

Trevellion nodded to the helicopter controller. 'Tell *Perdix* to carry out a radar visual search to the south of our sector,' he ordered. 'Stand by to execute vectac.'

'Aye, aye, sir.'

Trevellion looked up, catching McKown's eye. 'Funny thing is,' he remarked casually, 'none of our nukes are in the area.'

Bernard Towke relished his supplementary duties of flight deck officer: the responsibility of holding the lives of the pilot and observer in his hands, and of safeguarding the handlers, was stimulating after the grind of the ship's office. But he was beginning to feel weary: *Perdix* had been away on radar/visual searches most of the night.

Night flying was an exciting business, but the glamour tended to wear off in the early hours. The drill was so professional now that the flying-off and recovery became routine ... but Bernie realised what a nightmare his job would be with a less competent pilot. Hob was first class. He flew *Perdix* as if she was part of him, throwing her about like a shuttlecock.

Towke stamped his feet in the chill of the morning as Hob carried out his final checks on the Lynx. The handling party was scouring the flight deck for scraps of litter which could be sucked into the twin intakes of the engines. The handlers had taken off half the lashings, leaving the remainder and the harpoon to lock *Perdix* on to her grid. The refuelling was almost complete.

'Off tip socks.'

The handlers moved in the darkness like glow-worms, working with the aid of their shoulder lights to remove the luminous protectors on the blade tips.

For Bernard Towke, hard-bitten by his experiences in the constricted arena of remittances, allotments and pay, there was a touch of drama about night flying, a heightened excitement he would have found difficult to put into words. Here, isolated at the end of the ship and connected to the command through only a telephone link, a team of individuals was totally involved in launching a lump of metal into the air and in its safe recovery. In these moments, before the engines whined into life, he was overawed by the immensity of the heavens, by the impossible concept of infinity ... the scurrying team was about to launch their vital machine a few hundred feet into the air — and for what objective?

It was to defend the exercise of their free will that Hob and Rollo were prepared to haul themselves into the sky at night in an unstable flying machine, to discourage those enemies who wished to destroy their freedom. 'Better red than dead' cut no ice in the Navy, one of the three services whose function it was to ensure that the majority could at least make its choices without fear.

'Lower the nets,' Towke ordered.

The guard rails were slipped and the safety nets fell horizontally. Things were relatively safe at the moment, but on a bad night the deck was slippery and the nets were a comfort. He could see the faces of Hob and Rollo, shadowy behind their windscreen, as they carried out their pre-flight checks. The white lights were on in the cockpit as Hob checked his instruments. *Perdix*'s navigation lights were bright beneath the fuselage — and Bernie Towke checked his own illuminated batons with which he visually demonstrated his orders.

'Start port engine.' As Bernie gave the order, he held the glowing white baton of his right hand high above his head. He twirled the baton in his left hand, keeping the tip low, then the port engine was in accessory drive and running up until its whine had reached full pitch. *Perdix* was free to escape now, held by only her harpoon; Hob, engaging the rotors, forced the Lynx down on to the grille by adopting negative pitch.

Towke flipped down his right arm, twirled the baton and waited as Hob started the starboard engine. The flutter pitch changed, roughened, and then both engines were screaming at full power ... The weird, luminous parabola glowed above the cab, where the blades chopped through the darkness.

Hob had signed for the torpedoes which now hung snugly in their common carriers beneath each side of the cab. Operated by the observer, the solenoids would release the lugs and the fish would drop into the sea. Hob had accepted the pins of both torpedoes and the 4.5-inch flares; coloured ribbons were attached to the pins and to any other extraneous fittings which had to be removed before take-off, so that they could not be missed during the final checks.

The captain had asked that take-off should be confined to well within limits, the 40-degree restriction on each side of true wind. At twenty-one knots *Icarus* was opening out to close the reported sub contact, and tonight Hob was relaxed: the ship's pitching and rolling was minimal.

Towke watched the vertical edge of the superstructure cutting across the dark horizon, swinging into the glittering path of the moon, before settling to the take-off course. *Icarus* was turning into the wind.

'Stand by.'

'Stand by for take-off...' Hob came through clearly on the loop above the cacophony of the engines.

The ship had steadied and Towke's eyes flickered for the last time across the deck. His arm shot above his head, the baton tips touching.

Hob swivelled into wind; he released the harpoon, applied full power. The Lynx shook, shivered, and then she began to claw upwards, hauled vertically by her pilot, who had judged the moment perfectly. In seconds she was away, lunging to the south-west and gaining height at every second. Her flickering red light grew fainter, then vanished into the night.

A handler took Towke's batons from him and he switched off the loop system. Then he noticed the bulky figure in the anorak, a rating he had not recognised in the darkness. Osgood was up here, helping when they were short-handed. There had been rumours that he was slapping in his notice, so what was going on?

Hob revelled in flying his Mark VII Lynx in these conditions: the weather was right, and *Icarus* and her HCO (Helicopter Control Officer) were doing all the work. All he and Rollo had to do was to obey orders. The captain had wasted no words on their mission: 'Relieve *Jesse*'s LAMPS chopper. The course of the contact is 275 degrees, her speed thirty-one knots, from her furthest-on position, working from *Jesse*'s datum. Carry out a Jezebel and hang on to the contact by MAD until the three Sea Kings from *Glorious* relieve you. I'm ordered to remain on screen for the time being.'

Kids' stuff — and here they were within three minutes of the drop position. It was difficult to believe that down beneath that silver surface a hundred or so Russian sailors were sweating it out ... Suddenly Hob felt the elation of reality. What was the submarine's purpose, steaming at speed into the Atlantic? Normally she would have been tailing the NATO exercise...

He glanced at Rollo, waiting for orders. The observer was busy, setting out his position for latitude and longitude on one chart, and his position on the grid for easy reference. He had sorted out his plot and had identified the other ships in the force, in addition to the other choppers in the area. *Glorious*'s three Sea Kings would be airborne soon: *Perdix* had taken off at 0354 and was just approaching the furthest-on position of the contact: the time was 0401.

'Ready on heading,' Hob said.

'Lowering the MAD bird,' Rollo reported.

So Rollo was starting his MAD run now.

'Two hundred feet,' Hob said. He watched the pointers on his dials as he took *Perdix* at cruise speed along the heading. The torpedo-shaped shell of the MAD bird was streaming astern, fifty feet above the surface of the sea.

'Heading two-nine-o,' Hob reported. So often had they practised this drill, the whole business a monotonous chore ... now Rollo was reporting *Perdix*'s position back to *Icarus*. The HCO in the ops room had been kept in the picture but, for real, Rollo would have remained silent. So far, things were running to form — *Jesse*'s LAMPS report must have been a false echo, or one of their own boats.

'MAD contact hot!'

Hob twitched in his seat when Rollo shouted, the report deafening the pilot inside his bone dome.

'*Hot*, Hob. Hold where we are while I get out an enemy report. Yippee!' Rollo's fingers were flicking at the switches, scribbling across the plot with his chinagraph pencil, his eyes scanning his instruments. 'Stand by to lay an ASRB pattern,' he ordered. 'Heading three-one-five, Hob.'

Seven minutes later, the ASRBs laid, the observer reported tersely to his pilot: 'Nuke confirmed. She's going like hell. I'll get out an enemy report before we refine.' Rollo turned briefly, grinning all over his face. 'She's a goer, Hob! We mustn't lose her. Hope to God she doesn't alter course.'

'She doesn't even know we're here,' Hob said.

'FLASH — FLASH — FLASH. Firm nuke contact grid two seven decimal three, four eight decimal six. High speed. Refining ... out,' Rollo ordered. That was all he had time for at the moment. Hob glanced again at Rollo, working furiously trying to localise the contact. That was the first priority: to hold on to it until the Sea Kings arrived. It was 0409 already. *Glorious*'s choppers had been airborne since 0406 and Rollo had said that they should take nineteen minutes, if they homed on *Perdix*'s IFF. Rendezvous should be at 0425, sixteen minutes...

'Come to port: heading two-nine-o,' ordered Rollo. He could not contain his excitement as he localised the data from the ASRBs: position, course two-eight-o, speed thirty knots, signature confirmed nuclear submarine. He passed the information back to *Icarus,* knowing that the whole force must be listening in. 'Probably a ... Charlie II.'

Rollo turned to Hob, a look of amazement on his face; for months and months they had dreamed of such a moment. Then the observer was crouching again over his plot, determined to hold on to the contact until the Sea Kings took over. The Charlie was going like a bat out of hell. Then he called up 864, *Glorious*'s leading Sea King.

'864. This is 491.'

'Roger 491. Three big dippers joining from the east at two hundred feet, one hundred knots. We carry six Reptiles and have no restrictions.' His voice was matter-of-fact; it sounded like Tony Hall, *Glorious*'s senior pilot. If it was, the nuke would have to be good to escape. 'We have four hours endurance, Charlie time 0800.'

'Roger 864,' Rollo acknowledged. The Sea Kings would have to quit at eight, but by then they would have been relieved, if this was to be a major effort. Rollo had passed 864 all the data she needed.

'Roger 491. Many thanks. We're ready to dip as soon as you're clear.'

'Okay. We'll clear right.'

At that moment, Hob saw them, the first of the flashing red lights winking in the night sky. The Sea Kings were dashing in from above his port side; he could see the flame from their engines.

'Clear right,' Rollo shouted.

Hob lifted *Perdix* and soared for height. As he was reaching six hundred feet, his HCO cut in from *Icarus:*

'Carry out fresh radar/visual search, fifteen miles due west.' The grid reference was passed, then Hob recognised the captain's voice.

'491 — act as longstop until your Charlie time. Operate in concert with the Big Dippers, keeping fifteen miles ahead of them. Understood?'

'Roger, sir.'

'Out.'

On their way to their new datum position, Hob heard 864, coming in loud and clear.

'Hell ... he's altering. New heading confirmed 210 degrees.'

The Sea Kings were hot, and hanging on remorselessly. The contact was confirmed as a Charlie II, a nuclear fleet submarine armed with eight SSN 7 cruise missiles, weapons which had a range of thirty miles. With eight 21-inch torpedoes, and with cruise missiles which they could launch while the submarine was submerged, the Charlie IIs were a formidable challenge to any surface force — which was presumably why they were deployed in the Mediterranean to cover the American Sixth Fleet. The nuke must have picked up the Sea King's active transmissions from out of the blue, after steaming for hours since passing through the Straits. Submariners disliked helicopters — they were unpredictable.

'Three minutes, Hob.'

'Roger.'

At 0456, having dropped from six hundred to two hundred feet, *Perdix* began her second search. Methodically she crisscrossed the square, Rollo glued to his Sea Spray radar. Hob, with little to do, was relaxing and listening to the chat from the Sea Kings. *Perdix* had twenty-six minutes remaining before her Charlie time.

'491 — Bravo One leaving the force,' the HCO cut in. 'Joining you and Big Dippers.'

'Roger.' Rollo looked up, a weary grin on his face. 'I knew they couldn't keep their fingers out,' he said. 'But it'll be nice to have her around with all this talent about.'

'Increases our Charlie time,' Hob said.

'Ain't much use,' Rollo said, switching off the external loop. 'The Sea Kings have all the fun, now the sub is heading southwest.'

'She might double back.' Hob was beginning to feel the strain now that the pressure had eased. Black clouds were building up from the west, and the wind was getting up with the dawn; below him, the first white horses were breaking, flurries of foam speckling the dark surface of the sea where the first wavelets broke.

There had been a long silence from Rollo, and Hob turned to see how he was getting on. The observer was crouched low over his plot, his eyes were fixed on the radar. Suddenly his back stiffened.

'Christopher!' he shouted suddenly. 'Hob! That was an echo. There ... again!' He tensed, re-tuning.

'Riser ... it's fading ... Alter left to heading two-zero-zero. See anything?'

Hob felt the hairs prickling at the back of his neck as he pulled *Perdix* round. He strained his eyes, peering down at the dark surface. 'On heading two-zero-zero,' he reported.

Then Rollo picked up the echo again. 'Riser confirmed!' he shouted. 'Just like the other, Hob... and he switched to the Sea Kings' frequency.

As he frantically prepared to drop the first of the ASRBs he began passing his enemy report back to the HCO. Minutes later, Rollo had laid his pattern, and up came the contact: firm.

'864. Contact confirmed and hot,' he reported, trying to conceal the excitement in his voice. 'We're holding her.'

'Roger 491.'

But then Rollo was unable to keep the amazement from his voice as he passed his amplifying report: 'Probable nuke contact position grid two nine decimal two; five three decimal eight. Refining ... out.' He worked feverishly to localise again, to classify, plot and report.

At 0517, nine minutes before Charlie time, Rollo confirmed the contact: another fast nuke, her signature indicating a Victor II, the fastest submarine in the world. It was pointless for *Icarus* to try and chase her.

'Return to mother,' the HCO ordered. 'Two Sea Kings are being diverted. 864 will take over your contact until their arrival.'

Rollo handed over the contact to 864 on the common loop, but Hob had to break away before the Sea Kings could be sighted.

Captain Trevellion was on the flight deck to greet them when Hob finally put *Perdix* neatly on the grid. The harpoon banged home and they clambered from the cockpit as soon as the handlers had her lashed. The tall figure ranged towards them.

'We seem to be redundant with you lot around,' he said, grinning. '864's tailing your Victor II. We're rejoining the screen now that I've got my main armament back. Come up to my cabin a moment.'

Hob struggled with his bone dome. Minutes later, still in his overalls, he was ensconced in one of the captain's chairs, Rollo in the other.

'I've news for you both,' he said. 'While you've been away swanning, I've announced to the ship's company that the country is now at Alert State Three and that a period of tension exists. Their Lordships must have suspected something — and now our nuke reports will certainly give them food for thought. We'll be breaking off "Clear Lane" to maintain contact and to report any Soviet forces.' Trevellion fixed them both with his level gaze.

'I'll be conserving *Perdix* and your hours as much as I can, but arm your torpedoes with warheads immediately.' His face twitched in a half-smile. 'Whether we still get our Christmas leave depends on the Soviets.'

Hob caught Rollo's eye. It was already Tuesday morning, and the ship was due back in Plymouth on Friday the 21st of December.

CHAPTER 12

London, 18 December.

It was with a sigh of relief that Vice-Admiral Peter Hawke reached the calm of his office. The Second Sea Lord sensed a strange unease, a foreboding that today might be a landmark, not only in his life, but in that of the nation.

That morning, Hawke had been forced to attend the Combined Procurement Meeting with the senior civil servants because Andy Kemp, who had only recently taken over his new appointment as Controller to the Navy, needed support for this vital meeting. The army and RAF were also batting their First Eleven: the buzz was circulating that the Treasury was putting the screws on their executives again. Once more the services were having to fight for every farthing.

Hawke had known Andy, now Admiral Sir Andrew Kemp, KCB, FBIM, for a long time, but never had he seen him so worked up; he was white with rage after the blistering attack which he and the other service officers had launched. It was left to the Air Vice Marshal to deliver the annihilating blow — but Andy had wished the honour could have fallen to him.

Andy had batted first. There were several important developments coming forward, improvements on existing weapons and the furtherance of vital countermeasures against hardware which the Soviets were now producing in quantity — in particular, the laser developments and improvements to the Sea Harrier concept by using container ships, as MAC ships were used in World War II.

Then, in the afternoon, Peter Hawke had attended a briefing given by the Director-General of Intelligence personally. His exposition spread a universal gloom that was spiced with a certain quickening of the adrenalin.

Hawke extracted from his pocket the jottings he had made. First, the overall American sitrep, based on their latest SOSUS reports: the trickle of Russian submarines through the northern gaps had grown to a deluge, many more outward than inward bound.

Then the RAF's Nimrods: particularly significant had been Nimrod Tango's report, from the Greenland Gap. These LRMP (Long Range Maritime Patrol) aircraft had the best long-range surveillance: without the initial LRMP detection of Soviet submarines, ASW frigates — even with their Lynxes — could not get out there in time to foil a determined Soviet submarine. But there were far too few Nimrods in the air — and if things went hot, they would be hurled into the air battle off Britain's coasts; the RAF would have no choice with the ludicrous numbers of aircraft at its disposal. Nimrod Tango, using her radar, sonar and MAD (Magnetic Anomaly Detector) had tracked no fewer than three nuclears.

The third bit of news was that the Fleet Submarine HMS *Safari,* shadowing a Delta II, had stalked the enemy for over eighteen hours until ordered to break off and to resume her billet.

Perhaps the most worrying incident had been the fourth on the agenda: the British master of one of the VLCCs, *Celtic Warrior,* early this morning had identified a Russian cruiser as *Azov,* one of the latest Karas. The master's telex had, between its lines, told a remarkable story:

Celtic Warrior, fully laden with crude for Milford Haven, was clearing the southerly end of the Mozambique Channel when she was ordered to heave-to by the Russian cruiser. Captain Morgan had no option. Under the shadow of her guns, *Azov* had brazenly sent a boarding party across in her pinnace and demanded to see the ship's papers. Explaining away his contravention of international law, the Russian had stated his suspicion that the oil was intended for South Africa, contrary to the sanctions imposed by the United Nations. *Celtic Warrior* was ordered to follow the Russian cruiser into Lourengo Marques. Evidently feigning acquiescence, Captain Morgan had pushed out an immediate Mayday which had alerted the US Fleet units to the north. As soon as the Russian boarding party jumped back into its pinnace, Captain Morgan had put his wheel hard over and telegraphs to full ahead. To avoid collision, *Azov* had been forced to get out of the way. *Celtic Warrior* had removed a touch of Russian paint in a glancing blow aft, as the tanker churned ahead. The British master, refusing to be bullied, had won the day. *Azov* shadowed for an hour, then broke off.

What Captain Morgan did not know was that only five days ago the Russian fishing fleet off Cape Province had been so exasperating the South Africans that a South African Fast Attack Craft had arrested a Soviet trawler and escorted her into Simonstown. The *Celtic Warrior* incident had underlined the Russian's point: the oil route to Europe was very vulnerable.

Another incident in this potentially explosive area was a recent brawl between American sailors from the *Ike,* on a courtesy visit to Mombasa, and a posse of Russian Merchant sailors in a bar on the waterfront. The incident was losing nothing in the telling over the radio nets of African states. It was all the more embarrassing because the Soviet matelots' behaviour was undoubtedly more inhibited than the traditional, happy-go-lucky attitude of the doughboys.

Hawke studied the sitrep: the enemy was winning without firing a shot. And nearer home, the tension was mounting — the Kremlin was certainly pushing it at the moment, the first real aggression since Brezhnev had departed from the scene. A lone Soviet ship, always hove-to on the edge of the limits off Shetland, had been replaced by a standing patrol of anti-submarine ships. They flaunted their presence, perhaps to advertise their deep-sea trawlers off the Brent field who, with their bottom trawls and gear, could clobber Britain's oil line from the rigs to Sullom Voe or destroy it with divers, if they chose.

The telephone on Hawke's desk trilled.

'ANCS here, sir. VCNS has asked me to get through direct: he's just been called by the Chief, sir. "Clear Lane" has been cancelled.'

'What's happening to the force?'

'Dispersing, sir. STANAVFORLANT is ordered back to its operational area; *Icarus* was detached earlier because she's due for Christmas leave on the twenty-third. *Glorious* and her group are rejoining EASTLANT, sir.'

'Thanks, Brian.'

Hawke replaced the phone, feeling a numbness spread across his lower abdomen. The pain materialised more often these days, now the pressure was on.

CHAPTER 13

London, 22 December.

Geordie Baines, Senior Security Officer, slammed shut the inside rear door of the blue Princess, then jumped into the seat beside the Wren driver.

'Step on it, Sue,' he muttered. 'We're running late.' He slipped into his safety belt, then half-turned to keep one eye on his charge, who was sitting in silence on the inside back seat. Admiral of the Fleet, Sir Anthony Layde, GCB, MVO, was strangely quiet this morning. He usually had a word for Geordie Baines and his Wren driver.

Sue glanced at Geordie in surprise: the clandestine meeting at Number Ten and the departure from the rear entrance pointed to unusual goings-on — exasperating, with only three days before Christmas and this the last Saturday.

Sir Anthony had become First Sea Lord at the right moment. He was a communications man, Geordie knew that. It was rumoured that the considerable effort devoted to jamming and electronic warfare was due largely to Layde's influence and drive ... that secret world, a sinister twilight domain where espionage and security forces clashed ruthlessly across their frontiers; amorphous, undefined frontiers of spy and counterspy. Geordie Baines half-lived in this secret world; he was told no more than he needed to know in order to guard his protégés. He felt the reassuring bulge of the Smith and Wesson beneath his armpit. The nation's serenity depended on the protection of the First Sea Lord against an IRA or other murderer's bullet.

Sue glanced at her route plan, slipping the Princess down to third as she swung the car through the gates of NATO's and Fleet's headquarters, the First Sea Lord unsmiling as he returned the sentries' salutes. The car glided to a standstill. Baines jumped out, opening his passenger's door. The swifter he propelled the Old Man down through the steel door and into the underground bunker, the sooner he'd breathe a sigh of relief.

Sir Anthony's cup of coffee awaited him, his naval assistant hovering in the background. In the dim lighting, the First Sea Lord recognised the familiar figures as they rose to him while he found his way to his desk. From this operations room deep underground, the Defence Chiefs could be in touch within seconds with any unit around the world.

He nodded to Hawke and Andrew Kemp. The First Sea Lord felt a twinge of satisfaction: he had picked a good 'un when selecting the new Controller.

'Please carry on,' he said quietly. 'We've a lot on our slop chit this morning, gentlemen.'

The emergency meeting began, the staff captain standing by the projector as he presented the briefing. Sir Anthony's heart sank as the chap methodically went over the dismal catalogue of the week: *Celtic Warrior*; the exodus of the Russian nukes from the Med; the movements in the Baltic and Kola. The voice droned on in the semi-darkness…

The First Sea Lord realised once again how much easier his task was because of the far-sightedness of his predecessors. But he needed time, a few vital years for bringing to fruition the plans they had fought for so long, supported by so little.

The grit of those misunderstood admirals of the seventies, officers who had to persevere against an impossible economic and political climate had ensured continuity, disproved the theory that the Royal Navy was merely a legend. But the race was touch-and-go, much as it must have been after Munich in 1938. He and his friends in the other services knew how narrow was the margin for survival.

Sir Anthony sighed to himself. Britain's survival depended upon retaining control of the Atlantic and the North Sea. With one ear he picked up the thread of the briefing, which had still not reached the previous Tuesday.

If the Soviets could restrict the conflict to the Atlantic, they need not start a hot war in central Germany, nor on the southern or northern flanks: the results would be too catastrophic, even for them. If NATO were to lose this second Battle of the Atlantic, the Soviets would slap down their edict: 'You've lost so far, so we'll stop any further Atlantic reinforcements from America; accept our conditions.' Even if NATO attacked and destroyed their naval bases, it was conceivable that the war could be restricted to the Atlantic.

The slides flickered upon the screen, as the staff captain began briefing them on world dispositions. STANAVFORLANT was steaming to its war station in the Northern Sea; *Glorious* and her group were moving north, to be detached home for Christmas leave; and, for the sake of prudence, 'Clear Lane' had been curtailed early so that some ships at least could be granted Christmas leave before any balloons went up.

The First Sea Lord felt pleased as he watched the careful planning working so smoothly, the ships of the Fleet steaming without fuss to their war stations. This was the peacetime phase. How many Britons, huddled around their tellies tonight, had an inkling that a few miles to the north of Sutherland, their countrymen in the Orkneys and Shetlands were pawns in the Russian game? The Orkneys-Shetland gap; the Shetland-Faeroes, the Iceland-Faeroes and Greenland-Iceland gaps were the Clapham Junction of the sea lanes in this area; the Russian Northern and Baltic Fleets had to slip through these gaps to reach the Atlantic Ocean. The monitoring of these movements through these gaps had alerted the NATO politicians; they could not shut their eyes to what was happening this week. The Prime Minister had given the First Sea Lord *carte blanche* this morning, but had insisted upon being informed immediately should the Defence Chiefs decide to go ahead. Sir Anthony promised to use the hotline before coming to a final decision.

There was, the First Sea Lord thought, an air of unreality in the bunker this morning, as he listened to the briefing: this historic moment was the culmination of forty years' developments in common communications, of exercising, time and time again, the international, administrative machine of NATO, and training politicians to cope with rapid military decisions. Confrontation was the politician's primary headache; he must be able to control events by denying the enemy command of the sea, the land and air spaces vital to our defence. Communications were such that the politician and the commanding officer of the ship at sea now understood each other's problems. The First Sea Lord had so often hammered home this fundamental: the marrying of the politician's control with the captain-on-the-spot's understanding equated resolute action. Military power was only an extension of the political will. He had rammed this home at every staff course he had addressed. Sir Anthony was convinced that confrontation and escalation could be halted by resolute action at sea, but, however sensitively the rules of engagement were framed, the first CO to be fired upon would be an unlucky bloke.

Peter Hawke's voice grated from the gloom, his questions crisp.

'How many submarines are out?'

'We've logged 141, sir.'

'What general area?'

The Vice-Chief of Naval Staff took over from the staff captain, now that discussion time was approaching. He indicated the traditional Greenland-Iceland-UK gaps, then shifted his spotlight to the western approaches, the areas south of Ireland and north of the Azores. The Soviet submarine movements could give an indication of what the enemy was up to.

'We're waiting for the feints,' VCNS continued. 'From the most recent reports, especially after the incidents earlier this week, we can assume that the enemy is not playing this time.'

Sir Anthony spoke up, his first contribution so far.

'The Chiefs and I had a meeting with the Prime Minister early this morning, gentlemen. The FO consider that these incidents and movements represent real probes by the enemy: as we have been expecting, he is not playing to NATO rules. He's testing us seriously, beyond the Tropic of Cancer. An hour ago, two Delta IIs, a Charlie II and a Victor were reported north-east of the Falkland Islands as the Argentine fleet put to sea with its amphibious backup. As you know, political pressure's hot there from the Argentinian oil lobby.'

'You wish to bring up the Indian Ocean, sir?' VCNS prompted.

'No, Charles. Would you remind us, please?'

The spotlight wavered to the trouble spots: off the Cape of Good Hope. Mauritius — and now, to provide the pincers

Tristan da Cunha in the South Atlantic. VCNS continued: 'The Soviet fishing fleet is still behaving enigmatically. A minor group is fishing off Durban, supported by Kashins and a backup force of AS ships in the deep field, at the southern entrance to the Mozambique Channel. Four Victor IIs have been positively identified working out of Mauritius.' The Vice-Chief of the Naval Staff cleared his throat. 'You'll see why this is significant, gentlemen.' His spot flickered to the Aldabra islands off the northern tip of Madagascar. 'The American Indian Ocean Strike Fleet is taking care of things here, but we are concerned at this morning's developments.' He turned towards Sir Anthony. 'Would you care to comment, sir?'

Sir Anthony's voice growled from the centre of the room, 'Go on, Charles — let's get nearer home. All this is bad news, but let's get to the nitty.'

'Very good, sir.' He touched a button, and the area they all knew so well glowed across the wall map. 'Satellites are reporting major sailings from the Kola Inlet: a 56 per cent increase in submarine traffic. Norwegian Maritime Patrol Lockheeds are doing their best but have been swamped: they have been reporting four Soviet submarines a day, but yesterday the count went up to nine. We'll soon be running short of sonobuoys.' He laughed shortly, and glanced at the Controller before continuing. 'Our Nimrods from Kinloss are fully stretched in the Greenland and Faeroes gaps. The sonar picture tells the same tale: the signature printouts confirm major Soviet effort. About 36 per cent of enemy submarine sailings slipped through our first line of surveillance patrols; they were presumably making their departure dived and were screened by the noise of surface ships.'

The First Sea Lord listened to the summing-up, glad to hear the serious situation being repeated. 'As you all know, the

Icelandic elections are impending and the communist party poised to take over again. Their main election plank is that they will revoke the Keflavik base agreement with the United States and throw out the Americans.'

The VCNS paused, and Sir Anthony could hear the blower of the projector whirring in the silence. 'The Americans flew massive reinforcements into Keflavik two days ago to pre-empt Soviet landings, should they be invited in by the communists. Yesterday evening, the Soviets gave the Americans twenty-four hours to start evacuating their reinforcements.'

Sir Anthony was always faintly amused by Charles, who enjoyed his moments of drama. When he had finished the briefing, the VCNS turned towards his boss. 'That's as far as I can go, sir.' He raised his eyebrows in anticipation and stood aside for the First Sea Lord to take over.

Sir Anthony Layde rose briskly from his desk. A burly figure, with his characteristic purposeful stride, he had nearly reached the briefing desk when the red telephone on his desk shrilled. In the silence that filled the large underground room, only the purring of the ventilation system was audible. Sir Anthony glanced up from the instrument at his key officers. He nodded, murmured his thanks, then slowly put down the phone, returning briskly to the briefing desk.

'The Prime Minister, gentlemen.' He glanced at the other two Defence Chiefs. 'The Americans are standing firm in Iceland. The Soviets have just informed the United States that they consider the American move to be one of aggression. The Soviets therefore have to review their relationship with NATO's ally closest to the Soviet northern frontier. They also state that the communist minority element in Finnmark is demanding Soviet protection. As a precaution against similar

NATO aggression in Northern Norway, the Soviets are starting their winter exercises forthwith: in the Murmansk area, the Kola Peninsula, and on the central front.' He faced them all, folding his arms. 'The Americans are calling for a show of resolution from the North Atlantic Alliance. The United States will begin reinforcing Europe across the Atlantic by air lift the instant that NATO shows its resolve to resist.' He paused. 'The Prime Minister has ordered me, as Chief of the Defence Staff, to bring the fighting services immediately to Alert State Two, gentlemen.'

He turned towards the VCNS. 'Get the fleet to sea, Charles,' he ordered coolly. 'Quietly, without fuss. Inform the major NATO commanders what you are doing.'

CHAPTER 14

Plymouth, 23 December.

A pallid sun dodged from behind the sombre clouds building up from the tors above Yelverton. Margaret Burns pulled the blanket up around the dark head nestling in the hollow of her shoulder. Corporal Roderick Burns, Royal Marines, her Roddy, had come home at last, a day earlier than expected. She sighed with contentment as she glanced at her man lying in her arms.

These two hours would slip away too swiftly: she and Rod were on their own for two hours, the children being out until six o'clock. She smiled to herself at the memory of his telephone call from the dockyard yesterday morning. He'd just caught her before she left for the Saturday market.

They had been very good to her. The Royal Marine Barracks had somehow organised a sergeant to call round to tell her that *Icarus* was anchoring late in the Sound on that Friday night. In spite of the hour and the cold, she had wrapped up the kids and taken them down on the bus to the Civic Centre. She would remember for ages the excitement as they hurried up Lockyer Street to the Hoe — then Cherry's cry as she saw the navigation lights of the frigate stealing slowly into the Sound. The green and red lights glowed so brightly, seemed so close — then from the stillness on the Hoe they had heard the rattle of cable and her anchor splashing into the water.

'Is Daddy in that boat?' Cherry had asked, wide-eyed. She was Rod's favourite, Margaret knew, though he would never confess it: he loved their two sons, but his only daughter, just beginning to boss her elder brothers, was very special.

Now he was stirring beside her and she thrilled to his touch as he slowly re-awakened: he always enjoyed the second time better, after these long partings. She was waiting impatiently, longing to give him more even than he craved: she gloried in these reunions, these fresh honeymoons when he came home. She half-turned, waiting for his eyes to open…

It was Rod who had had the idea of parking out the kids this afternoon — tonight his mother and father were arriving for the Christmas weekend, which meant that she and Rod camped out in the living room. She had thought of Merle Osgood, who was always keen to have the sprogs, as amusement for their spoilt little Debbie. Merle was a bit shallow, but Margaret remained friendly with her because of their mutual friendship with the Fanes. Poor Gwen — she was knocked sideways by Niv's death. After the shock, she had let it be known that she preferred her own company for the time being, and her friends had respected her wishes.

Merle had not been at home, judging by the three bottles of milk stacked by the back door, so Margaret had gone round to her own parents. Giving her a huge wink, Dad had jumped at the chance of taking the kids for the afternoon. So she and Rod were sharing these two hours together ... but now she saw that the hands of their bedside clock were already creeping to half past three. She climbed over him and began brushing her lips across his mouth ... he was reaching for her, loving her, when she thought she heard the chimes of their doorbell.

Margaret stiffened, listening for a repetition of the chime; then she heard it, definitely ringing again. She pulled herself from him, flung on her blue housecoat and pattered down the stairs. Through the stained glass she could see the shadow of a man, a big fellow, standing on the step outside. She smoothed her hair, glanced in the hall mirror and opened the door.

'Oh…' She felt her heart slump, but forced a smile. 'It's you, Sergeant Phillips. You want Roddy?'

The sergeant saluted, shifting from one foot to the other.

'Won't you come in? I'll fetch my husband.' She opened the door wide.

'No, thanks, Mrs Burns. I've come officially…' He hesitated, glancing at the house next door. 'We don't want to advertise it, but your husband has to return to his ship at once.'

Her hand flew to her mouth, but the little cry escaped her lips. 'What's he done?' she asked softly. 'Is he in trouble?'

'No, Mrs Burns, 'course not. It's just that his Commanding Officer is away in another ship. Corporal Burns is in charge of the Royal Marine detachment in *Icarus*.'

'What's he got to do, then?'

'Report immediately on board, that's all I know. The ship's ordered to sea. Exercises.'

He saluted again, awkward, hesitating. Then he let himself out through the front gate and disappeared down the pavement.

Gwendoline Fane folded the cloth and threaded it through the drying-up arrangement Niv had made for her during his last leave. Hot and sticky after the Sunday dinner, she glanced at herself in the mirror: was the drawn face staring back at her really that of the same Mrs Fane who, ten days ago, was longing for her husband's Christmas homecoming?

She touched her black hair, swept up at the back as he had always liked it, even though the grey flecks showed more that way. Although she was only twenty-seven that haggard face was ten years older, with grey half-moons beneath her eyes.

And the eyes he had loved filled with tears, despite herself, for any little thing which reminded her of him, still triggered the agony of emotion.

She had stopped feeling sorry for herself, knowing how he would have despised her lack of guts. Mass this morning had helped: Father O'Connor had been understanding, giving her the strength she needed. Thirteen days since Niv's death in the fire — eight days since the funeral on that terrible Saturday morning in the mizzling rain. They'd buried him in the naval cemetery, done the thing properly, as he would have liked.

Niv's parents took care of her for a couple of days, but she had wanted to come home, in spite of the memories; and today she'd done her best for the kids — they wouldn't get a joint like that again for a long while. Gwen had cancelled Niv's order for a telephone, and the neighbours were helping to find a smaller place close to the kids' school.

One ordeal she could not bring herself to face again for a while was to read those wonderful letters from the ship. Captain Trevellion was coming to see her when he could manage it.

Gwen was filling the kettle in the kitchen when she thought she heard a knock on the door. She turned off the tap ... there it was again. She slipped out of her apron, smoothed back her hair, slicked her eyebrows with her fingertips, and hurried to the window. Through the lace curtain she could see a man outside, a sailor in uniform, with his back to her. Her heart began racing as she hurried into the hall and opened the door.

'Who—?' she began, and then she recognised the unshaven, bedraggled man as Tom Osgood — Niv's friend Oz. 'What's happened, Oz?'

She stood aside and let him into the hall. She took his muddied raincoat, guided him into the living room and made him relax while she brewed the tea. Then she went into him, sat by his side, waiting for him to talk. The kids were quiet, happy upstairs, parcelling up their presents for Christmas.

'I've got this for you, Gwen.' He took the ring from his pocket and pressed it into her hand. 'Thought you should have it.' Before she could answer he was fishing an envelope out of his pocket. 'The Master-at-Arms asked me to give this to you from the lads.' He handed it over awkwardly, as if it was burning a hole in his palm.

Inside was a cheque for £350 and a crumpled sheet of paper bearing a few lines of model longhand. *To help you over a difficult time,* was all the note said, *from the ship's company of* Icarus.

Gwen broke down and hurried into the kitchen. When she rejoined Oz, he was standing at the window, his raincoat hung neatly across the back of a chair. He had smoothed back his fair hair and was tidying up his suit. There were blue shadows beneath his brown eyes.

'Thanks for this,' she said softly. 'I'll write when I can.'

He came close to her and put an arm about her shoulders, saying nothing. She and Merle had often swapped confidences, and she knew she was safe with him. 'What's happened to you, Oz?' she asked. 'You look done in. It's kind of Merle to let you come down: it's an awkward bus journey from Roborough.' She watched him closely, upset by his wild appearance. Oz was normally a fine-looking man, someone any woman could be proud of, but at the moment he looked muddy and dead beat. 'What's happened, Oz?' she repeated softly. 'Tell me.'

'Oh, Christ...' he whispered, his hand clutching at her shoulder.

'Oz,' she asked, *'what's wrong?'*

'Merle's left me.' Gwen felt the shaking of his body as he was wracked by an outburst of uncontrollable sobbing. She let him break away from her and quietly slipped into the kitchen. She selected two glasses from the cupboard, pouring him the last of the sweet sherry and tipping a few drops into her own.

When she returned to the lounge, he was himself again, the same, strong Oz. Gwen went to him, touching his hand. She said nothing, waiting.

As Oz stood up from the sofa his brown eyes were on a level with hers. He looked as hurt as a whipped spaniel. 'When I got home on Friday evening…'

He hesitated, glancing at her for assurance. She sat down on the sofa and patted the cushion beside her.

'I found our flat locked. The caretaker told me that Merle had left three days ago; she left the key with him in case I got home before she did.' She listened to his half-whispered words, hearing the bitterness in them. 'I never knew, Gwen, honest, I didn't, whether she was speaking the truth or lying.'

He was staring at her, hesitating. She had never before seen a man so stripped of his pride. It was not a pretty sight, and she was glad when Oz held up his head again. His chin jutted obstinately, and there was an edge to his voice as he continued.

'There was a note on the kitchen table, just a note, saying she'd left me and taken Debbie with her … taken Debbie, just like that.' He choked and could not go on. 'My little Deb,' he whispered to himself, over and over again.

She stroked his forehead with her fingers, and suddenly he laid his head on her shoulder.

'She gave no reason, Oz?'

'Yes, at the end of the note — she said she couldn't go on with these long separations and being skint all the time. She'd had enough of Navy life. She's going to find happiness with someone who can give her a decent week's wage and who'll be at home. Oh, God, Gwen…'

His fingers were crushing hers, so hard that she wanted to cry out.

'I never really understood Merle,' she said to him. 'She seemed never to have grown up. She revelled in men's admiration — and with her figure she got plenty of it.' Gwen bit her tongue, wishing she'd kept quiet.

'It's Ray — Ray Bolt, I'm sure. He was always in the boozer when I was last home.' He looked her squarely in the eyes. 'You know, Gwen, I'm glad it's finished... I've been unhappy about things for a long time. She was never satisfied, we never had enough lolly, she was always moaning about our way of life. I realise we're getting a raw deal in the Navy, but it'll get better soon. On this last trip I decided to chuck my hand in so that I could save our marriage. I've been blaming the Navy, but she'd have been the same whatever I was earning — never bloody well enough, mate.' He swore beneath his breath. 'Gwen...?'

'Yes?'

He took her fingers, crushing them again in his huge hands. She allowed him to lean against her, his head on her shoulder as gradually the pain drained from him. He would talk when he wanted and, somehow, sharing his torment was helping her to forget...

The door burst open and two little figures tumbled over each other as they fought their way to the TV set. Oz did not move or take his hand away.

'You remember Mr Osgood?' Gwen said. 'He's come to see us for a little while. He'll be staying for supper.' She glanced at Oz, her eyes inviting.

'Yes, Mum.' The elder one gave Oz a friendly, fleeting smile. 'Can we have *The Grimbles* on, Mum? It's just after the news.'

Oz pulled himself to his feet. He leant over and flicked the switch. The black-and-white shadows zigged, then swung into focus. The newscaster was reaching the end of the local news.

'You don't want to be bothered with this, Oz,' Gwen said.

'It's okay by me,' he said, glancing at her. 'The news is almost finished, and they won't miss their *Grimbles*.'

So they watched the newscaster as he adjusted the prompt cards in front of him. The friendly face looked up at his invisible viewers. 'And before I wish you all a very good evening,' he was saying, 'I have a special announcement from the Plymouth Command for the Royal Navy: All officers and men from the following ships should report back on board as soon as possible. The police have asked us to stress that this is an exercise and is no way an emergency. Here are the names of the ships…' and, as the newsreader read from his list, the names were superimposed across the screen. *Icarus* was fourth from the top.

'Not my lucky day,' Oz said, as he rose from the sofa. He turned to Gwen and hugged her, kissing her on each cheek.

He looked at Gwen steadily, taking her hands in his. 'Thanks,' he said. 'I'll be in touch.'

'Take care of yourself, Ozzie,' she said softly. 'There's always someone here if you need any help. I'll keep you posted when I move.'

He took his cap from the hall stand and slipped on his raincoat. Gwen opened the front door and watched him walk down the path, closing the gate behind him. The reflections of the orange street lights shone on the wet pavement; a steady mizzle, driving in from the west, was slatting across the street. Tom Osgood pulled up his coat collar and leant against the wind.

Hob and Allie Gamble tottered out of bed at eight, Hob wondering if he had enough strength to go over to his mother's for lunch. They had done their Christmas shopping in Wendron on their way back from a long walk over the moor yesterday evening, a hilarious hour before returning home. Last night had been a night of heaven, warm in their tiny cottage, but they did not want to waste this Sunday. Hob had to be back in the ship for the flight inventory next Thursday. Allie was deliciously happy, and not taking life too seriously yet.

'All in good time,' he'd whispered into her ear that morning. 'We've a lot to do first.' She'd then suggested driving up to the north coast. 'Why do you want to leave home?' he asked.

'To get out and smell the cliffs and the sea,' she said. 'You love it up there.'

'I've seen enough of the bloody Atlantic to last me my life,' Hob replied. 'I've got other ideas...' And he had loved her again before getting ready for church.

'I'm thinking things out a bit, Allie,' he said quietly, as they drank their coffee afterwards. 'In choppers we get used to casualties, but that death we had in the ship ... and the fact that we've now got a bloody good CO, a man who makes us think about *why* we're really flogging about the Atlantic...'

'Well, if you *will* fly those rotating machines...' she had replied softly, leaning across the wooden table to kiss him. 'I don't want my lovely husband taken from me.'

He'd told her not to be so bloody silly, and they had gone up to the little chapel. It was warm inside as the Cornish voices lifted to the Christmas carols. 'Who said the church was dead?' he asked afterwards, as they drove off to lunch with his mother.

She had never been so happy.

They left Hob's mother when the light began drawing in. He had switched on his headlights just after Wendron.

'Here we go,' he shouted above the revving of the engine as he changed down to swing into the home straight. 'Tea and bed, Mrs Gamble.'

The kettle was simmering even before he had locked up. Mascot, their black-and-grey setter, wriggled off his wetness from nose-tip to tail. 'Filthy animal,' Hob shouted, before drying off the bedraggled hound.

'Cornish cream,' she said. 'Your mum gave it to me.'

'She's happy about us, isn't she?' he said. 'You know she's longing for us to have a family.'

She nodded, stared into his eyes. 'Are you changing your mind, Hob ... about our family, I mean?'

'Do you want our child?' he asked. 'My parents' separation has made me cautious. I want to be absolutely certain.'

He tried to take her into his arms, but she held him off. 'Why *did* they break up, Hob?'

'Dad became obsessed with his questionable politics. He only held on to his civil service job through influence and bloody good luck. He's a bitter, twisted little man, they say. It's all washed up...'

'That won't ever happen to us,' she said softly, sliding into his arms. She hauled his sweater over his head and began unbuttoning his shirt. 'We're wasting time,' she said softly. 'It takes time making babies.'

'Not so very long...' he said.

As he came towards her, she heard the scrabbling of gravel outside in the lane. She drew away from him, listening ... there, the clunk of a car door.

'Bloody hell,' he muttered. 'Who the hell's this?'

She zipped up her jeans, then opened the green door between the bay windows. A black-and-white police car was stopped outside. One of the policemen was already trying the gate.

'Mrs Gamble? Is your husband in?'

'Yes — what is it?'

'We're sorry to disturb you on a Sunday afternoon, but Culdrose have got through to us. They couldn't raise you on the telephone this morning.'

'We've been out most of the day.'

'Sorry, madam ... but Lieutenant Gamble has to report back to his ship.'

She felt Hob's hands on her shoulders. 'You want me?' he asked, an edge to his question.

'Yes, sir. Your Commanding Officer wants you to report back to your ship.'

'Immediately?'

'Those are our instructions, sir. We are to drive you back to Devonport, if you have no transport. We can wait while you pack your things.'

She could sense his anger. She felt uneasy, aware of his quick temper.

'Can I see your papers, please?' he asked curtly. 'This doesn't make sense.'

The policeman fumbled for his identity card. 'Police Constable Trelawny, sir. PC Penfold is the driver,' he said tersely.

Hob sounded weary. 'Okay — but I'll put a call through first. Come in.'

She poured them lukewarm tea while she listened to Hob's resentful voice in the hall. 'Right, Number One. Bloody hell ...

I suppose so. There's no train now, but the police are being obliging. I'll pick up Rollo.'

He was pale and dragging at a cigarette when he returned to the kitchen.

'I'll drive you,' she said firmly. 'I can stay with Lucy for the night.' She glanced at the policemen. 'Thanks. We're sorry you've had to come out all this way.'

They picked up their chequered caps and moved awkwardly to the front door. 'Sorry, sir,' the driver said. 'But we often have to do this around here — your search and rescue squadron is on our beat.'

She glanced at her husband, pride warming her. He remained silent as he closed the garden gate on them. He put his arm about her, pushing her gently back into the cottage. Something choked in her throat and she could not speak.

There were nine others in the church on that Sunday, 23 December; nine regulars, not counting Miss Bakewell, who was wrestling with the harmonium. Rowena Trevellion lowered her head as the vicar pronounced the blessing. She heard him rustling down the aisle and then she climbed to her feet, shivering from the dank cold of this little church, Wesleyan in style, towerless, ugly, but of rugged granite which befitted so well the Cornish character.

She turned to help Pascoe with the wheelchair. Ben had behaved as well as was within his power; the parishioners were used to him and appeared to ignore his ceaseless grunts and jumbled laughter, which were such a part of Rowena's existence. The Trevellions passed the time of day at the door, then they were out in the bitter wind, past the white latch-gate and into the lane for the walk back to the house via the pretty way. Pascoe enjoyed the glimpse of Carrick Roads, but they could not be too long today, because Rowena was worried about the leg of lamb she'd left in the slow cooker.

She watched the tall, stooping figure she loved so much, jogging down the lane ahead of them and jostling the chair back and forth as Ben chortled his delight. Pascoe cherished these moments, walking together as a family when he was home on leave. 'This gives me the stability I need,' he had told her once after the accident. 'I want to bring up our family the way *I* want, not the way our modern society tries to make me.' She had not forgotten his words, and had never allowed the housekeeping chores to intervene, to separate her from him during these precious days.

'Over there, Ben ... look, just above the rushes,' he called excitedly.

As she caught up with them, she sighted the geese, a pair which had arrived last winter. Their white feathers were bright among the bulrushes at the head of the creek. Tears sprang to her eyes: why couldn't these golden moments last for ever? And why did there have to be so few of these interludes, only once or twice a year when he was on leave?

Rags, their old Springer spaniel, suddenly burst upon them and floundered around them with frenzied barking.

'Ben, look, here's Rags. *Down,* old boy, down,' and Pascoe quietened the dog, allowing him to lick Ben's outstretched fingers. Ro hurried past them into the warmth of the hall; she had left on the gas heater for his homecoming yesterday. Without removing her coat, she went straight into the kitchen. As she lifted the lid of the slow cooker, she heard the telephone ringing in the hall. Still holding the oven cloth, she moved to the door.

Pascoe's back was turned to her, as he stared through the windows overlooking the bare beeches. He seemed to be listening, saying little, nodding his head. Then she heard his words: 'Yes, sir, right away. I'll phone the first lieutenant.'

She hurried into the hall, threw the cloth on to the bench in the corner. 'No, Pascoe, no. Not today, Pascoe.'

He turned to her, his gaunt face strained.

'Merry Christmas,' he said, kissing her. 'That was my duty officer. Fleet has ordered *Icarus* to sea with all dispatch.' He put his arms about her, holding her tightly. 'If you'll drive me to the dockyard, I can be there by four.'

She dragged herself from him, rushed into the kitchen, blinded by her tears. She couldn't talk to him now: all her anxieties, the bank manager wanting to see her, the first instalment of the fees for Ben's residential home...

She dashed the hot tears from her eyes, itching to hurl the spuds through the window.

'Lay the table, dear,' she called without turning round. 'I'm dishing up.' They'd have their Sunday lunch together before tackling the icy roads.

CHAPTER 15

HMS Icarus, 24 December.

Captain Trevellion, having spent Monday afternoon with the staff of C-in-C, Plymouth, was shifting into his sea-going uniform. It was 1725 when Jewkes tapped on his cabin door.

'Lower deck cleared, sir. All hands on board, except for Able Seaman Foulgis. I'll report him absent on sailing. We've been sent seamen reliefs for our Marines — it seems we won't have to put up with the scrum for too long.'

'Thanks, Number One, I'll follow you down. I expect they have ideas for our Royals — and the ship can do without Foulgis.'

The hangar doors were shut and they had switched on the heating, but the draught cut to the marrow. There was barely space for them all, even though the engine room watchkeepers — who had flashed up an hour earlier — were absent. He returned the salutes of his officers (he had not had time to see them all yet) then went straight to the point.

'Considering the pier-head jump we've all suffered,' he began, 'I'd like to tell you how good it is to have a ship's company that does not let you down. There's only one man adrift.' He glanced round his ship's company, squashed into the hangar and peering through the doors, eager to learn what was happening. The Master-at-Arms stood at the front with the chiefs and petty officers; the leading hands (Osgood amongst them, he noticed) in a group together.

'There are better ways of spending Christmas Eve,' he went on. 'But the sooner we show the Russians that we mean business, the sooner we'll get back to our homes.' He glanced down at his notes.

'First, you all know that our American friends have called on NATO to show its resolve. A Period of Tension has been officially declared. We are ordered to Alert State Two and to rejoin STANAVFORLANT, taking up station on the edge of the Arctic Circle just about now.

'You've been working flat out since rejoining on Sunday night. We're now ammunitioned, fuelled and stored — again, I'd like to thank you for getting down to it. We've been ordered to be as discreet as possible about our recall and the fact that the Fleet's putting to sea, but the dockyard are bound to know about it by tomorrow.'

He paused, looking around him.

'I want to put you fully in the picture. The Soviet Union have replied this afternoon to the American's firm stand in Iceland. The Soviets have said to the United States and to NATO: "Okay, so you are acting aggressively in Iceland to safeguard your defence. We are entitled to do the same. You have secret installations in northern Norway which are threatening our security and our territory, particularly our Northern Fleet's base at Murmansk. We have friends in Finnmark who don't like this aggressive posture, comrades who wish us to free them from the oppressive Norwegian government imposing its will on the Finnmark people. We are disturbed by these warlike threats on the part of Norway, one of NATO's allies, so we reserve the right to take what defensive steps we believe necessary to protect ourselves against attack."

Pascoe could feel the tension in the hangar; he did not have to raise his voice now. 'So,' he went on, 'the Soviets declared this morning that they will start their winter manoeuvres immediately in the Kola and Murmansk areas — they are already moving, according to our satellite intelligence. They've two divisions there, complete with massive tactical air support — and a dedicated amphibious force to lift 1,700 men of their Naval Infantry Regiment. That's a total of about 35,000 men.' He paused to allow this reality to sink in. 'They'll be ready to attack across the border within four days.'

He faced them, watching the reactions of the older, married men who would bear the brunt of it if the going got tough. The only sound was the whistling of the draught through the doors.

'NATO is reacting with a flexible response to this Soviet threat. First, we are showing the Soviets that we *shall* resist any Russian attack upon one of our NATO allies. We are immediately landing 45 and 42 Royal Marine Commandos in northern Norway; they've been exercising with the Norwegian Army and their Home Guard for years. *Glorious* is embarking 45 Commando here in Devonport as we speak, and she'll be sailing on tomorrow's tide. *Furious* is being brought forward in Portsmouth as rapidly as possible, to embark 42 Commando which is now fully trained for Arctic fighting. If we had enough amphibious ships, we could land the whole lot together.

'We're asking the Merchant Navy for help in landing our troops in Norway. *Fearless* is bound for the Faeroes with troops. When *Intrepid* is ready, she'll be taking a force of Ulstermen to Jan Mayen Island. The Norwegians are taking care of Spitzbergen but the Russians may attack there, on the pretext of defending their miners.

'The job of the troops is to bring up the Russians with a round turn. If the Soviet Union attacks Norway, the Royal Marines will hold the line until reinforcements arrive. The

ACE (Allied Command Europe) Mobile Force is assembling at the moment for air and sea lift into Norway.'

He glanced again at his notes. 'We are sailing now to join *Gloucester,* as the second Area Defence ship for STANAVFORLANT whose job it is to stop any Soviet Amphibious Force from landing from seaward upon the Norwegian coast — probably in the Tromsø area. We reckon they don't want to go further south, because if they take Tromsø, they will have achieved their objective: they will have chucked us out of the North Cape Area, from where we monitor the movements of their Northern Fleet.

He glanced round at them all before continuing. 'I've nearly finished. NATO is also showing its resolution in its Anti-Submarine role. If they attack Norway, we shall sink every Soviet submarine we can find. As you know from our experience in "Clear Lane", the Soviet submarines are on their way out to their war stations — where to, and for what purpose, we don't know. If they decide to go hot, we'll sink 'em. If they play it cool, we'll tail them.

'The Yanks are taking care of the Greenland-Iceland gap; America and NATO, the Iceland-Faeroes gap; NATO and ourselves, Faeroes-Shetland; and the Royal Navy on its own, the Shetland-Orkneys gap and the Pentland Firth.' He looked up. 'I need hardly add that our task is also to sink any ship or aircraft threatening our platforms in the Brent and other oilfields.' He glanced about him, then asked, 'Where's Corporal Burns?'

'Here, sir.' Then he spotted the solid figure of the Royal Marine, his green beret conspicuous in the crowd, his 'Booties' grouped around him.

'Corporal: reliefs have been embarked for your ship's duties. Be prepared for anything. Get yourselves ready for landing.

Captain Stoddart told me that most of you are Arctic trained. You've loaded your Arctic gear?'

'Yes, sir — all of us except Gregg and Allan. Can we pick theirs up in Norway?'

'I expect so, Corporal. I'll signal Captain Stoddart in *Gloucester* when we get there. You'll remain in charge of the contingent until he joins you. I don't know *how* he'll join yet.'

Burns gave him a half-hearted grin.

'Before I dismiss you,' Trevellion continued, 'I want to ask all officers to make certain that their departments are on a war footing. All gear's to be properly stowed — no inflammables about the place. Our rules of engagement have been upgraded, and, as always, we have the privilege of being allowed to open fire on any ship after she has opened fire on us. At action stations wear your life jackets and keep them inflated.'

He grinned, glad of the light relief.

'When *Glorious* has finished her amphibious job, she'll revert to ASW and probably be sent by CINCEASTLANT to operate in the gaps. STANAVFORLANT may have to screen her, but that depends upon whether our through-deck cruiser, *Invincible,* is out of refit on time. If *Illustrious* had finished her trials to schedule there would be no problem.' He said no more, for the labour troubles in that yard were notoriously bad.

'That's all. The barracks berthing party should be on its way to slip us. We'll steam at maximum cruising speed up the Irish Channel and we should be off Lough Foyle by 1500 tomorrow, if the navigating officer's got it right.' He smiled at Brian Neame, then added, 'We shall listen to Her Majesty's broadcast at 1500. I want as many of you as can be spared to watch because, after the Queen has talked to us, the Prime Minister will be talking to the nation. This will be the first time that our people will really know what's going on, because we've been trying to play down the crisis. The media hasn't yet reported today's problems in getting *Splendid* out of Rosyth — we had to use troops.'

He turned to the first lieutenant. 'Special sea dutymen,' he barked. 'Single-up. Let's get to sea and on with the job.' He turned and smiled at his ship's company. 'And a Merry Christmas to you all,' he said.

Returning the salutes of his officers, he was surprised by the cheer that rang about his ears as he disappeared through the doorway to the Burma Road which led for'd to the bridge.

Oz stood alone in his favourite vantage point abaft the bridge. Wrapped in his anorak, he was watching the soft colours of Ulster slowly mounting above the horizon.

Since returning to the ship on that Sunday night, L/RO Osgood had kept himself to himself. He had briefly shared his news with Rod Burns, but had been too busy to stop and natter: his feet had barely touched the ground since *Icarus* had put to sea.

Since clearing the Lizard last night, the ship had kept one-in-four. Oz had got his head down until the morning watch, which had been uneventful as *Icarus* steamed at twenty-four knots up the Irish Sea: peaceful, the weather still tolerable, though the barometer was falling. He was up here for a breather after watching the Queen and the Prime Minister. The lads did not show their feelings; they never did.

Perhaps because Mick Foulgis's corroding influence was missing, they had all listened in silence to the Queen. It suddenly struck home that this was no longer an exercise; they might all be at the start of something beyond imagination. It was as if the first gusts of an approaching hurricane were bearing down on them.

The mauves and blues of the Irish hills were merging with the drear winter sunset as *Icarus* steamed up the head of the lough. The pinpoints of light along the Lisahally jetty shone brightly in the gloom as men of the Royal Ulster Constabulary moved into position, guns in their hands. The silent dockies stared upwards, then took the lines as the frigate slid alongside. Minutes later, the Chief's boys opened the valves; the hoses bulged, pulsing with the precious fuel.

After supper, Oz went aft to watch them working on the Lynx. The flight was flat-out arming the torpedoes, checking the Sea Skua missiles, flares and securing for sea. Oz gave them a hand running *Perdix* into the hangar. Lieutenant Gamble came up to him.

'You're often down here with the flight, L/RO Osgood,' he said. 'The Lynx interest you?'

'Yes, sir. Makes a break from the office.'

'Ever think of transferring?' Hob Gamble said, then put his finger to his mouth. 'Shouldn't have said that. You're going outside, aren't you?'

'I've requested, sir.'

'The Navy can't afford to lose good men, Osgood — not just now.' The lieutenant walked off to inspect the brightly painted tail rotor with his critical eye.

CHAPTER 16

HMS Gloucester, 27 December.

Captain Richard Stoddart, Royal Marines, like many of those off watch in HMS *Gloucester,* was up on the bridge making the most of the last half-hour of semi-daylight. Here on the edge of the Arctic Circle, the sun never rose above the horizon at this time of the year: only a lugubrious twilight dispelled, for a few hours, the gloom of perpetual night. November until January must pass before there could be hope of better things…

Dick Stoddart felt adrift away from *Icarus.* He had been 'lent' to this DDG, a cracking good ship, but he could not settle down. *Gloucester* was worked up and able to fulfil her role as an Air Defence Ship to STANAVFORLANT. In comparison to dear old *Icarus, Gloucester* was in a class of her own; she was the next-generation destroyer.

He moved to the forward window and peered into the semi-darkness. Only one or two blurs were visible — *Jesse L. Brown* and *Oileus,* probably — the rest of the force being dispersed in loose formation around the horizon.

Stoddart missed his Royal Marine detachment in *Icarus,* the men he and Corporal Burns had trained to such a pitch; they were a good lot, and raring to get back to the snow.

Captain Stoddart had spent seven winters on Arctic Express exercises, and he could not wait to get ashore — this time perhaps for real, under wartime conditions. He pushed aside the memories of his wife Sally and their two-year-old daughter, tucked away in Kendal for Christmas. He had known for some time that he would never be able to get home for the festive season. Already it seemed another life since STANAVFORLANT had swept up from the sunny climes, keeping clear of Ireland, on passage to their secret billets. On the night of Christmas Eve, Rockall had been sighted as *Gloucester* steamed north towards the Faeroes-Iceland gap, where the north-east gale struck them.

Dick Stoddart glanced at the bridge clock: 1445 on this interminable Thursday, the third day of this gale which still showed no signs of decreasing.

Gloucester had arrived on her billet twenty-four hours late. The captain had knocked her down to twelve, but even at this speed, and with her four stabilisers, life was uncomfortable; if it had not been a head sea, existence below would have been miserable. Most of the younger rates and officers were seasick from the pitching, and he braced himself again for the crash as Gloucester sawed through the next big sea thundering down upon them from the Pole. She trembled along her whole length, shook herself free as she sprung upwards, climbing, climbing ... poised in the air, then slamming down into the trough again to confront the ceaseless battering from those dark merciless frozen wastes.

The force was hove-to, barely maintaining steerage-way, trying to minimise the icing-up from the freezing spray. Once in every watch the force turned downwind so that the hands could chip off the worst of the ice. Dick was the officer of the watch, but the captain had taken over for the turn when *Gloucester* almost broached. She rolled to her beam-ends and hung for a lifetime before catapulting back. Thankfully *Gloucester* was not crank, but the driving blizzards and darkness did not help during those first days before they realised that the designers merited the trust placed in them. Modern ships tend to pose stability problems for the naval architects because of the new propulsion installations, but *Gloucester* had no massive boilers mounted low in her structure.

Dick had been down to the engine room during his second day on board. The Olympus engine was the same model as that used in aircraft, and those gigantic power units generated such power that the man on the bridge could feel the acceleration as she responded automatically to the orders passed from the two levers mounted on the bridge consol. Her variable-pitch propellers controlled her speed, controls which — like others in this ship — could be operated either hydraulically or electrically. The engines could even continue to function if all electric power was lost. The Agoudi system — the technique of ejecting air through the barrel of the shaft onto the propellers — had been perfected to confuse any listening submarine, and was giving no trouble now.

Dick braced himself as the deck came up to meet him ... his knees and every muscle in his body were aching from the continuous struggle for balance. Everyone was tired, bad-tempered, craving sleep. He peered out from the port wing of the enclosed bridge; from here he could see the whole sweep of her side, down to the flight deck. Seas were swirling across the flat surfaces, half-moons of froth seesawing and curling with the motion. Dick wondered what she would be like without her stabilisers and twin rudders. Even in these hard conditions she was giving little trouble to the Chief and his boys; only No. 3 stabiliser had 'fallen over'. The marine engineers ran the ship from their cosy, centralised control room, where push buttons and computers did the work. The ship was designed to fight with as few men as was necessary. A future war would not last long, they said...

Dick smiled sardonically. No planner (as most admitted) could envisage what a hot war would be like. He suspected that sea warfare would revert to traditional hard slog, decided by who could hold out longest, whose morale would crack first. That depended upon the quality of sailor fighting the ship — and, even more, upon those leading him.

Gloucester's spirit was infectious: they were an enthusiastic team, from the compact, humorous man who was their captain, down to the most junior rating. They all knew where they stood, because discipline was firm, and the effectiveness of this finely tuned, superb weapon — a ship costing thirty million pounds — depended upon instant and efficient reaction to any threat the enemy might hurl at her. There had been criticism of these ships, but now that they had been modified the Type 42s were as efficient as any warship in the world.

The morning's sitrep had stated that *Glorious* and her amphibious force would be off Tromsø at 1600 this afternoon, ready to disembark 45 Commando. Dick smiled ruefully: at least he had won the Old Man's permission to land somehow, to prepare for the arrival of his detachment from *Icarus*. He hoped that Corporal Burns had prepared the detachment for what was coming to it — *Gloucester*'s captain had broadcast to his ship's company a lucid explanation of STANAVFORLANT's and the Navy's role up here.

The Russians had built up their Northern Fleet for two objectives: firstly, to cut NATO's Atlantic sea lanes so that America could not reinforce the free nations of Europe — and that meant one million tons of stores had to be convoyed across the Atlantic during the first few days of war if NATO was to survive. For this reason, the Soviets had built their huge submarine fleet, a nuclear fleet able to roam the vast ocean of the Atlantic; able to lie in wait below the horizon, choosing the moment to fire their missiles at the stream of modern ships, each one on average four times larger than those of Hitler's war. To realise this objective, Russia must first take out the exasperating thorn in her flesh — the surveillance and counter-threat of NATO's presence at North Cape.

The enemy's prime objective, of course, was to destroy the retaliatory threats, the widely deployed ballistic missile submarines — their missiles beamed on the Soviet naval dockyards — and the American carrier strike forces cruising in the Mediterranean and the Atlantic. But so remote was the chance of countering all these in time that both objectives would, and could, be pursued simultaneously.

'And that's why,' the captain had concluded, 'we are sending our Royal Marines alongside the Norwegian army, to show the Soviets that NATO will resist to the death any invasion of its territory. Our chaps and the Dutch Marines are on their way now to Norway in *Glorious;* and with the consent of our Norwegian and Danish friends, a force to Spitzbergen and Jan Mayen islands. The ACE International Mobile Force will soon be on its way from Europe, and will be landing its troops and aircraft two days after 45 Commando.'

Dick had forgotten the importance of ice-bound Jan Mayen and Spitzbergen: they also overlooked the Russian bolt-holes into the Atlantic.

STANAVFORLANT was keeping radar and radio silence. The Russians would have a job pinpointing the force in this weather, though its Northern Fleet frequencies were monitored to catch every transmission. *Gloucester*'s EW team were watch-on, watch-off at the moment, receiving and analysing the data, both from the enemy and from Northwood.

The ops room was building up a considerable plot but, due to the radio and radar policy, no overall picture was yet possible.

STANAVFORLANT was standing by as a longstop, secretly patrolling the second line of defence, detecting and monitoring any Soviet warship sailing from Murmansk. The first line, the SSN Fleet submarines, were maintaining their Iron Ring off North Cape; they were on their stations, watching, reporting, shadowing, ready to strike. Deep-field in the Atlantic, south of the Greenland-Iceland-UK gaps, the third line of defence — the American strike fleet — was forging to its war station under SACLANT's orders.

It was 1530 and darkness was gradually shutting down again upon another wild night, another night of bitter weather; another twenty-four hours of chipping, officers and men together, fighting the insidious invasion of black ice. Frozen hands and feet, the cold eating right through them — it was not surprising that men were asking themselves what the ship could achieve in these frightful seas. The weapons gave the answer, provided they could stand up to these harsh conditions.

The bo'sun's mate was preparing to make his pipe to call the dog-watchmen. Dick Stoddart slipped from the bridge and hurried down the ladders towards the ops room. There was time to bring himself up-to-date and sight the met forecast before he took over his watch.

Leaving his anorak and gloves outside, Stoddart stepped into the gloom of the compartment which was the combined brain and heart of this fighting ship. He glanced at the 'State' board on the port side: there they were, ships of the force. *Athabaskan,* the Senior Officer in the centre and coping with the 'Up-Threat', with the oiler and the replenishment ship disposed five miles astern of her, three miles between each. To the north-west, *Goeben;* away to the south-east, *Gloucester,* covering both RAS ships and the eastern half of the force. When *Icarus* arrived, any hour now, the western section would also be covered, though her Sea Cats could not give long-range cover. Frigates, frigates ... never enough of them, as Nelson had complained.

There was a chance that the weather might moderate tomorrow for a brief twenty-four hours. The Commodore had approved the captain's suggestion that *Gloucester*'s Lynx might lift Stoddart to *Oileus* and that her Sea King should fly him to Tromsø to prepare for *Icarus*'s detachment. Conditions were too hairy for *Gloucester*'s Lynx to lower him by wire on to *Icarus*'s lurching flight deck.

'Stoddart ... all set for Saturday, if I can get you off?'

The captain was looking across at him, the customary cheerful grin on his round face. He was slumped in his chair at the Command Display, where every scrap of information, after being filtered and analysed by the computers, appeared on the PPI in front of him. On the captain's left was the Advanced Principal War Officer taking care of the air battle and every action above water. On the captain's right was the other PWO, junior to the AWO, who was responsible for the battle beneath the surface. The ship was organised into two defence watches, so the two AWOs and two PWOs were watch-on, watch-off. Life down here was as boring as hell at the moment, with nothing much from the EW room and little more from CINCEASTLANT. A Soviet passenger ship was coming up from the Skagerrak steering north-north-west; that was all, except for numerous 'sub' enemy reports from long-range maritime patrol aircraft.

'Yes, sir,' Dick answered the captain. 'I'll pick up my Arctic gear in Tromsø.'

'You'll leave a gap, soldier.'

'I'll miss *Gloucester*, sir.'

He meant what he said. It had been a revelation to serve in a 'latest generation' destroyer. This was one of the most up-to-date ops rooms in the world: totally computerised, data-linked to the rest of the force by modern inter-command communications. The captain had discarded his headset because of the silence policy.

The force was data-linked through its UHF system, so that each ship could follow the battle wherever she was in the force. The captain and each of the ops room team were provided with boom mikes; a foot-switch cut out the internal circuit and allowed the team to listen with their right ears to the external voice circuits, while the left ear absorbed the internal chat. A strict 'circuit discipline' made sure that things worked. A hardened PWO never raised his voice, but listened for his opportunity to break in.

When Stoddart was officer of the watch, he appreciated the chat line, for he could anticipate what might happen next. When things got hairy and the escorts too close during a submarine hunt, it was the OOW's job to override the command's instructions. The OOW was the captain's safety man. When consorts came too close, the Command Display could not react swiftly enough to a neighbouring ship's change of bearing during rapid alterations of course — seconds counted. The officer of the watch's heartfelt cry: 'Bridge Override — I'm not happy, sir. Suggest coming to starboard...' was the nautical ejection seat.

Dick Stoddart felt happier keeping a night rather than a day watch, because for him the picture seemed less confusing at night. How the hell had the PQ convoys coped during their runs to Murmansk during World War II? If STANAVFORLANT ran into a hot war tomorrow, how would he react? Over in seconds, depending upon who fired first — even one bullet through this lot and they could be helpless, if it hit the one vital item of equipment. The SAGA stores system, a comprehensive miracle which was able to find in a few seconds any of its thirty thousand items, was as vital to the ship's efficiency as her weapons. Its compartment ran athwartships from one side of the ship to the other. What would those PQ men think of this?

'Going on watch, soldier?' the captain was asking.

'Last dog, sir.'

'You're going to be late. Keep your eyes skinned. *Icarus* should be joining us soon on the western flank. It's a rotten bloody night.'

'Aye, aye, sir.'

Stoddart slipped out of the snug compartment. Elbowing himself into his anorak, he wrapped Sally's scarf about his neck and clambered up the ladders to the bridge.

At 1714 precisely the communications rating picked up in the darkness a winking light, a yellow smudge flashing its message. *Icarus* was in station on the screen. *Gloucester* relayed it by blue lamp to *Oileus,* invisible to the naked eye for over two hours; and so, back to eyeball methods, the Commodore in *Athabaskan* finally received the report. STANAVFORLANT was complete.

Stoddart sighed with relief: his detachment was here. The day after tomorrow, 29 December — if the weather eased — he and Corporal Burns would be ashore and fixing things up for the detachment's hop north to the base camp. It would be good to be on skis again but not such good news to be shacked up in snow-holes, waiting on the blizzards to blow themselves out...

He crossed to the starboard side of the bridge, waiting for the white-out to improve. For the hundredth time he lifted his night binoculars; even though the force was so dispersed, he disliked the feeling that a close consort could suffer a steering failure and make an error in her zigzag. Station-keeping in this weather, with visibility down to half a mile, tended to keep officers of the watch on their toes.

It was lonely here, the helmsman and bo'sun's mate his only company. The one break in the monotony was calling the watch to chipping stations twice a watch when the force turned downwind, keeping the seas on the quarter to avoid broaching.

Stoddart glanced at the clock for the umpteenth time ... fifty minutes before the end of his watch. He wanted to get a letter off to Sally before supper. He lowered his binoculars, his arms cramping from his perpetual searching. The two lookouts were on hourly tricks, a discipline brought back from the past by the captain who was a submariner. Wartime experience had taught that an hour's binocular watch was long enough for ratings — two hours for officers — when sighting the enemy first decided the issue.

Stoddart's eyes had been aching for the last hour, but he would take one more look on this side before returning to the other. He straddled his legs wide and wedged himself into the corners of the starboard after window. The shock of the ship's pitching had already bruised the socket of his right eye, so he gingerly raised his binoculars to begin another sweep. Starting aft, he slowly cut across the invisible line where the sea was supposed to meet the sky.

It was impossible keeping an efficient visual watch with this bloody pitching. The gale was battering at the bridge windows while sheets of water streamed across the bridge, even when hove-to like this. It was the noise that strained his resilience: the continuous roar from the breaking seas, the howl and shriek of the hurricane-force gusts as they tore through the aerials and radar mounts. After two days of this devil's orchestra, nerves began to fray: would this pounding cacophony never cease?

Stoddart compressed his lips and tried to concentrate — the essence of a good eyeball lookout. It was crazy to be using binoculars — even with light intensifiers — when the ship was fitted with millions of pounds worth of radar equipment, navigation aids, IFF, radio communication links, the lot. When his eyes were tired he always suffered hallucinations and imagined he saw things that weren't there, and his vision was becoming jumpy from constantly registering the rollers stampeding towards the diminutive *Gloucester.*

Then, the seas crashing upon her, she shivered, shook herself, began swooping upwards; poised an instant, then plunged again into the gaping valley below ... Stoddart was reaching Green 130 when the horizon line seemed to take on a strange luminous whiteness. He jammed the eyepieces more firmly into his eyes, stared until they ached. His heart suddenly missed a beat.

A mountain of breaking, lunging seas was foaming in confusion; above it he saw a white plume, a silver scimitar scything into the night sky, its height impossible to guess. Through this veil of drifting spume, the blurred outline of a giant vessel emerged, a gigantic ship careering down a quartering sea.

'Captain on the bridge!' he yelled, keeping his eyes on the apparition. 'Quick, Signalman, call the captain…'

There, at less than a quarter of a mile distant, was this gigantic spectre, the pride of the Soviet Navy: one of their latest carriers, a Kiev.

'Yes, soldier, where is she?'

The captain grabbed at his binoculars, half-strangling him with the straps. 'Where is she?'

'You're about lined up on her, sir. Look! There.'

He watched the darker blur of her starboard quarter disappearing into the night. The captain had picked her up.

'Got her … my God, she's the *Kazan*. Look at that modified top sail. Sure of it … damn, she's gone.' He flung the glasses back to Stoddart, grabbed his own, began searching, talking aloud to his officer of the watch. 'Her bow, soldier; did you see her bow?'

'Yes, sir…' How could he ever forget it, that graceful clipper bow lifting to the swell? The silhouette which burst through the maelstrom was familiar to every officer in the Royal Navy. She had been at only a few cables: Stoddart had recognised that castellated superstructure with the 3D top sail radar at its peak, the radome forward and just below the truck. The huge ship had rolled slowly towards him, her great flat expanse of flight deck gleaming in the darkness, an expanse of shimmering water sluicing across the surface like a motorway during a downpour. She rolled away; then, in the confusion of that furious cauldron, she vanished as swiftly as she had emerged. It seemed to Stoddart that the apparition had flashed into view for only a few seconds, though afterwards the signalman said he had timed its presence as lasting forty-seven seconds.

'I've lost her, sir!'

Dick swept back again for a final look. At first, he thought he was seeing *Kazan*'s wash again, waves breaking in all directions. But then the grey furies seemed to divide. The seas were flying into the night, cascading high into the blackness, across something thicker, more opaque than the curling seas. He felt the kick in his guts again…

'There, sir! One of her screening destroyers!'

The captain was standing by him, feverishly searching. 'Where, soldier, for God's sake?'

'I'm on now, sir. Green one-two-o.'

'Got her…' the captain shouted. 'She's bashing straight through … Christopher! Look at that, soldier. Her main deck, right aft to her quarterdeck, is underwater. See the gap between her bridge superstructure and mainmast? She's no destroyer.'

Dick had picked her up for a few seconds, holding her in his circle of vision. He held the spectre momentarily, watched it merging into the spray that was swallowing her again.

'It's their relative sizes, sir,' Dick shouted, trying to steady his voice. 'A cruiser, isn't she?'

The captain was snapping his orders at the signalman. 'Send out a flash report,' he commanded briskly. 'One Kiev carrier, probably *Kazan*, escorted by one Kara cruiser in position — quote our DR — course 280 degrees, estimated speed eighteen knots.' He turned to his navigating officer who was poring silently over the chart table, his pencil and parallel ruler flying as he traced the enemy's track.

'Where's that taking her, Pilot?' he shouted against the battering of the storm.

'Doesn't make sense, sir. Jan Mayen, if she holds that heading.'

The enemy report was cleared in seconds. The Commodore repeated it to CINCEASTLANT, then relaxed radar silence and used UHF to manoeuvre his force. STANAVFORLANT turned in a forlorn attempt to hang on to the Russian ship, who probably had not even sighted *Gloucester*. Within minutes, it became obvious that the chase was futile: the enemy's radar echoes soon vanished as *Kazan* and her escort disappeared to the north-north-west.

For the remainder of the last dog watch, little was spoken on *Gloucester*'s bridge. Stoddart sensed the frustration, the intense disappointment: the superior speed and the excellent sea-keeping qualities of those superb Soviet ships had never been brought home in such a traumatic manner.

Gloucester was a formidable warship: her dual-purpose missile system, her Foxer and sonar; her chaff rocket-launchers and STWS torpedoes — and, above all, her Mark VII Lynx helicopter system — would force a Russian to think twice, wherever she was encountered throughout the world. At last NATO was catching up — but did they have the time? The bogeyman always had the initiative…

Stoddart handed over his watch to the sub. He had only three minutes in hand before his divisional meeting with the Royal's contingent at 1815. He wanted to be there to help the lieutenant who had only recently been appointed to *Gloucester*. Stoddart felt that the chap could cope now, because the drill had been standardised with the other frigates and destroyers. *Gloucester*'s contingent was not being put ashore, because few of its Marines were Arctic-trained and also because the contingent was vital to the manning of the destroyer.

The divisional meeting went well, cooped in the fug and warmth of the Royal Marines' mess. The bulkheads and lockers dripped condensation: the Arctic was no respecter of comfort.

They had tried everything, but nothing dried, the dampness permeating everywhere.

The Divisional Officer closed the meeting: 'And I know you'd like to thank Captain Stoddart for all he's done for us during his enforced stay. Good luck, sir, in Norway.'

They rose to let him edge past them. The stench of sweaty feet and stale vomit was getting even Stoddart down. 'Thanks,' he said. 'That's if I can get ashore. Depends on this bloody weather. Good luck to you lot in *Gloucester.*'

It was 1925 when he reached the wardroom. He still felt queasy, so he paused to read the bulletins pinned on the notice board outside the canteen. No one knew when the next mail could be expected, so the BBC news provided the only means of guessing what was happening at home. Propping himself against the bulkhead, he tried to focus on the news-sheets swaying backwards and forwards with the rolling of the ship.

So the Soviets were keeping up the pressure? Divisional troop movements on the Central Front yesterday — Boxing Day — while the Western world snored in front of its tellies, had been confirmed by SACEUR, and meanwhile the Murmansk Divisions were concentrating on the Kirkenes frontier.

The atrocious weather was preventing accurate reports on the movements of the Soviet Northern Fleet, although more outward sailings than normal of ballistic submarines from all their fleet were suspected. And then the home news caught his eye: the usual disquieting stuff to which Britain had become accustomed during these locust years.

The various European transport systems were struggling to cope with the chaos of cancelled bookings all over Europe — skiers were shuffling back and forth in both directions, unable to decide whether it was prudent to risk a few more days in the snow. By all accounts, it was a case of the survival of the fittest on the railways. Anarchy prevailed as usual at British airports; the weather and a festering go-slow of traffic controllers in Britain and France ensured the customary farrago. Not many servicemen would be suffering those frustrations, thought Stoddart.

The Home Office had its hands full, dealing with riot fever spreading in the big cities ... was it too late, this time, to rise to the challenge as Britain had succeeded in doing before? And could the politicians give a lead now, after years of fostering the politics of envy? Would the Deputy Leader this time loyally back up his Prime Minister as that chap Attlee had done in World War II?

Dick Stoddart shook his head and pushed open the wardroom door. Avoiding the chattering group of officers in the anteroom, moved straight into the dining annexe: a quick supper and then straight to his pit. He had the morning watch, which he shared with the first lieutenant.

CHAPTER 17

Norway, 29 December.

It was very dark when *Oileus*'s Sea King dropped to the lights glimmering from the black abyss below the shuddering cab. Dick Stoddart returned aft, to his seat next the observer: the two pilots were concentrating on their approach drill into Harstad airport. He clipped on his safety belt, then tried to focus his thoughts on the job that lay ahead.

Gloucester's chopper had managed to transfer him to *Oileus,* as the gales had begun to moderate. COMSTANAVFORLANT could not spare his principal air defence ship to approach the Norwegian coast in order to fly off her Lynx, so the superior range of *Oileus*'s Sea King had been exploited. These two imperturbable Dutch pilots were good news. They had just signed off from Andoya air strip, the most northerly and seaward of the Vesteralen islands; the observer had homed on the Andenes radio beacon and had picked up this wicked coast exactly where he expected it.

Through the window in the door, Dick spotted the white snowflakes flashing past the dark backdrop of the Hinnoy heights, mere hills of three thousand feet — and now the Sea King was dropping prudently between the peaks of Hinnoy and Grytöya, which loomed darkly against the night sky.

'Going in.'

The guttural English came clearly through the intercom, and then there was the slight bump as she touched. The motors slowly unwound and the engines growled to a stop. The door was opened by the aircrew and then Dick was tumbling out and on to the hard snow. The senior pilot held out his hand.

'Thanks,' Dick said. 'Thanks very much.'

'Okay ... see you, soldier.' And the Dutch pilot grinned from within his bone dome as he unharnessed himself. He'd refuel, and then he'd be off again into the night to find *Oileus* — but there'd be no beacon for him on the way back: STANAVFORLANT had re-established silence.

Stoddart sucked in his breath when the cold hit him. He slung on his gear, flipped up the collar of his jacket, pulled down his earmuffs, then stomped across to the Royal Marine who was doubling across the field to meet him.

He returned the driver's brisk salute, and then they lugged his gear into the back of the Land Rover; they drove off beneath the brittle glare of the road lights heading for the Naval Headquarters at Ramsund.

The Commander, 42 Commando Brigade, was striding into the briefing room when at 1600 precisely, Ian Dixon, a buddy of Dick's, shovelled him into a seat at the back. 'When the OC's finished, I'll take you to Staffie,' he whispered. 'Everything's fixed, but you're not getting all you asked for.'

A blown-up map of northern Norway was projected on to the wall behind the commander. Colonel Backhouse was a tough-looking character, but he spoke quietly, unemotionally, presenting the day's briefing to them as if this was just another exercise. He too had discarded his Arctic gear, and was beret-less and relaxed in his woolly pully.

'Evening, gentlemen. I'll be brief, because time's against those of you in 42's rearguard who have still to deploy tonight. Fortunately, we can't tell night from day, so you shouldn't be feeling the strain.' He faced them all, the tip of his pointer tapping the cleft in his chin. 'Before starting the main brief, I want to remind the more junior of you and the newcomers of the reason we're here.' He cleared his voice, spoke clearly, precisely, choosing his words.

'The objective of the Royal Marine Commandos is summed up in one word — deterrence. That's why we are deploying with full publicity, why we are broadcasting to the enemy that we are taking up our battle stations alongside our Norwegian friends; that's why we're taking no deceptive or security measures with our amphibious operations. Our job, gentlemen, is to buy time for the NATO politicians, so that they can make up their minds. We're here to show the Soviets that our side means business; if the shooting starts, we've failed in our primary objective. Until you deploy to your prepared positions, you can make as much song and dance about it as you like. No restrictions on radio, but don't clutter the air. And now to recap on the enemy's objectives ... He cleared his throat and turned to the map, his pointer indicating each area as he referred to it.

'Tonight, gentlemen, some of you might be excused for feeling that, after so many years of Arctic training, you may at last be called upon to use it. 45 Commando is taking up its advanced positions, in conjunction with the Norwegian Sixth Division and Brigade North, and you will be taking up your own lines tonight and tomorrow. So what is the Soviet line-up at this moment?'

His pointer flicked to Murmansk.

'At 1000 this morning, the Russian strengths were as follows: The customary two motor rifle divisions totalling twenty-four thousand men on the border, in the Kola inlet; the Naval Infantry Regiment of seventeen hundred men, a complete package with its thirteen amphibious ships. Add to this total their 400 tactical aircraft and their logistic backing and we've counted somewhere around forty thousand men. Of course, they can also throw in their airborne forces from the Leningrad area.'

He turned to regard the silent rows of officers before him. 'The enemy may try to move his forces by road, but don't forget that he can't, any more than we can, shift more troops than the capacity of the two routes will allow: one division of twelve thousand down the E6; the other division across the Finnish Wedge. If he decides to go all out and violate Finnish neutrality, then, of course, we'll have plenty of warning. His first wave is bound to be his armour and motorised riflemen; the second, his backup ammunition and logistics.'

Several hands were raised. Colonel Backhouse grinned as he anticipated the inevitable questions. 'Yes, I know, gentlemen, he doesn't have to come by road…' He paused to take a scrap of paper from his pocket. 'I have news for you, a flash report: *Leningrad Fourteenth Motor Rifle Division confirmed 28 December rail junction Kandalaksha, probable deployment Kuolayarvi.*'

The commander's pointer jabbed at the focal frontier town where rail and road communications met, a quarter of the way down the Finnish-Russian border.

'You may or may not consider that this is a feint, gentlemen, to distract us from our main deployment in Finnmark and Troms; but they've also announced their Northern Fleet manoeuvres into the Barents Sea. Their main units sailed north from the Kola inlet less than an hour ago. Simultaneously, their "Woodpecker" jamming procedures began, so all radio communications and radar systems are blotted out to the south of Mo-i-rana. Satellite surveillance continues, but a white-out has been reported from Novaya Zemlya. These reactions are a deliberate escalation of tension.'

Dick could hear his neighbour's breathing; the silence in the room was complete.

'Gentlemen, we've been beaten to the gun by our enthusiastic Danish NATO friends: at 1600 yesterday, without consulting us, they declared internationally that, for their own protection, they had activated their controlled minefields to the boundaries of their offshore limits.

'The Soviets have reacted by coming to Full Alert on the central front, announcing at the United Nations that they consider the Danish action — that of a NATO member — is one of aggression and of escalation. The Russian Kuolayarvi deployment can be considered as a reaction to NATO's firm posture, I believe. But don't forget, gentlemen,' he added quietly, 'that our six-day warning period expires this evening. Our planners have not been far out.

'HQ is convinced that the enemy, as always, is interested in only the Troms region — anywhere below Narvik is unimportant to him. He needs to take out our installations in Finnmark, destroy our dominance of the Barents Sea.' The colonel glanced at a Norwegian Air Force colleague. 'Our Air Force chums are flying aggressive patrols off North Cape, but are being buzzed by Kola MIGs.'

He turned to the officer sitting directly below him. 'Come on, Jake… The brigade major will now give you your orders.' He sat down, taking the brigade major's chair when the second-in-command took over.

The brigade major was a stocky man, bristling with self-confidence. 'Right.' He jabbed his pointer towards the left-hand corner of the map. 'Because of STANAVFORLANT's enemy report two days ago, the Norwegians have asked us to send a company of Royal Marines up to Jan Mayen Island … and as you'll see, this has meant sorting 42 out a bit.' He pinched his ginger moustache. 'First, the political situation here. Our Norwegian friends are as angry as hell over the Americans' bleating that NATO should pull out from its northern flank because our position here is untenable. I'd be as angry if I was in the Norwegians' predicament. But, as you all know, gentlemen, our friends mean to fight it out to the death, if the Russians invade.' He lowered his voice, then added, 'There's no need to add that 45 and 42 Commandos will stick by its allies.'

Then he continued, 'We may be overwhelmed by lack of anti-air missiles, lack of any tactical air force in the skies above us, or by lack of mobility because we have no dedicated amphibious shipping.' He slapped the table. 'But we're going to stick in our holes,' he said. 'Marine Bloggs will kill as many Russians as he can with his rifle before he is killed himself. His tenacity will give time for the backup to arrive.'

His pointer hovered over Narvik, then moved to Harstad and Tromsø. 'HMS *Glorious* began disembarking 45 Commando last night; 42 should be in position by this time tomorrow. *Furious* has been delayed by strikes for so long that she can't be brought forward in time, so the private enterprise ferries have been helping out with 42. The first ferries got in this morning, but the gales have left the troops the worse for wear.' He flashed his cold smile. 'Marine Bloggs is a quick recoverer: I'm told that 42's first convoy is already on its way north, to back up 45. The E6 is like a crawl to Brighton on a Bank Holiday. But we've never been given a dedicated amphibious lift and so we're having to extemporise: we're using every swinish dodge I know to move our Marines about.

'We've always known that the decision to use *Glorious* and *Furious* was a political compromise. The ASW carriers can be used for the amphibious role only in a quick dash operation.

But now, gentlemen, make the best of it; there are plenty of submarines for them to chase when they've dumped us.' He glanced at his audience. 'Fortunately, our Norwegian friends are right behind us: you won't find any fishermen or anyone with a boat who won't help you. If the weather's okay, use them to your utmost for moving along the coast.

'Backup.' For the first time he raised his voice. 'It's on its way, while the politicians brace themselves. The Royal Netherlands Marine Corps' Amphibious Combat Group — Whisky Company — is landing tomorrow, ACE's (Allied Command Europe) Mobile Force — our Fire Brigade — was to have deployed but cannot now be spared.

'Remember to hot up on your procedures: ACE has as many Canadians, Americans, Germans and Italians as Brits.'

Dick Stoddart smiled to himself as he listened to the subdued chuckle in the room. Ghosts still lingered.

'Don't forget, gentlemen, the Norwegians' sensitivity,' the brigade major continued. 'We're in their country. Though all forces are under the command of the Norwegian Commander, North Norway, overall command is exercised from Kolsas by our Royal Marine General, and our brigadier controls us. You can't ask for more than that.

'Tactical air ... tactical air, gentlemen, is at a discount. Hoard your anti-air missiles like gold. You won't be getting any more; hopes for promised tactical air support from the UK or from anywhere else are as Alice-in-Wonderland as the promises of those who made them. The best thing is to pray for bad weather, when the Russians' overwhelming superiority will be reduced by Mother Nature. For light lifts, our own flights are already deployed: you all know the communication procedures. There won't be many elements of 845 Naval Air Squadron around, because they're up with 45. The Navy's short of pilots because *Glorious* and *Furious* are likely soon to be resuming their ASW roles.

'For transport, most of you will have to rely on snowshoes and skis. All units are being kitted up as soon as they land. Base camps are holding spare stocks and rations are scaled for thirty days. Mercifully, we've got our hundred and fifty Volvo over-snow tracked vehicles in time — about a tenth of what we could do with — so go easy with your requests. The "bandwagons" will be restricted to the frontline, and today that means 45 Commando.

'Ammunition, gentlemen: a dirty word.' He paused momentarily. 'That knotty one has been solved, due to the guile, if I may use such a word, of our Brigade HQ. Once stockpiling was accepted by the Norwegians, we were able slowly to build up our stocks. But be thrifty; fire discipline is essential, because getting ammunition to you without transport is going to be tricky — and that's the reason why all depots have their bulk stocks topped up.'

Stoddart groaned mentally at the memory of pulk-pulling loads across deep snow on snow-shoes. Sledge-dragging was not as easy as it looked.

'Weather and survival.' The brigade major was hurrying on, trying to beat the clock. 'Stick to the drills. Deception is always vital, particularly if the weather remains fine. Don't forget that snowshoes conceal tracks more easily than skis if the patrol is of any size. Remember how difficult it is in the assault, to climb out of your planks smartish.' He looked around his audience. 'Of course, there's the old argument: some of us prefer to assault in snowshoes, rather than with only boots, if we've discarded skis.

'Do all you can to avoid asking for transport. After fifteen years of using a heavy-lift chopper, we've still nothing yet to replace the old Wessex. And remember your hygiene and buddy-buddy drill. Remember that a frost-bitten man is not only one less in the unit, but can render the whole troop ineffective if the casualty has to be returned to base medical care. Your Arctic clothing is the best in the world: that and each man's ski, snowshoe and winter kit costs nearly a thousand pounds. Look after it.

'Anti-tank remains a problem for 42, I'm afraid. You'll still have to make do with your old friend, the 84 mm gun, but 45 and a few of your companies have now got the Milan. It's a good weapon, gentlemen, as you know, though complicated.'

Dick noted the nods of approval about him.

'And don't forget your "do-it-yourself" kits, gentlemen. The 66 mm Law disposable anti-tank weapon is still a good bet. Remember, it requires a crew of three in a section of nine men, but the weapon weighs only just over four pounds.'

'Sounds like a sales rep,' Dick's neighbour, a major from 42's HQ, muttered irreverently.

'If it comes to the heavy stuff,' the brigade major was continuing, 'don't forget how much mobility and general chaos you can cause by using your Raiding Squadrons, the Rigid Raiders and the SBS (Special Boat Squadron) to the full. They're trained to play foul, the cunning swine…'

There was an outburst of laughter. Dick smiled broadly, remembering his early days as a subaltern in the Royal Marines' version of the army's SAS. Highly trained in every lethal art — parachuting, canoeing, diving, espionage and reconnaissance, fast Gemini handling — these special units had supreme confidence in themselves as being the elite of the Corps. Parachuting into the Arctic fjords, to swim ashore and fight it out; to canoe in freezing gale-force winds, then dive in their shallow-water diving-gear to calmer conditions below the surface in order to reach their objective; and to be landed, disguised, from submarines or from Norwegian fishing boats were natural projections of the original SBS which had been born in 1942.

'On the domestic scene, gentlemen, we're still getting mail coming through and we're distributing it to the units.' He looked about his audience, his eye finally catching Stoddart's. 'Captain Stoddart, *Icarus* is coming in to Fuglöyfjord tomorrow with your detachment. Could you transfer STANAVFORLANT's mail?'

'Certainly, sir. Where'll I pick it up?'

'Captain Throwleigh, my GSO, will brief you: he's taking care of your operation.' The brigade major began collecting his bits and pieces. 'Before I finish, you ought to be brought up to date with news from the home front.'

He glanced at the notes in his hand. 'After Parliament's declaration of a State of Emergency on Thursday, Regulation 18B was approved yesterday. Suspected traitors are being rounded up and interned in detention camps.' There was a cheer around the hall, followed by good-humoured laughter at the news that the Peace Watch group had been refused permission by the Home Secretary to march down Whitehall. 'There have been riots in the docks, notably in Southampton and Dover. The Territorials got the ferries away all right, and the troops are learning to use the giant container cranes. There have been more deaths amongst travellers trying to get back from the European ski resorts ... and Heathrow has finally seized up ... There we are, then, everything's normal at home.

'That's it, gentlemen. It's no use griping: we just haven't got the anti-air, the tactical air or the coastal amphibious lift. Your job is to stop the Russians by using what you're carrying, by fighting delaying actions and by using the terrain to the best of its advantage until ACE's Mobile Force and Whisky company arrive.'

He jumped from the stage and the assembly broke up. During the melee of climbing back into Arctic clothing, Dick was taken aside by the staff officer, Captain Throwleigh.

'I've got it all in writing for you,' Throwleigh said, whisking through Stoddart's field orders. '42 will be in its defensive positions north of you by tonight. You are to divide your detachment into two sections, the first, Zulu, under your command to establish ambush positions at Skibotn. From the mountains there, you can command the junction, where the only road from the north meets the E71 from the Finnish Wedge. Don't blow the bridges until you're ordered. Your second section, Sierra, with an NCO in command, is to take up its ambush position, here, above Helligskogen on the E78 near the Finnish frontier post. Here —' he marked the ambush position with his pencil — 'nine men can close this pass by the lake for a hell of a long time. We've dumped ammo, and food for Zulu at Skibotn. That's okay for your section, but I haven't been able to scrounge transport to get the stuff up to Sierra. I've scrounged a shaky Land Rover for your detachment, complete with driver. It's waiting for you at Sørkjosen airstrip, at the head of Reisafjord. It's carrying spare Arctic gear, in case *Icarus*'s pusser hasn't been up to scratch — and you've enough juice to keep you going for a couple of days. There's a good military ski and snow-shoe depot at Sørkjosen.'

'Communications?' Dick asked. 'Local frequencies once *Icarus*'s Lynx has rejoined the ship?'

'Roger — but reception is bloody awful around here in these mountains. Try the local pigeon.' Throwleigh held out his hand. 'Good luck, Dick,' he said. 'They're waiting for you at Åsegarden — one of our Kangaw Flight, so you're in good hands. Tony will have to refuel at Bardufoss before taking you on. If the weather doesn't shut down, you ought to be touching down at Sørkjosen by 2100 at the latest. Your driver's expecting you.'

'Thanks.' Dick was grateful to the staffie who was helping with his pack and gear. 'What's *Icarus*'s ETA, Kagsund?'

'0500. I'll signal if she's delayed, but she'll be in a hurry. She's rejoining STANAVFORLANT off North Cape to forestall any Russian amphibious attempts.'

'I reckon the enemy heavy units will back up his amphibious forces,' Dick said as he pulled on his mitt. 'It'll be warming up a bit off North Cape.'

As he strode across the crackling snow, he turned to wave at the figure framed in the doorway of the hut. Stoddart wondered when he would be enjoying the comforts of civilisation again.

CHAPTER 18

HMS Icarus, 30 December.

'Grimsholm lighthouse 237 degrees. Noted the time, Pilot?' Captain Trevellion sang out from the bearing repeater to Brian Neame. Trevellion's eyes ached from the long search for the landfall off the island of Vannöy. The entrance to the fjord was difficult to identify in this jagged coast; even in this calmer weather the long swell which followed the gales was pounding against the lee shore to catapult huge tapestries of spume hundreds of feet into the air. In this darkness, the breakers seemed an endless army of spectres whose shrouds twined and leapt ceaselessly.

'0425, sir. Radar range, four decimal three miles. We're just south of our line, sir: suggest course, 154 degrees.'

'Steer 154 degrees. How far to our heave-to position?'

'Twenty-four miles.'

They had picked up Fugloykalven's white group occulting light at fifteen miles, but Grimsholm, only five miles off in this darkness, barely showed, shaped as it was like a trimmed-down nuclear submarine. Neame had never sighted the Gasan shoal, which, even at high water, was supposed to break white: it was dangerous here, because the lethal tip of these seaward shoals remained in the white isophase sector of Fugloykalven light.

Captain Trevellion turned as the helicopter observer and pilot clambered on to the bridge.

'Ready to take off, sir,' Hob reported, saluting. 'Corporal Burns and his detachment are standing by.'

'Right.' Trevellion turned to Daglish. 'Happy about your orders?'

'Yes, sir: take off as we approach The Leads. You'll be using Lyngskjer light beacon, on the reef at the head of Lyngenfjord, as your datum. You'll be anchoring just clear of the channel in Kagsund, between Kaagen Island and Arnöy, to be in the lee: the wind normally blows up or down Lyngenfjord, apparently.'

'Right — visibility acceptable?'

'Yes, sir, but I can use the air strip's radio beacon,' Rollo said. 'We'll keep to the water, following the coastline.'

'Roger. I'll send in the boats with the heavy gear when I heave-to under Arnöy. If I have to get out in a hurry, I'll show my emergency recognition lights and wait for you in Vannöyfjord. I assume you'll land ashore.'

They saluted and left the bridge. Pascoe leant with his elbows on the ledge of the starboard window. He sighed with relief at entering the sheltered waters of The Leads after these few days. Rough it had been, but the discomfort and tension of these past thirty-six hours, instead of producing the expected bloody-mindedness, had in a mysterious way welded his ship's company together. Hacking ice from the superstructures, officers and men together in those appalling conditions might have had something to do with it ... even the Sick Berth Tiffy, Morgan, had come into his own: there were queues of suspected frost-nip cases outside the sick bay during those early days.

Number One, too, was turning up trumps at last. The tauter discipline, where each man knew where he stood, had shaken them all up, officers and men. Gradually they were growing proud of their ship and themselves...

The captain took off his cap and ran his fingers through his hair. He would fly off *Perdix* in ten minutes and then Neame could take the ship up the fjord and into The Leads. By the time *Icarus* reached the head of Lyngenfjord, to turn up into Kaagsund, Trevellion could have washed and shaved; the ship could go to breakfast while the Royals were flown ashore. *Perdix* would make four trips to Sørkjosen airstrip: she would lift five booties, plus rifles, Arctic clothing and packs, per trip. Ammunition and food stores would be landed by the motorboat and the three-in-one at the fishing haven of Hamneidet on the Reisanfjord peninsula.

The message had already been passed to Dick Stoddart, who had been at Sørkjosen airstrip all night, waiting for his detachment. (Trevellion was looking forward to meeting his Royal Marine captain one day…)

As he waited for the Lynx to fly off, he flicked through the first lieutenant's daily orders. Jewkes had found the right touch now, keeping the ship's company up to date with events: the prospect of a mail delivery today had sent morale rocketing. At 0900 he would be seeing requestmen: there were no defaulters, and this hour's break provided an opportunity to catch up with the important details in men's lives — two advancements; one good conduct medal; and a request from L/RO Osgood to see the captain privately. Lochead, the divisional officer, had passed on the request directly to his captain, so presumably Osgood needed help with his private affairs. Campbell, the Master-at-Arms, had hinted as much in Trevellion's cabin yesterday: Osgood had taken an emotional hammering.

There was the familiar roar, the sudden flutter and the blue flames from *Perdix*'s engine exhausts, as she swung across *Icarus*'s bow towards Arnöy and the Sound of Kaag. A couple of hours to unwind, and then *Icarus* would be on her way back to rejoin STANAVFORLANT, to keep the Red Banner Fleet's head down, until *Glorious* and *Furious* could resume their ASW roles.

Hob Gamble lifted Perdix from Sørkjosen's brightly lit airstrip. He hauled her up and away, then steered north for the gap in the hills. He was orientated now and Rollo was happy, so he could short-cut by flying across the neck of the peninsula and following the western shore which showed sharply against Kaagen Island. This, the last of the lifts, was satisfactorily completed.

'That's it, then,' Rollo chipped in. 'Breakfast, shave and shower.'

'More than our poor old bootie'll get,' Hob replied, grinning inside his bone dome — but Corporal Burns had seemed in good nick.

'No nonsense about him,' Rollo said. 'He's done well while Dick's been away. Burns was last out of the final lift.'

Hob nodded. 'Pity we couldn't have found the time to sort the mail for them,' Hob said, nodding towards the bag at the back of the cab. 'Would have done the booties good.'

'There she is, the lovely girl,' Rollo said. 'Dear old *Ic* shows up well on the screen, even amongst this lot...' He nodded towards the sheer faces of the mountains which hemmed in the fjords from all sides. The peaks were concealed by those lowering clouds, where the mountains reared to six thousand feet — truly alpine terrain. Dick Stoddart and Corporal Burns would be out in that lot, battling to survive in this Arctic cold, waiting for the attack which, please God, would never come...

'Here we go.' Hob revelled in throwing this machine about. The toy ship beneath them lunged into shape, magnifying each second as he allowed Perdix to fall from the sky — and then he was swooping into the hover for the landing.

There were the blue lights of her flight deck, dimming as Bernie Towke, the flight deck officer, switched on the glide path indicator and the horizon bar. *Bit of old rope, this, after the recent ocean flying,* Hob thought, resisting the temptation to relax his concentration. He glanced through his window, pushed her gently, held her, then plonked her down on to the grille, before stabbing at the harpoon button.

Outside the cockpit, the freezing wind snatched at his ears when he levered off his helmet. Bernie Towke was waiting for him, a message pad in his hand — not a bearer of good news, by the look of him. Without a word, Bernie shoved the pad in Hob's hands.

The signal was 'Immediate' and from MoD. A hairline crack had been discovered in the tail unit of another Lynx at Yeovilton. All Mark VIIs were grounded.

'Bloody disastrous,' Hob said. 'A tail failure is catastrophic enough, Bernie. But what's the Old Man going to say, now that his ship's lost her main armament?'

CHAPTER 19

Norway, 30 December.

They watched the Lynx's flashing light until she disappeared behind the shoulder of the peninsula.

'We've work to do, Corporal.'

As they loaded the Land Rover and trailer Corporal Rodney Burns realised how vital his nine years' training in the Corps had been: the next few days, out on his own and in charge of his section, would show how thorough the training had been...

Burns accompanied his captain on the first trip to the fishing haven of Hamneidet, tucked into the mountainside under the lee of Kaagen Island. The little port was still drowsy from another winter's night, but sleepy Norwegians were already about their daily errands and shuffling along the snow-packed road which joined the E6, fifteen kilometres to the south. An old fisherman was gazing bemusedly at the pile of gear which *Icarus's* crew had dumped on the rickety, ice-encrusted jetty. Gulls screamed overhead as a solitary youth, muffed to the eyebrows, tried to brush down the decks of his fish-scaled inshore boat. He looked up as he heard the doors of the Land Rover slamming above him.

And that was the moment when things began going right. The fisherman grinned beneath his fur hat, tried out his schoolboy English ... ten minutes later, the old boat's decks were laden with the weapons and gear of *Icarus's* RM detachment.

'I'll take the signalman and four, Corporal. If we get to Skibotn before you, I'll start my recce of Zulu position. Keep in touch on the working frequency.'

The corporal saluted, watched the cloud of exhaust condensing above the Land Rover's roof as its headlights snaked like glow-worms along the twisting road. The fishing boat's diesel was thumping and, as Burns jumped down across the gunwale, the young Norwegian flicked off the for'd warp.

The moon had not yet set behind the film of high cirrus which was spreading across the bowl of the morning sky. As the boat chugged to its maximum eight knots, the breeze bouncing off the slab sides of the islands brought down the temperature: Burns and his men congregated in the warmth of the saloon below. The forty-year-old skipper spoke no English, but they grinned at each other and knocked back the ritual tot. An hour later they were into Rotsund, and at 1130 were well into Lyngenfjord. The pale brightening of the sky behind the overpowering backdrop of the mountains, which plunged sheer into the hundred fathom depths of the fjord, cheered the rumbustious marines, who were now beginning thoroughly to enjoy their escape from shipboard monotony.

Burns was glad to be among them, secretly chuffed at having the responsibility of his own section. But it was reassuring also to know that the captain was at his back, in position Zulu overlooking Skibotn. From Zulu, Captain Stoddart's section could cover the E78, which linked up with the E6 on the only road to the north. The ambush was a prepared, mined position and easy to blow. Stoddart was keeping the signalman at Zulu because Burns's communications training would stand them in good stead up at Sierra.

Burns could not stomach the smoke, the stink of fish and diesel oil, so he climbed out to the letter-box wheelhouse, where the skipper had taken over from his young crewman. With the engine thundering below them, the tough Norwegian pointed out the landmarks as the boat chugged up the sheer-sided fjord, a miniscule water beetle in these majestic surroundings. The islet of Aroyholmen slipped down their starboard side and then they were crossing the head of Kaafjord, where its deep waters, ebony black, gleamed from the lights of Olderdalen which nestled under the mountainside. The western side of Lyngenfjord was much steeper and the immense scale of the fifty-mile fjord was awe-inspiring. The skipper was pointing again through the starboard window. Even after three winters in Norway, Burns had never seen such majestic beauty: a glistening glacier drifted like a silvery curtain down the Wagnerian cliffs which plunged into the black fjord.

'That's Storfjord,' the skipper grunted, as Lyngseidet, a town nestling high on a plateau which was covered by Christmas-card chalets, slipped past them on the western shore. The two smiling fishermen insisted with that they should all share their midday meal. As they munched the salted fish, Kvalviknes passed to port, and then, five miles south, the vibrations ceased as the diesel died. They slid past a black spar buoy marking the dried-out bank. Burns could see the white surf of the boat's wash breaking across a rock a couple of hundred yards from the beach. Seconds later, the boat was nudging alongside the stone quay, where the headlights of the Land Rover were flashing a welcome.

'Spot on,' Captain Stoddart hailed from the quay, as his party took the lines. '1405. We've settled in at Zulu. Come on, Corporal. We'll get you up to Sierra.'

While the captain drove off the first batch of his section, Burns loaded up the trailer. By 1415 the Land Rover was trundling along the E78 which led up the valley towards the

Finnish border. As they crossed the Skibotn bridges, Stoddart pointed to the cliff brooding down upon them from the right. 'We're up there, Corporal. Uninterrupted arc of fire, first-rate cover.'

'Hope we're as lucky in Sierra as you are,' Burns muttered.

'We're soft, sir, after all this time in the ship.'

Stoddart grimaced beneath his fur hat. 'You're not beefing then, for the compulsory doubling around the upper deck? The fish-heads enjoyed watching us, even if you lot didn't appreciate my concern for your fitness.'

The lift to position Sierra took four hours: two trips each way, carrying the nine-man section with its weapons and Arctic gear. Considering that time had been spent drawing skis, boots and snowshoes from the depot at Sørkjosen, eleven hours for the day's evolution without adequate transport was good going, and would have been impossible without the fishing boat. Burns set his first four men gouging out the snow-hole as soon as Stoddart and he had decided upon the ambush position. There was no difficulty with the choice: one jagged snow-covered peak completely dominated the E78 where it crossed the river running from the small lake above the town of Helligskogen.

'Up there,' Captain Stoddart said, pointing, 'you can spit on 'em if they try to force down the E78.'

While the Land Rover returned for the last load, Burns set up his gun positions and organised the camp. The road ran alongside the river some seven hundred feet below. Those birch trees, bending beneath their weights of snow, were sited right, wooding the ambush position from the road. The GPM/G, or General Purpose Machine Gun — though it demanded a third of his section — could command the bridge from here; and the two-inch mortar could lob its bricks directly upon the road, like tossing a cricket ball from the deep field. It was a pity the GPM/G was being phased out, because it was a good gun.

A couple of hours after the last glimmer of the dreary twilight had merged into darkness, they brewed up for the first time on the fire outside. Burns had insisted on spending a full hour collecting birch wood, because wood stock always disappeared too damn quickly — the eight-foot-high stack should keep them going for a day. He repeated again, for the benefit of them all, the rules for Arctic survival, so that even the thick 'uns could not forget: a frostbite casualty would be on his own, a menace to all concerned, because no one could get him down to Zulu if the action got hot. The best bet would be to ask the village to take in the casualty, if he could be slid down to Helligskogen in time: from what Burns had seen, the natives seemed friendly enough.

'Gather round, you lot,' he shouted. The eight men dropped what they were doing and circled round the fire with him. Their rifles were stacked out in the cold, where the temperature was already down to minus 30 degrees. The skis were rammed into the snow, ready for instant use; around the camp, they used their snowshoes.

'I'll remind you about survival drill,' he said, 'before the captain gets back. These are your priorities.' He methodically checked off his list.

To fight in this hostile environment a man had first to survive when the going was tough — and on his own, if he had to. Conditions were brutal: each year a percentage of trainees had to be shipped back to the UK as 'unfit for Arctic warfare' — the silence and the loneliness of these unfamiliar, harsh conditions wore a man down, affecting his psychology if he was poorly led. There was only one way to fight in the mountains: to attack the difficulties with an aggressive determination never to give up — that way, Marine Bloggs would get back to fight another day. Severe cold had a sinister effect, and Burns never knew how men would react to it: some became bloody-minded, querying every order; other men became maddeningly rumbustious and jolly — more irritating, sometimes, than the aggressive cases... Unless well led, men would withdraw into mental cocoons, craving nothing else but to crawl into their sleeping bags. This attitude inevitably killed them.

Moving across the terrain in the ice and snow was often impossible. During white-outs the only safe drill was to hole up immediately and wait for the blizzard to end. Continuing the march was insane: men would either disappear over precipices or become totally lost. When the cloud shut down and merged with the snow there was no horizon, and a man became disorientated. He was entirely dependent on his compass and his pace-judgement: possessing only poor maps (out of date because they had not been re-surveyed since World War II, during which time forest plantations had changed the landscape), it was suicidal to continue. Compasses were unreliable due to the proximity of the pole and to iron deposits. These stark conditions affected the Russians as much as themselves.

The section listened to Burns in silence, the logs crackling, the spitting embers sizzling in the snow and sending up wisps of steam. 'When on your planks,' he reminded them, 'don't forget that it's a long time since you used them. Take it steady.' They grinned amongst themselves at the painful memories. Teaching a Royal Marine to ski was an experience. Raw novices, they hurled themselves down slopes for a fortnight until they were competent — they were magnificent.

They waited for the Land Rover to return; only another two hours working on the snow-hole and they could turn in for the night, except for the sentries. Burns hammered home the fundamentals about moving in this terrain: 'Don't get in a muck sweat working on these slopes — once you've sweated inside your clothing, it'll lose its insulation and you'll get frostbite. Keep track discipline by skiing in only one track, so the aircraft can't spot us. When you're working, don't forget plenty of ventilation stops to prevent sweating. Don't drink or eat heavily, but little and often. Our rations are scaled for forty-eight hours, but you're lugging seventy pounds on your backs, as well as carrying your rifles and our weapons. And when the action gets close, remember your grenades.' He glanced at Keith Hudson, the youngest in his section. 'How many seconds, Keith?'

'Four seconds, Corp.'

'And keep out of the road when you've chucked it — clears a fifteen-yard circle.' He watched them feeling for the grenades at their belts.

When fighting, the weather controlled everything, though the principles of war still applied. That was why he and Stoddart had taken care in choosing this tactical position, sited behind this outcrop, well in the lee from the wind which was certain to blow from the valley. Once the wind got up, temperatures dropped dramatically: at minus 15 degrees the nose hairs began to freeze; at minus 25 the brain began to slow down, and at minus 30 it could take half an hour to don skis, two hours to break camp. At lower temperatures than that, fighting stopped: survival was the priority for both sides.

'And don't forget the care of your weapons,' Burns said, as Paddy O'Malley dished out the hot tea. Paddy was the troop comedian — nothing got him down, but he was accident-prone and Burns had to watch him.

'Keep the snow out of your rifles: when it freezes, the ice will jam up the working parts. Constant thawing and freezing affects even the toughest steel, so watch it. Don't take your rifles into the snow-hole, or the condensation will freeze when you come out ... and what about your gloves, O'Malley?' The Ulsterman had once lost a glove on the top of a crest. If you touched the cold steel of your rifle, the skin of your fingers remained on the barrel. 'So keep your gloves on and leave your rifles, weapons and optical gear outside. And when you go into the assault on skis, if you can't fire from the hip, take your skis off before you go down to the prone position.

'We've set up camp, but the snow-hole's not finished. Our deceptive plan's okay: our tracks come up behind this escarpment. We can hold this spot for days.' He turned to O'Malley. 'Okay, Paddy, organise the sentry roster. We'll set sentries as soon as the captain's finished his brief.'

'Right, Corp. D'you want a buddy-buddy list?'

Burns nodded. Each man, paired off with an 'oppo', was responsible for checking him regularly for the first signs of frost-nip or frostbite, when the evil-looking waxiness began showing on the extremities: nose, fingers, ears. If one man fell out on patrol, his buddy would be watching, but he had to get himself up if he fell.

Then they heard the whine of the Land Rover churning the snow at the entry to the defile. O'Malley had already prepared tea; they saw the two shadows stumbling on their shoes up the slope. Burns saluted and showed them to the fire.

'Gather round,' Stoddart ordered. 'Saves time.' They listened in silence as he brought them up to date. 'The Soviets are moving up to their no-go lines on the central front in Europe. Their third motorised infantry division is now poised on Finland's eastern frontier at Kuolayarvi. It arrived by rail and is only three hundred miles from us. The Russians are telling the world that the Finns are asking for help to save them from Norwegian aggression. My latest bit of bad news is that their northern fleet is out; it sailed into the Barents Sea for exercises yesterday.

'45 Commando is at Red Alert, and in its prepared positions up north. Backing them up, from Kaafjord southwards, is 42 Commando, of which we form a minor part.' Captain Stoddart glanced around at them all: his detachment, men he had known since they had all joined *Icarus* from Poole. He had trained them, worked them up to their present efficiency. 'These, Corporal, are the orders for your section: Sierra section is to stop the enemy advancing down that road.' He jerked his head towards the drop overhanging the E78, the main road dividing Skibotndalen which ran down from the Finnish frontier to Lyngenfjord.

'We'll get plenty of warning, because the Russians can't enter Finland without violating her neutrality; unless, of course, they persuade themselves that they've been invited in. They'll have to come down the E78 from Rovaniemi, the rail terminus in the centre of Finland. That means a two-hundred-mile trek up the E78, which is just on the Finnish side of the Swedish border, until they reach Lake Kilpisjärvi, just on the other side of the Norwegian frontier post. If we haven't heard of Russian movement up the E78 by then from our Finnish intelligence or satellite reconnaissance, something will have gone wrong somewhere.

'Corporal, your job's the same as that for all the Royals: if the Russians attack with their thousands of tanks — if they come flowing down that road —' He pointed to the ravine below — 'let them roll over you; let 'em go. Then halt the infantry, who'll be coming up behind the tanks — zap their stores. Zap their supplies, their centralised organisation — and later, if need be, their army of occupation. Our job and 45's job is to hold the bastards up for twenty-four hours to give the reinforcements time to deploy. If we've succeeded in delaying them, then we've justified our existence. Our little lives, Corporal, will have been well spent.'

Burns watched the men around him. By the glow of the dying embers their faces were immobile, blocks of granite, each with his own thoughts. Burns had heard Stoddart's harsh message too often — okay for single men who didn't have women depending upon them, okay for those who didn't know what it was to nurture a loving family…

But Stoddart's spiel was not finished. 'After that, *if* there are any survivors, disperse to the mountains. Survive off the terrain. Organise resistance groups to cause the enemy as much damage as you can: supply lines, communications, anything — then our Commando's existence will have been justified…' Captain Stoddart hesitated, then stood back abruptly from the dying fire. 'Good luck,' he said. 'Get in radio touch at a quarter past the hour. Good luck, all of you.' He gazed wistfully at the red embers. 'And this must be your last fire. We're not playing any more.' They watched him disappearing into the night, a flurry of snow shrouding him as his head and shoulders vanished beneath the steep slope.

They kicked out the fire and prepared for the night. While the others finished off the roof of the snow-hole, O'Malley and his buddy, Lenny Holmes, started throwing the supper together. The naphtha double burner was efficient but dangerous — it flared too easily.

'Here, Grant and Tucker: get your planks on,' Burns ordered two marines who were standing idle. 'Before I set the sentries, we'll make a last recce before the night. We'll ski down to the road, then make our way up on shoes to the border.'

It was good to be on skis again, their rifles slung across their shoulders. Burns led, taking it gently through the birch wood. The going was relatively easy after the first two hundred feet, down which they sideslipped. Then after a gradual schuss down to the road they broke off to fix their snowshoes by the light of a hazy moon.

A small lake half-filled Skibotndalen, which led up to the Norwegian-Finnish frontier post. Burns kept below the lip of the road, then flogged along the edge of the lake. The going was hard, but he was glad to find the rhythm returning to his legs. The exercise was doing them all good. It was uphill going to the plateau above them, where his map showed a vast tract of water: Lake Kilpisjärvi, on the Finnish side, a lake four kilometres wide and seventeen long. It would be frozen solid like all the others, but he would take a look at the frontier to orientate himself in case bad weather hit them.

They moved on in silence, each in the other's tracks. They saw the yellow lights of the Customs barrier; the snow-mantled chalet; and further back, the desolate encampment which was the northern fringe of the iron curtain separating the two different worlds. The Norwegians got on well with their neighbours, though fraternisation was discouraged by the Finnish officials. It was difficult, Burns imagined, to prevent the interchange of locals from the town of Kilpisjärvi, six kilometres further up the E78.

They remained motionless a few minutes, orientating themselves, the vapour of their breath freezing, mini-stalactites forming on their eyebrows. The picture was one of utter desolation, nothing moving, no traffic on the road. All good men were inside their homes, snug with their womenfolk — the nearest Russian was three hundred miles away to the east. It was the poor sods in 45 Commando who were shit-scared tonight, sentries stamping numbed feet in the cold, less than ten miles from the Russian hordes who were swarming along the northern frontiers of the Finnmark plateau. It was eyeball-to-eyeball stuff up there, glaring at each other across frontiers which ran only twelve miles from the sea. There'd be no fires in the ambush positions up there...

'Look, Corp.'

Tucker was pointing towards the invisible lake, a vast snowfield covering the ice, which stretched into the distance. A mysterious grey sheen, tinged yellow at the edges, was reflected upon the base of the cloud covering the Finnish slot, abutting Sweden and poking like a finger into Norwegian territory.

'Must be the lights from the causeway,' Burns said, remembering the narrow isthmus which cut Lake Kilpisjärvi into two. 'Swedish Customs post, likely.' He turned, impatient to set the sentries, so that he could turn into the snow-hole for an hour or two. He could strip off inside and get some real sleep. 'Get your planks on,' he told them. 'We'll cut across the small lake.'

He was becoming irritable, waiting as Grant fiddled endlessly with his boots. Grant was a good Marine but desperately slow: he was always holding up the others, even across country when they tried to crack on the pace.

Burns led off down the open valley. He sheered off to the right, hearing the hissing of the others' skis behind him. He slowed, gliding towards the bottom end of the small lake; step by step he moved down the bank until he could walk upon the snow-packed ice. He waited for Grant and then they were off again, poling their way across the head of the lake, where the river began its course down the valley to Helligskogen.

It was hard work here without the slope. He moved rhythmically, his arms swinging, shoving with his sticks. Glancing over his shoulder, he saw Grant diverting to the left, where the snow seemed less deep. Irritated, the corporal shouted at him to get back into line.

Burns was reaching the head of the lake when he heard a sudden yell from Tucker, just behind him. There was a sudden crack like a pistol shot, and then the sound of splintering ice. He slewed round in time to see the dark, unwieldy shape of Grant, complete with rifle, snowshoes and sticks, disappearing beneath the collapsing ice of the lake.

'Help! For Chrissake help!'

The frenzied cry shattered the stillness. The hoarse croaking of a ptarmigan echoed from somewhere behind them, and then Tucker and he were frantically clawing off their ski bindings. 'Take the rope,' Burns yelled, tossing one end to Tucker, who was already slithering on his belly towards the black hole. The ice was crackling and exploding around them, long splits splintering as Tucker approached the floundering Grant, whose mitts were reappearing above the ledge.

'Quick, round your shoulders, Grant.' Burns tied the bowline and flipped it to Tucker, who looped it over Grant's shoulders. 'Heave ... now, Corp ... now...' They both leant backwards with all their weight, gingerly digging the heels of their boots into the slippery snow.

It seemed an eternity before they got him out, and each second that passed brought death nearer for Grant. At any instant the ice could collapse completely, drowning them all in the icy water. Then, panting and exhausted, Grant emerged, his dripping clothes suddenly freezing solid where he stood shuddering in the Arctic night.

'Quick, Tucker, on with your planks. Nip like hell and get the fire going in the camp.'

Burns took no more notice of Tucker, but concentrated on forcing the shocked Grant into movement. With mitted fists Burns pounded at the immobile man who was freezing to death before his eyes. If Grant had been naked he could not have been in a worse predicament, because the water was freezing inside his clothing.

'For God's sake, get cracking, Grant! Get moving, or you'll be a survival case. Move, man, move!' Yelling at him like a maniac, Burns tried to get him back on his skis; but the dazed marine fell, clambered to his feet, then stumbled again as he tried desperately to synchronise his limbs with his failing brain. Burns fought to help him, crawling under him to support his weight.

'Get your planks off!' He was shouting at him now, trying to make him register. At least they had reached the edge of the lake safely. Tucker had disappeared.

The snow felt deep and solid beneath them as Burns looked at the river bed running down the valley to his left. Unclipping his own boots, he floundered in the snow while Grant looked on dumbly, trying futilely to aid Burns's frantic endeavours. Then Grant's skis were off, and he slumped into the snow. Burns fitted his own snowshoes, then began fumbling frenziedly with Grant's boots. He had finished slipping on one snowshoe when he heard shouting from the trees above him.

Tucker was in the van, skiing down between the birches, four marines at his heels. Seconds later, they were swarming around Grant, pummelling him, ripping off his clothes. They dragged sweaters over him, shoved him into a sleeping bag, inserted it into another. They left his skis where they lay, slapped him on to the pulk, whipped on their own snowshoes, then thrashed their way back to the camp.

Burns did not know how long the emergency had lasted, but Grant had lost consciousness before the flickering flames of the fire showed through the birch line. They placed him on the windward side, two men pummelling him, chafing his cheeks, his ears, his nose, his hands. As soon as he came round, life restored by the heat of the crackling fire, they took him inside the snow-hole, his buddy Marine Hughes yanking at the sleeping bag to get it through the narrow tunnel entrance. They slapped Grant on the lower shelf, then Hughes unzipped the bag and crawled inside, his body transferring the life-saving warmth. There was no ribaldry this time: this was for real.

Burns watched, praying as he had not prayed for a long time. Slowly, as they carried out the survival drill they had so often exercised, the waxiness disappeared from Grant's finger tips, the edges of his ears, the tip and bridge of his nose; the spasms which shuddered the length of his body gradually became less frequent. His terrified eyes began to take on a semblance of intelligence. Grant seemed okay; he need not be pulled down to the town or to Zulu that night.

Corporal Burns watched the flickering candle; they'd have to evacuate the hole bloody quickly if it petered out because they were using up all the oxygen. He crawled outside into the night. 'Get going, O'Malley and Holmes ... what you waiting for? Get your gear on, you skiving layabouts — you've got your sentry posts, haven't you?'

The cold hit Burns as he clambered to his feet outside the tunnel. He was shaking inside his clothing, shocked by the accident which had nearly claimed more than ten per cent of his section. He was a bloody lunatic to have taken them so close to the lake's exit; he should have known better. As he waited in the silence, he heard the howl of a wolf, and then another, down in the pine forest a thousand feet below. The hairs prickled at the back of his neck. Perhaps Stoddart wouldn't leave them too long here, marooned in this desolate spot. Though it was isolated, the lemmings — those peculiar Arctic rats — would soon be keeping them company, burrowing into the snow-hole.

CHAPTER 20

HMS Icarus, 30 December.

On that same day, when Captain Stoddart's troop was deploying to its ambush positions in the mountains of Troms, HMS *Icarus* was steaming at twenty-five knots towards her rendezvous at 1800 with COMSTANAVFORLANT. The weather had eased and Captain Trevellion felt that he would be well up to time.

'Clear of the minefield, sir.'

Trevellion nodded at his navigating officer. Even Brian Neame seemed to have got the message: he was anticipating events, and no longer could Trevellion complain of the pilot's slackness or slipshod methods. If Neame continued as he was going, he could be taken off the Captain's Report...

Icarus left the swept channel buoy astern, then, taking his departure from Grimsholm lighthouse, Neame set his mean line of advance towards the rendezvous. It would be good to gain sea room and, perhaps, to clear the enemy's effective blanket jamming. 'Woodpecker', as it was known in STANAVFORLANT, blotted out everything, radar and radio, so that communications were now impossible. Fortunately, Woodpecker was a two-edged sword affecting the Russian communications as adversely as NATO's. Electronic warfare was a military science on its own; whoever won EW supremacy would be the victor in a clash at sea. For the past twelve hours the Russians had been blotting out the south-eastern sector of the Norwegian sea and the North Cape area, presumably to conceal the movements of their Northern Fleet into the Barents Sea.

The first lieutenant appeared on the bridge, spruced up after his morning watch. He'd had much to do reorganising the watches since the departure of the Royals.

'Ready for NBCD exercise, sir. You'll be RAS-ing port side?'

'Can't be sure yet. I'll let you know definitely when we get a bit nearer.'

'Will you see requestmen now, sir?'

Now that *Icarus* was on war routine, Trevellion found the mundane, everyday routine a reassurance: normality continued in men's lives. At the table, two men were for rating-up, one for his first good conduct badge. Even under war routine and after a night's watch, they had smartened themselves up.

'Leading Radio Operator Osgood, sir,' Campbell, the Master-at-Arms rasped. 'First request, sir: "Permission to withdraw his notice to leave the service", sir.' Campbell shot a glance at the tall divisional officer on the opposite side of the table. 'Second request, sir: "To see the captain privately."'

Trevellion met Osgood's gaze, then turned to the divisional officer. 'Lieutenant Lochead: you've seen this man?'

'Yes, sir.'

'Do you recommend the withdrawal of his notice? Once a man has made up his mind upon such an important issue, it's no light thing to renounce the decision.'

'I recommend that he stays in, sir. He's a good leading hand. His request is bound up with his request to see you, sir. I thought your experience would be more helpful to L/RO Osgood than mine, sir.' Lochead had clearly matured.

'First request granted,' Trevellion said, nodding at the Master. He faced Osgood. 'You realise, Osgood, that a man can see me privately only if it's about his personal affairs. Complaints don't come into the category.'

'Yes, sir, I understand. I want your guidance, sir.'

Trevellion hesitated. He had already made up his mind about Osgood — a leader amongst his peers, but unstable sometimes: he might steady down if given the chance. He turned to the DO. 'Thank you, Lieutenant Lochead. I'll see L/RO Osgood in my cabin at 1500.'

'Aye, aye, sir.'

Requestmen was over.

Captain Trevellion returned the salutes, then turned away to climb the ladder back to his bridge. Perhaps, after the NBCD exercise, he could snatch a moment to read Rowena's letter again. If she did not write so fully, life would be bloody. It was bad enough leaving her to cope alone during these frightening days.

So Thomas Osgood had got it off his chest — and as he watched warily for any sign of cynicism in the older man's eyes, he knew then that he had come to the right fount. Captain Trevellion had listened, easing Osgood's ordeal by occasionally adding a word here, finishing a phrase there. And now it was finished, this interview which Osgood had expected to be so difficult and, perhaps, humiliating...

'I'm afraid tragedies such as yours happen every day, Osgood,' Captain Trevellion said kindly. 'But that doesn't make it any easier for you.' He smiled, an uncomplicated smile of sympathy. 'The conditions under which, up to a few years ago, we were existing in the forces — conditions which men like you accepted loyally — too often meant a marriage breakdown. Some of the wives couldn't take it — and your Merle is one of those, I'm afraid.'

Osgood nodded his head. 'In some ways I'm glad it's over,' he said. 'But I don't know what I'll do without my kid.'

The grizzle-headed captain faced him squarely. Osgood had a strong face, stubborn, tenacious; this man would not be submerged by life's handouts. That open face with its dark-brown eyes was one which could be trusted.

'You love your daughter, don't you?' the captain was asking quietly.

Osgood nodded.

Trevellion murmured, 'It's the same with me, Osgood — but I've got a different sort of problem. We all have them, you know, one way or the other. It's how we cope with disaster which makes the man.'

'Perhaps, sir. But it's bloody difficult.'

The captain nodded. 'I'm glad you're staying on — right thing. The Navy takes care of its own these days.'

'Thanks for seeing me, sir. Kind of helps.'

'I haven't done much, Osgood. I'll put the welfare people on to tracing Debbie's whereabouts.'

Osgood choked and looked away, ashamed. The Old Man had remembered her name, then? He bloody well cared.

'Is there anything else we can do?' the Old Man asked. 'You can forget about the Bermuda episode. I'll fix that, now that hostilities are imminent: perhaps even Bermudian pub keepers will recognise on which side their bread's buttered.'

Osgood could still not face his captain. Staring blindly at the bulkhead, his head averted, he asked, 'D'you mean I've got nothing to pay now, sir ... nothing?'

'Scrubbed. And, of course, Mrs Fane can forget it all too. I've written to her.'

Osgood rose from the soft chair. He picked up his cap and faced the captain, his composure restored.

'Sir?'

'Yes?'

'I'd like to make a clean break, sir. Start again.'

'What d'you mean?'

The L/RO tapped his thigh with the rim of his cap. 'I'd like to join the Fleet Air Arm.'

Lieutenant Hob Gamble was the first in the wardroom for supper on Sunday night. Now that *Perdix* was grounded he and Rollo felt frustrated to the tits, like unemployed passengers. He shoved back his chair, did without his coffee and retired like a hermit in his cabin. He would console himself by answering Allie's letter. He slid her envelope from his desk drawer and slumped on to his bunk. Her ragged handwriting, reflecting her warmth so accurately, was good to see. He began re-reading, for the fourth time, her letter which had come in this morning's mail.

Leat Cottage
Christmas Day

My Beloved,

Just a little note on this lovely Christmas Day. You're probably beating it up with the Eskimo dolly birds somewhere up in the frozen wastes ... but wherever you are, my darling, this is just to tell you that all is well at Leat Cottage. Your mum's here, sitting opposite me, finishing off the horrid blackout curtains she's hanging over the kitchen window tonight. Dear old Mascot is snuffling away, his head on my lap, wondering why his master isn't sitting in the chair opposite — he's not the only one who's missing you, darling Hob...

Your mother is full of beans, trying hard to make it a good Christmas. She's frail, of course, but glad to be with me in the warm. We're dreading the idea of rationing.

What can I tell you, dearest, except that I miss you like hell? You said you liked sex-starved women — well, you've got one panting for you, down here in Cornwall. Hurry up and settle the Russians then fly your whirly bird down here.

I went into Plymouth and stayed the night with Peggy so that I could do some shopping. (I managed to collect that tea set you'd ordered for your mum — and she's delighted with it.) It was odd to see how the worthy citizens of Plymouth are facing up to the imminence of doom. A few people were self-consciously digging holes in their gardens — and volunteers were attacking the parks with picks and spades. The Volunteer Citizens' Force (they're already known as the VCs) are good news — two days ago they helped the police to break up a Peace Watch march around the Hoe — people are getting fed up with them. The 18B internment of those you call traitors is being accepted as good news, and call-up dodgers don't get much sympathy in spite of the Peace Watch's attempts. But the most depressing thing to me is the blackout they are going to start next week.

Mum and I are going to collect our gas masks (sorry! Anti-Gas Respirators) on Monday in case chemical warfare is launched — it's all a horrible nightmare, Hob, isn't it? But when I wake now, it's all too true — and the bed's empty by my side.

Take care of yourself in your rotating machine, my darling husband.

I love you

ALLIE

Hob laid down the crumpled sheets of paper. Should he answer it now, allow his pen to pour his thoughts out to her?

'Excuse me, sir. Captain's compliments, but he'd like to see you on the bridge.'

He nodded at the bo'sun's mate and reached for his cap.

When he reached the bridge the seas were flying over the bows, the spray lightening up the dark fo'c'sle. *Icarus* was pushing on, scything cleanly through the long, undulating swell. Captain Trevellion turned, then handed him the message. Its filing time was seven minutes ago, 1806. Hob began reading it, wondering why he'd been summoned.

'Our nuke has made an amplifying report,' Captain Trevellion said. 'A heavy force is steering 264 degrees, speed twenty-eight. STANAVFORLANT has been ordered to make contact and to shadow. The Commodore has ordered us to rendezvous at 2200, further north. He's disposed the force on a line of bearing across the enemy's track. Contact should be at any time after 2230. A white-out has clamped down in the Barents Sea, but its depression shouldn't be with us for a few hours yet. The electronic emission policy has been relaxed, so there's a good chance we'll find 'em if their jamming eases up.'

Hob had not known the Old Man to be so loquacious for a long time. The blue eyes glinted, but he was holding something back...

'Yes, sir?' Hob asked doubtfully. He wanted to add, 'So what?' Without her Lynx, *Icarus* was as vulnerable as a sitting duck.

'You'll be pleased to know, Hob, that the rules of engagement are becoming realistic. I can open fire if I believe the enemy is about to attack.'

Hob nodded. That was comforting, but without *Perdix*, *Icarus* would be blown out of the water as soon as the frigate's frequencies were picked up.

'Who's in the enemy force, sir?' he asked. 'Do we know?'

'A carrier and full supporting programme.' Captain Trevellion pulled a scrap of paper from his pocket. 'Read that.'

It was from MoD, originator Westlands, info COMSTANAVFORLANT. Westlands considered that it was operationally safe for all Mark VII Lynx to continue flying for a maximum of another twenty-five hours.

'We don't have to disobey orders, after all,' the captain said. 'Get your whirly bird out of her shed and kit her up.'

Hob turned to leave the bridge. 'What armament, sir?'

'Sea Skua missiles. Be prepared for anything. The Commodore may have other ideas.'

Hob saluted and scrambled down the ladder for Rollo's cabin. So there *was* work to be done: he must check that the Mark VI torpedoes and the sonobuoy kit were ready for action.

CHAPTER 21

Norway, 31 December.

Corporal Burns slept fitfully during that night. In their snow-hole they stripped off to their underclothes, each man taking an hour's trick at remaining awake to watch the candle flame. By the early hours they were suffering the usual headaches. Burns never slept for the first night in a snow-hole, the unique existence being alien even for a Royal Marine.

Grant eventually drifted into a restless sleep, but fears for his recovery were soon dispelled when the colour came back to his limbs. Only luck and swift survival drill had saved him.

At 0554 Burns slid from his sleeping bag and dressed. Trying not to wake his snoring companions, he crept past the heavy-lidded watchman and crawled through the tunnel. He was used to the candlelight — he would remain here a few minutes to restore his night vision — but he wasn't used to this cold. The thermometer hanging from a branch outside the tunnel entrance was showing minus 38 degrees. Burns felt hungry; he might as well mentally check the rations remaining while he waited for the day's first radio check with Zulu.

Twelve hours gone now, and a quarter of their rations already devoured. They'd had one good evening meal — a tin of soup, biscuits, minced beef and gravy, apple sauce and chocolate pud. O'Malley was a dab hand at cooking, which made all the difference to the morale of a troop. He'd be getting the breakfast in half an hour, a meal which they craved in this cold. Even the dreary old oatmeal block, the hamburgers, the biscuits, the marge and jam, rounded off with tea, put heart into a man when he couldn't tell the difference between night and day.

Burns shoved back his sleeve with the edge of his mitt: 0610. He scrunched to the wall of the snow-hole and picked up the radio telephone. After the third attempt, Signalman Budd, Stoddart's communications man, came on the air. His voice was heavy with sleep as he accepted Burns's sitrep.

'Come in Sierra. You're very weak: strength three to four, over.'

'This is Sierra,' Burns repeated. 'Wait one.' He clumsily pushed up the control to full power, but the output needle quivered at only two decimal five.

'This is Sierra. Any better, Zulu?'

'This is Zulu — my sit: four-two all quiet.' There was a snick of the switch, but then Budd came back. 'We'll bring up the batteries on our milk run. We'll replace and put yours on charge, over.'

'Roger. Own sit. No change. Weather overcast, minus thirty-eight. Admin, nil. No general info, over.'

'This is Zulu. Next check 0710, out.'

'Roger. Out.'

The message had been barely intelligible, but Burns would be glad of the charged batteries. He stamped his boots, scraped the packed snow from soles and heels, slipped on his skis. After testing the release on his bindings, he slung his rifle about his shoulders and shoved off down the slope. He'd call on Tucker, the dawn sentry, then make up towards the frontier post.

It had not snowed during the night, and the going was iron hard. Last night's frenzied tracks were still very visible, their flurry winding upwards towards the ambush's rocky escarpment. When he got back, he'd have them obliterated before the captain came up for his daily rounds.

'Okay, Tucker?'

'Fine, Corp. What's for breakfast?'

Tucker's white shadow had drifted from behind the snow-capped rocks, his rifle cocked. The white ski uniform gave good camouflage in these conditions. It was said that the Russian soldiers disliked moving in the snow ... Burns smiled to himself. They might take an aversion to these conditions, but Marines had developed a love-hate relationship with the Arctic — sweating it out in Guyana or freezing in the ice was all part of the job. He didn't wear the Royal's badge on his beret for nothing: the laurels surrounding the globe and the motto 'By Sea and Land' couldn't be more appropriate for the Corps.

As he pushed his way upwards, the image of Margaret invaded his mind. She was as proud of the outfit as he was, which was the whole battle. Even if he wanted to slap in his notice, Margaret wouldn't let him. Once again her sweet face floated into his mind. She'd be getting up soon, seeing the kids were ready, before nipping down to Harry's little shop on the corner. He could see her so clearly, round and soft and comfortable, as exciting to hold now as she had been those seven years ago ...

He was puffing as he reached the crest overlooking the Finnish frontier post. Huge snowflakes were beginning to tumble from the darkness, gently, silently, like feathers.

What must it be like to be vassals of the Russians? Impossible for a Brit to conceive; the British took freedom for granted. If he had his history right, the Finns under Mannerheim had fought to the death, holding up the Russian colossus for over six weeks across those frozen lakes ... He screwed up his eyes to peer into the gloom of those eastern ranges ... over there, three hundred miles away, the monstrous beast squatted, waiting to lumber forwards across defenceless nations.

Then his attention was drawn to the increase in activity at the frontier post. A dozen or so individuals, impossible to distinguish in their winter clothing, had appeared and seemed to be interrogating the pair of sleepy Customs men. The two Norwegians, on their side of the post, seemed to be enjoying the argument. A lighter flared, and by the light of its flame he could see that the Norwegians were laughing their heads off.

Tucking the tops of his sticks into his armpits, he leant forwards to take a breather. Between the road and the near side of the broad snowfield which was Lake Kilpisjärvi, he watched the headlights of several trucks, yellow glow-worms in the distance, threading their way through the falling snow as they approached the frontier post. They were a noisy lot ... then, suddenly he realised that the growl of engines came not from the road but from overhead, reverberating across the valley.

He braced himself, glanced upwards at the snowflakes drifting down. To the south, a ribbon of arc lights suddenly switched on, the swan-neck light standards illuminating the E78 where it ran along the eastern shore of Lake Kilpisjärvi. The whole area was transformed into a luminous bowl, while above it the giant snowflakes tumbled down in the eerie reflected light.

Burns went rigid as the unmistakeable roar of a jet aircraft exploded above him. Then another, and another, their engines screaming in the snow-filled sky — there must have been a dozen of them.

As he jerked round to follow them while they terrain-hopped down the valley, he heard another sound, the rumble of numbers of large aircraft. He held his breath, listening: no way could he be wrong. These were large turbo-prop aircraft, flying quite low. The sky above him began throbbing, the whole valley reverberating with sound; the sky was stacked with aircraft, circling, turning back on themselves, away from the range rearing up at them from inside Norwegian territory. The dark night pulsated above him as each wave flew in, seeming to circle above his head, then slowly lumbering away again, into the darkness whence they had come ... another wave, then another and another...

Corporal Burns executed his kick-turn. As he pushed off down the hill, he glanced in the direction of the receding aircraft. The snow was falling faster now. He wiped the back of a mitt across his eyes, blinked, then stared again.

Those huge frozen crystals — he'd never seen such bloody great flakes ... and as they spiralled downwards, dodging, floating, drifting from the night sky above his head, he suddenly recognised them for what they were: airborne troops, floating from the darkness on their parachutes, swinging downwards in the snowstream and tumbling on to the frozen lake.

The air hissed as Burns sucked in his breath. He'd be cut off from the small lake, where the paratroops were also dropping thickly. Thousands must be landing on Lake Kilpisjärvi, touching down at this moment; they must be highly trained in Arctic warfare, if they could carry out a drop in these conditions with such precision...

His skis hissed through the snow, the flakes scalding his cheeks as he stabbed the ground frantically with his sticks. He did not know how he reached the bottom of the defile without falling but, as he crashed into the bank at the bottom, he saw that the leading paratroops were already on the move from the small lake. He could hear the cries of those trapped in the weak ice, shouting, whistle blasts and the commands of officers...

Burns shoved on to the foot of Sierra's ambush position, tore off his skis, snapped on his snowshoes. Trying to subdue his mounting panic, he began scrambling up the face of the escarpment. He could hear the echoes of Russian orders in the valley below him, the crackle of walkie-talkies ... then, far away by the Customs post, the staccato coughing of tank engines roaring into life. But unseen hands were grabbing him and he was being dragged up the last shoulder, which concealed the ambush position.

'Last night's tracks,' he gasped. 'We've not covered them.'

'It'll take a while for the snow to hide 'em,' O'Malley said. 'Worse than a signpost.'

'Man your fire-posts,' Burns ordered. 'Tucker, O'Malley, Grant: stand by to engage with the Law. Wait for the first tank and don't fire until ordered.' He swung round on the others. 'Here, Budd and you lot. Man the GPM/G — stand-by sustained fire. The rest of you, get a load of grenades ready. Watch our rear...'

As he scrambled for the radio, the first shots began plummeting into the snow around their heads. Lying prone, he watched the tanks jerking down the road with amazing speed, throwing up clouds of flying snow. He saw the shadows in the birches, white blotches against the blackness, gliding like spectres ... and the red flashes spitting from the flame guards of their automatics. He could hear the cries of their officers, urging them on. From here, Sierra section could take care of them, picking them off like flies until the tanks came within range...

'Target: riflemen on the slopes in front of you,' Burns shouted to the GPM/G group. The crew waited, immobile, like a dummy run for the Royal Tournament. 'Open fire!' he yelled.

The stuttering of the machine gun drowned all efforts at raising Zulu on the radio. The screams and yells of the enemy echoed up from the cliff beneath.

'Check — check — check!'

No. 2 tapped the gunner's shoulder and the sudden silence brooded with the stillness of death. He picked up the mike again.

There was a crimson flash from their right and a shower of snow drifted over them; a group of Russians was concentrating in the birches.

'See 'em, Tucker, right front?'

'On target, Corp.'

'Independent fire: open fire!'

At that moment the first of the tank missiles plunged into the rock behind their heads — a whisper, a flash and an ear-splitting explosion...

'This is Sierra, this is Sierra. Do you read, Zulu, do you read, Zulu...?'

He looked at his watch: 0707. Zulu was due on the air in three minutes. For Christ's sake, how could he warn them?

A dual crack, a shattering roar. A grey plume, an orange flash at its base, leaping at their feet. O'Malley was yelling, 'Within range, Corp! I've got the leader.'

'Shoot!' Burns roared.

The agonising wait, the muttered curses as the Ulsterman aimed his 66-milllimetre anti-tank weapon ... the long pause ... and then the bright flash at the base of the tank's squat turret (just like on the ranges) — a T-80, by the look of the bastard.

A cheer from the crew and then Burns was on the radio again just as the GPM/G opened up, scything the snow slopes at their feet. There was an inferno of sound all about them and then, again, the flutter of missiles, the blast of explosion. There was a yell from Grant and curses when the GPM/G jammed. In that second, Burns knew he could sacrifice his men no longer.

One of them — he could not see who — lay twitching in the snow by the charred embers of the fire. A dark stain was seeping across the snow from a severed artery. The machine-gun's crew were wrenching at their belts for the grenades.

Corporal Burns bellowed as the hordes began closing in from three sides: 'Follow me, lads! Let 'em have your grenades, then disperse and scarper for the mountains. Make your own way to the coast.' He sprayed the birds with a last savage burst. 'Get in among 'em and cause as much ... nausea as you ... well can.' His men were loping past him, grabbing their skis from the pile, crouching low as they retreated. He waited for Grant, then grabbed the radio again. *For Christ's sake...*

The black night exploded in his face. A flaming, whirling mist, a shattering roar overwhelming his world — Corporal Burns spun into the rumpled snow. He twitched once, then lay still, face down, cut in two by a burst from an automatic weapon.

The first of the airborne assault troops had reached the lip of ambush position Sierra.

This was not Dick Stoddart's day. Since the early hours he had lain awake worrying about his two sections. He had certainly slipped up in not checking that the radio batteries were charged.

But his anxiety went deeper: for so long, he had tried to bring small ships' detachments up to scratch in amphibious warfare. After all his wrangling to get his detachment ashore, he had been side-tracked to a couple of minor defensive posts in 42, miles behind the Commandos advanced positions, and 42 was secondary to 45, which was up on the northern border where the action was.

He was still trying to discover why the snow-hole collapsed. Just after 0300, when the relief sentry had returned, the entrance tunnel had fallen in. After the initial panic, they had managed to burrow out to the air from what had nearly become their snowy tomb. The incident certainly shook everyone, and the rebuilding at dawn had not improved tempers. It was an effort to get them all on the move again.

'Can't raise Sierra,' the signalman hailed. 'It's past 0725 now. Shall I go on, sir?'

'Pack it in,' Stoddart replied. 'We don't want to cane our batteries too.'

Damn. No contact with Corporal Burns, who was one of the best NCOs Stoddart had known. The sooner communications were re-established the better.

'Driver Hawkins.'

'Sir?'

The marine, who was cleaning his teeth, swilled out his mouth and tried to salute with the stump of his toothbrush in his hand. The chuckles of the section were a needed tonic this morning. In the snow, no one stood on rank, and this policy had amply justified itself. In the Arctic, an officer lived with his men — even cooking for them if he was the best cook — which was one reason why such comradeship existed among these magnificent men. Dick Stoddart felt proud of his section: what other bunch of guys displayed such loyalty, such versatility?

'Get the truck ready, Hawkins. Tell the signalman to load up the spare batteries. I'll go up to Sierra as soon as you're warmed up.'

Marine Hawkins disappeared, and minutes later the sound of a starter motor grinding to a halt disturbed the stillness in the valley.

'You bastard!'

Stoddard finished his own tooth drill. Land Rovers disliked temperatures of minus 35 degrees; by the time they had got the camphor stove going, heated the water and coaxed the truck into life, it was already past eight o'clock.

'Sir, will you wait for Sierra's 0810 call?' the signalman asked. 'They might have tried warming up their batteries.'

'Okay, I'll hold on.'

He waited impatiently until the fruitless exercise was over and then jumped into the Land Rover. The surface was crisp; no problems for the climb. 'Keep a constant watch,' he shouted to the signalman. 'I'll keep in touch through my set in the truck.'

'Aye, aye, sir.'

'Let's go.'

As the driver let in the clutch, he heard a shout from behind. 'Hold on, sir…' the signalman was yelling. 'Flash report, sir, from *Cornwallis*.'

Stoddart halted the truck and leapt out. Why was Ramsund HQ coming on the air out of routine? He heard the static of the signalman's receiver, then the measured voice of a staff officer, determinedly unflappable…

In the silence, the only sound was the coughing of the truck's exhaust and, from the birch woods below them, the croak of a ptarmigan. The carrier wave of the radio began crackling again:

'Flash — Flash — Flash,' the operator's voice snapped.

The signalman held up a hand. 'Stand by, sir. There's another coming up,' he shouted, adjusting his headset. In the loneliness of their ambush position, perched above the vital road junction, the men listened to the awaited code word; some dreaded, some relieved, others elated. 'Command 42: Red Alert.'

The enemy had to fight his tanks past their vital junction, even if he was overrunning 45 in Nordland. 45's Brazen had at last been broadcast; it would be interesting to see how long they could hold out.

'It's no good sitting about on our arses here,' Stoddart barked. 'Strengthen points of fire, while we take Sierra's batteries up to them. Stockpile the ammo, and see that it's easy to get at. Set up the Milan to cover both bridges, and nip down to the first bridge to check that the detonators are okay.'

He needed to jolt them into action: HQ's sitrep had shaken them. At least everyone knew where they stood now: out on their own, miles from anywhere, short of ammunition.

The Land Rover churned the snow, then settled to its four-wheel climb up the valley. By 0850 they were above Lulle; twenty minutes later they slid past the tributary from the lake westward of Helligskogen. The driver was hauling the vehicle out of a right-hand bend when he braked suddenly.

'Good God, sir, what's that?'

Through the frosted windscreen a yellow glow spread across the valley. The light jumped crimson at times, pulsing orange and throwing up cascades of sparks.

'Helligskogen's on fire,' Dick shouted. 'The town's ablaze.' He was turning towards the driver when he saw the loom of a tank swinging rapidly towards them, down the centre of the road. He picked up the mike as the driver swerved, wrenching the Land Rover round in two movements. They thrashed down the hill as the first missile streaked past them to explode in a puff on the rocks to the right.

'Flash — flash — flash!' Stoddart yelled into the mike. 'Contact Report. One: now. Two: three kilometres north Helligskogen. Three: enemy tank force: T-80. Four: proceeding north at speed down E seven eight. Five: withdrawing...' He paused to catch his breath; he could hear the signalman breathing at the Zulu end. 'Contact — wait out.'

'This is Zulu. Message received. Will relay to 42. Out.'

The Land Rover lurched, struggled round the bend. 'Unfriendly bastards,' the driver said as he flicked on his sidelights. 'Didn't even sound their bleedin' 'orns.'

CHAPTER 22

HMS *Icarus, 31 December.*

'Slip the jackstay.'

Captain Trevellion nodded through the window to his first lieutenant, who was standing in the starboard wing of *Icarus*. When the last line had gone and the telephone disconnected, he waved to the Dutch captain towering on his bridge above the diminutive frigate. 'Port ten...' Another RAS completed. He had lost count of the number, but *Icarus* had dropped below the acceptable fuel level after last night's debacle.

'You have the ship, Officer of the Watch.'

'I have the ship, sir.' The sub was on watch again, more reliable since the bollocking Trevellion had given him for passing too close under the oiler's counter. The captain could ease his tired brain for half an hour while *Icarus* took up her position again on the south-east flank of the force. To the north he could distinguish the dark blur of the replenishment ship, hull down on the horizon and silhouetted against the dancing lights of the aurora borealis. *Icarus* was also running low on provisions and would have to replenish tomorrow.

Yesterday's damage control exercise had been a success. Controlling emergency after emergency from his DC HQ, the Chief had been master of every complexity. Today's RAS had also gone well: refuelling had taken three-quarters of an hour, so he could nip down to his cabin for an uninterrupted spell in which to digest Rowena's long letter. She was coping in these difficult times but, reading between the lines, Ben was being very difficult.

He slumped in his chair, feeling the weariness seeping through his limbs: last night had been one of intense strain for him, with its frustrating disappointments and fears. It was all too easy to see now where the mistakes had been made.

At 2300 last night, after turning north-east to sweep towards our SSN's enemy report, the jamming had ceased as abruptly as it had begun. The interference had been directional, an arc blanketing the coast between the Barents Sea and a line of bearing of 210 degrees. On receiving CINCEASTLANT's new directive on radar silence policy COMSTANAVFORLANT had lifted the ban. Closing at speed on a course of 065 degrees, *Athabaskan*'s 265 radar had picked up echoes of what must have been the enemy's carrier group reported by our SSN off North Cape.

The Commodore had maintained his course, and for twelve never-to-be-forgotten minutes both forces were racing towards each other at a relative speed of over sixty-five knots; shifting from the tracking to the firing mods, the enemy's radar was illuminating STANAVFORLANT — and the pulse and scanning rates were switching. The NATO force was also in all respects ready for battle, their weapon systems at the first degree of readiness. The ECM boys were hard at it, and it had been a hairy few moments, with both sides' fingers caressing the triggers.

But, rules of engagement being what they were, a NATO captain had to be fired upon first before he could retaliate to defend himself. Trevellion could still hear the sigh of relief in his ops room when the plot showed the enemy turning away on a reciprocal course for the Barents Sea. He was thankful he had not flown off the Lynx with her Sea Skuas — her remaining twenty-five hours of flying time might be needed yet.

'Thanks, Rowlans.' His leading steward slipped the coffee cup between the fiddles on the tabletop: discreet and unobtrusive, Rowlans was a first-rate steward; Trevellion valued the sense of comradeship which was growing between them. 'Give me a shake in half an hour if I drop off, will you, Rowlans?'

''Course, sir — rough night for you last night.' The steward slipped away as silently as he had entered.

The enemy's carrier force had slipped back into the darkness of the Barents Sea. Even with calmer sea conditions our ships could not keep up ... *Kiev* (or she could have been *Minsk*) and her group had an edge of at least three knots, and so drew away rapidly. By 0104 on this Monday morning, having lost contact, the Commodore reversed STANAVFORLANT's course to resume its patrol line to the south-west.

The Commodore also wished to make a southing because the second old carrier, *Furious,* was at last emerging from the English Channel with her ASW group to support the second vital amphibious force of channel ferries which were crammed with troops for the northern flank. When *Glorious* finished disembarking her commandos at Narvik, she too would join STANAVFORLANT which, disposed on a line of bearing of 290-110 degrees, her RAS ships in the centre, was settling down again on its ASW sweep towards North Cape. Trevellion was fighting drowsiness when he heard the tapping on his doorframe.

'Communications Officer's compliments, sir. Flash report from CINCNORTH to Allied Forces Northern Europe.'

Trevellion held out his hand, took the message board. He motioned the radio supervisor to the chair opposite.

SITREP 0932 31 Z DEC: FOLLOWING IS
APPRECIATION OF CONFUSED NORTHERN
SITUATION. PARACHUTE ASSAULTS BRIGADE
LEVEL AT 0715 ON HARSTAD, BARDUFOSS AND
FRAMNES AIRFIELDS. AMPHIBIOUS LANDINGS
BEING ATTEMPTED FROM NORTH-WEST THROUGH
MINEFIELDS AND INTO MALANGENFJORD
THENCE ORLSBERG AND ANDSELV PRESUMED
OBJECTIVE TO ISOLATE BARDUFOSS FROM
TROMSØ AND RAMSUND AREA WHERE
NORWEGIAN SIXTH DIVISION ARE COUNTER-
ATTACKING. SITUATION IN OFOTFJORD REMAINS
CRITICAL WHERE TWO POLISH MERCHANT
VESSELS SUNK ACROSS MAIN CHANNEL. HMS
GLORIOUS CLEARED NARVIK AND OFOTFJORD AT
0615 FOR RENDEZVOUS WITH WHISKY COMPANY.
NORWEGIAN BRIGADE NORTH ATTEMPTING
LANDINGS THROUGH SOLBERGFJORD TO CUT OFF
ENEMY BUT OPERATION HAMPERED BY LACK OF
DEDICATED AMPHIBIOUS LIFT. ENEMY
INTENTION TO ISOLATE RAMSUND AREA WHERE
AIRBORNE REINFORCEMENTS ARE DEPLOYING
HOURLY. OWN TACTICAL AIR HITTING BACK
MAGNIFICENTLY IN CRITICAL AREAS BUT
OVERWHELMED. 45 COMMANDO HOLDING
MASSIVE MOTORISED INFANTRY ATTACKS IN
NORDLAND. 42 COMMANDO NOT YET COMMITTED
BUT DETACHED UNITS BELIEVED OVERWHELMED
ON E78 FINNISH BORDER. ENEMY OBJECTIVES
AND DEMANDS NOT YET PROMULGATED BUT
POLITICAL SITREP WILL BE ISSUED WHEN
SITUATION CLARIFIES. CINCNORTH'S OBJECTIVE

REMAINS UNCHANGED: RESIST TO END TO GAIN
TIME FOR ARRIVAL REINFORCEMENTS IN BATTLE
AREAS. MESSAGE ENDS.

Captain Trevellion glanced across to his radio supervisor, who had risen to his feet. 'Thanks, I'll talk to the ship's company immediately. Warn them on the broadcast, will you — five minutes time?'

'Yes, sir. It's war, isn't it, sir?'

'How can we avoid it? The Russians have got to withdraw — or it's hot, hot war.'

Trevellion remained in his chair long after the chief petty officer had left the cabin. He could see it now, the trap they had fallen into last night.

Last night at 2200, after receiving CINCEASTLANT's orders to make contact, COMSTANAVFORLANT had acted in the best traditions of the service: he had raced into the attack when the enemy's carrier force had turned away. The Commodore had done exactly what his commanding officers had expected him to do by chasing the superior force, determined to give the Russians a bloody nose if they were asking for one. By charging north-east after *Kiev* and her supporting forces the Soviet amphibious squadron, slipping away beneath the umbrella of ECM jamming, had been able to make its undetected landfall precisely on time off the entrance to Malangenfjord.

Trevellion heard the officer of the watch calling through the intercom: 'It's beginning to snow, sir.'

'What's the vis?'

'Down to half a mile, sir.'

'Quite happy?'

'Yes, sir. No problem.'

'Call me if you're worried.'

Trevellion wanted half an hour of uninterrupted peace, just a few minutes to read Ro's letter again — and he needed a moment of calm in which to weigh up the implications of CINCEASTLANT's depressing sitrep ... but the radio supervisor was back at the cabin door. A sardonic smile creased his grey face.

'From MoD, confirming our rules of engagement, sir — remain the same, pending political decisions.'

'Thanks.' Both men smiled at each other wryly.

Trevellion climbed to his feet when the curtain was drawn again across the doorway. He had better see how the sub was getting on. He disliked this tension, this fighting with one hand bound behind his back. There was little comfort, bobbing about in your lifejacket in the Arctic Ocean, in knowing that you had the right of self-defence once you were yourself attacked. No one doubted that a Russian captain would fire first: it was his privilege.

This was going to be a long day, and a longer night, waiting for the issue to be decided ashore by those gallant commandos and Norwegians. Patience was no quality of Trevellion's, and he sighed deeply as he pulled the heavy sweater over his head.

CHAPTER 23

HMS *Icarus, 1 January.*

It was a few minutes before the faint twilight finally dissipated when *Gloucester*'s flash report blistered through the radio. Convinced that a Backfire at medium height was carrying out a determined attack upon her, *Gloucester* shot it down with her Sea Darts seconds after the bomber fired her missiles. The DLG's ECM dealt with the air-to-surface attack, the missiles going wide, but the incident did not augur well for the first day of the year. There were no survivors from the Backfire, which disintegrated in mid-air. STANAVFORLANT was at extended disposition, dispersed across the horizon as it awaited the inevitable counter-attack.

Trevellion had kept *Icarus* at action stations; men remained at their quarters, fed with sandwiches from the galley. The captain remained in the ops room, waiting, alert, tensed. By 1400 that afternoon the picture on the Norwegian front was beginning to piece together.

Little definite news had emanated from the Norwegian battlefronts, only that the commandos were carrying out their duty as everyone knew they would, dying at their posts, refusing to budge as the Russian armour rolled over them, thrusting down the main artery of North Norway. The Royal Marine Brigade Commander had closed his last broadcast with words that would be remembered for years. 'We Royals shall stick where we are.'

Due to the sinking in Ofotfjord of the two Polish ships, *Glorious* could not now land her reinforcements at Narvik. The air was totally dominated by the enemy, and AAFCE (Allied Air Force Central Europe), faced by the Russian Air Divisions massing on the central front, had refused to be drawn, except to send two token squadrons of Phantoms. They had been torn out of the skies within hours, as much because of the unaccustomed severity of flying conditions as by the prowess of their adversaries; and so Tromsø was also denied to *Glorious* for the safe disembarkation of the vital backup force. The troops, existing under miserably crowded conditions 'tween decks, were becoming bloody-minded because of seasickness and the continuous shilly-shallying. At no time was a massive helicopter lift more desperately needed: but the squadron was either already airborne or non-existent. *Glorious* was now steaming south, bound for Trondheim, in the hope that the troops could be sent up by rail to Lonsdal, on the edge of Nordland.

Furious, at last freed from the dockyards, was on passage to Europe to lift more troops. With her five Sea Harriers, she was to cover the amphibious convoy which consisted of *Intrepid* and three Channel ferries about to sail from Antwerp. Neither *Furious* nor her squadron were fully worked up, but the convoy was a juicy target for the enemy's Backfires. These Mach 2.5 bombers heavily outnumbered the force; they were a major threat and a bloody menace.

Tonight, *Glorious,* hopefully having landed her mobile force, would be steaming northwards at speed: with her screen and replenishment ships, she would be resuming her ASW role, which was badly needed up here. The SSN's reports on westbound Russian submarines were wasted if the enemy was allowed to escape through the gaps for their Atlantic stations.

Poised up here, with STANAVFORLANT in support, *Glorious*'s Force Q was also an added deterrent against an enemy attack on the oil rigs. Trevellion pursed his lips: at this moment he would prefer any employment other than that of an oilman on those desolate, defenceless platforms.

'Nimrod *Lima* is reporting her position, sir,' said the PWO (Air), McKown. He shook his head. 'Wouldn't care to be in his shoes, would you, Julian?'

'They're a gutsy lot,' the PWO (Underwater) replied. 'Sitting ducks.'

'I wonder how long the RAF will be able to keep up the LRMPS?' the captain posed. 'But even one Nimrod's better than none.'

It was 1509 precisely when Force Q's radio link came on the air. *Glorious* was taking up her station, screened by the DDO, *Sheffield,* and the frigate, *Brilliant,* in company was her replenishment ship, *Regent,* and *Grey Rover,* her oiler. *Glorious* was flying the flag of the ASW Group Commander. Although operating now wholly in her ASW role eighty miles to the north-west, the Rear Admiral would not be taking COMSTANAVFORLANT under his command. Each force would act independently but in concert with the other. This resulted in a disposition signal from Commodore dispersing his ships over a wider area. *Icarus* was ordered forthwith to open twelve miles further to the south-east; this fresh disposition placed her nearest to the Norwegian coast but further than the remainder of the force from the expected encounter with the enemy's surface fleet. She was in station by 1605.

'Feel a wee bit lonely,' the first lieutenant said when he came into the ops room on his evening browse. 'We're a long way from home, sir.'

Trevellion smiled. 'But nearer to the action, Number One.' He tapped the command display in front of him. 'We're only 118 miles from Tromsø.'

The intercom from the radio office broke in:

'Captain, sir, Chief Radio Supervisor here. We've just picked up a special BBC announcement, one we missed last night. The Prime Minister is speaking to the nation in seven minutes.'

'Thanks. Relay it on the general broadcast.'

'Aye, aye, sir.'

They remained at their quarters, every man silent as the Prime Minister's voice issued clearly through the loudspeakers. Trevellion surreptitiously regarded his team.

'I have just been on the telephone with the Head of the Soviet Government,' the Prime Minister was saying without emotion. 'I asked him why he, in the name of the Russian people, was invading the territory of northern Norway. I will repeat to you, my British listeners wherever you may be, the seven main points in his explanation to me of the Russian aggression:

'One: the Americans have refused to withdraw their reinforcements from Iceland, which were landed against the wishes of the Communist government of the Icelandic people. We Russians warned the West that we would regard the American action in Iceland as provocation and as military escalation against the Soviet Union unless the American reinforcements were withdrawn within twenty-four hours. The United States refused.

'Two: the Soviet Government realises that everyone agrees on one fundamental fact: the peace of the world depends upon the strategic nuclear balance of terror between the two superpowers. The Soviet people know that the American SNBM submarines are based on the west coast of the USA,

236

four thousand miles away from Russia. But our Delta Is, Delta IIs and Yankee-class SNBM submarines are based in the Kola inlet only 150 miles from a major NATO power which keeps us under constant surveillance. We cannot tolerate this menace to our security; this inequality is upsetting the strategic nuclear balance. The only way to ensure world peace is to restore stability. It is essential for our security to have a *cordon sanitaire*. We *must* have the Troms region — so we've taken it.'

The silence in the ops room following the Prime Minister's words was profound: no one moved, no one spoke. The calm and measured voice continued:

'The Soviet President went on to enlarge his argument with me. Three: the Finnish people, who for a long time have been frightened by Norway's aggressive posture, have asked us for protection: we have given it to them.

'Four: if America continues to escalate the crisis, she must not be surprised if the Soviet peoples' massive military power is not used to its ultimate limit. The Soviet peoples, having won the Nazi war by the sacrifice of over twenty million of its citizens, are used to suffering.

'Five: the people of the United States should also be reminded that we have targeted thirty-five major unprotected American cities. In Russia, there are only nine comparable cities. These are all now "hardened" to withstand nuclear attack.

'Six: our terms are very reasonable: Accept that we shall remain in Northern Norway. We shall not advance further. We don't need to.

'Seven: if the West persists in continuing with hostilities we shall fight it out at sea with you. Neither side can gain by devastating Europe in a nuclear exchange.

'Eight: the issue *must* be decided at sea. All EEC nations would prefer this alternative to the total annihilation of their countries.

'Nine: if you use the nuclear deterrent against the Soviet Union, there will be world devastation. Even so, the Soviets will win. In one immense attack, one colossal effort, we will go all out for real and lasting world peace, universal and complete disarmament.'

Once more, only the whisper of the carrier wave disturbed the silence in the ops room.

'Her Majesty's Government is in unanimous agreement as to the response it should make to this blackmail. With the support of the American people, we will not fail our friends. We say to the Head of the Soviet Government: "Return inside your own borders. We shall do all in our power not to escalate this crisis, but liberty for us is of the spirit: freedom of worship, speech, of association between all peoples of the world; freedom from want, from fear, from war — we prefer to die rather than to live under the monstrous system you are determined to impose upon all peoples on this planet. We shall never surrender."'

There was a long pause before the Prime Minister went on, 'I must warn you, my fellow patriots, there's work to be done. Every step that we can take for our own protection must immediately be put in hand. With such terror loose in the world, we must be prepared for what our military leaders term "the pre-emptive strike". The British are at their best in adversity. Let us show the world we are of the same breed as that of our fathers who lined the beaches in the days of 1940. And now, may God protect us all.'

No one spoke. Finally, Julian Farge said, 'This is the test of will we've all been waiting for. Crunch time.'

'It wouldn't be the first time a dictator has miscalculated,' McKown replied. 'A pity it's such a profound error.'

'We're not at war yet,' Trevellion snapped. 'Back to defence stations, Number One. Tell everyone to get their heads down as much as they can. I'm going to my cabin.'

Though Trevellion was troubled when he reached his bunk, he was asleep in seconds. He didn't know what time it was that the Communications Yeoman shook him:

'Enemy reports, sir. One Delta II and two Charlies steering south-west from North Cape.'

He had barely dozed off again when a distress call was picked up from one of the Shackletons which had been pressed into service. An unidentified attacker had shot it down north of the Faeroes. Then a Nimrod reported that it was investigating a contact seventy-three miles north-north-west of *Icarus*'s position. Trevellion picked up the mike by the side of his bunk.

'Captain — bridge.'

'Bridge — Captain.'

'My compliments to the observer and pilot. Tell them to arm *Perdix* with ASW Mark 46 torpedoes, markers and the 196 ASR-buoys.'

'Aye, aye, sir.'

Trevellion turned on his side, switching off the light. The night promised to be gusty. He *must* sleep or he'd be unable to think straight. As he lost consciousness, he was aware that the seas were getting up: the wind was battering against the superstructure and *Icarus* had begun to pitch.

CHAPTER 24

Norwegian Sea, 2 January.

Zragevski was bored. For five days, his submarine had been patrolling her station, 210 miles west of the benighted North Cape. Captain Boris Ilyich Zragevski was a tough, squat, heavily-built officer, in the forefront for promotion to Rear Admiral — which was, he presumed, why he had been appointed to this boat, the latest of the new Victor IIs. As he tried to relax in the armchair of his cabin alongside the control room, his mind turned over those first days, three months ago, when he had started whipping SSN 329 into shape — some job, with the conscripts always on the move. He was satisfied now. SSN 329 was an efficient fighting unit, worthy of her frontline place in the Red Banner Fleet.

SSN 329 was a modified Victor II, a considerable improvement on the first of the Victor Is which he had joined as a Third Hand in 1967. 329's dived displacement was nearly two thousand tons greater to allow for her extra torpedo tubes and the improved twin nuclear reactors. Her three shafts gave her over thirty-four knots dived, when she banked on the turns like a fighter-bomber. Since Admiralty Yard at Leningrad had perfected the new welding techniques with the new high-carbon stressed steels, her tested diving depth was over six hundred metres, but she could probably go deeper. No doubt he'd find out one day, if the hydraulic telemotor pressure failed again, as it did last week — fortunately he had exercised drills 'in hand' only a few days previously, so they pulled her out, even with the fore-planes jammed at hard-a-dive... His only criticism of her was that she was still noisier than the enemy's boats.

It was pointless to criticise the British, because it was their technology that had produced the foundation upon which the Red Fleet's ASW was built. Now it was as good as — and in some areas better than — the Royal Navy.

The captain of SSN 329 glanced at the depth gauge on the outboard side of his cabin, the repeater upon which he instinctively kept an eye: though only a couple of hundred miles from land, even at her patrol depth of eighty metres there was still plenty of water beneath the keel. The depth of the sea bed had been meticulously charted by the surveying ships of the Red Fleet, who represented the largest surveying effort in the world. Creeping along at slow on the outer shafts, up and down her billet on a line of 320-140 degrees, was a soul-destroying business, but at least the sonar people were kept occupied: the department had been keeping 'passive' watches for nine days, the only excitement being during that Sunday night when the carrier Strike Force had turned away to draw off the enemy, so that the amphibious boys could make their landings.

There was a tap on the lintel of his door and the bearded face of the officer of the watch peered inside. 'Permission to come up to communication routine depth, sir?'

The captain glanced at his wristwatch: 1045 already? 1100 was one of the four routine traffic periods direct with CINCKOL (Commander-in-Chief Kola Inlet). But 329's indicator group had not been included yet, not in nine days...

'Checked the bathy?'

'Yes, sir. CR depth is well below the layer.'

'Have you checked the CSS?'

'No, sir.'

'Why not?' he snapped, exasperated at the feckless youth.

'You know my orders.'

'I'll check right away, sir.' The bearded wonder disappeared. A feeble officer, typical of the short-service entry which was doing no good to the submarine branch. This Schlovsky did not realise how careful he had to be with NATO's ASW forces — or how lucky he was to be serving in a boat fitted with a CSS (Combined SIRENE System). This anti-air system, one of the Navy's best-kept secrets, had been developed with astonishing speed by the Military Science Division in response to the request of the Flag Officer Submarines for such a weapon.

The Combined SIRENE System was a miracle of simplicity, consisting of two parts: the towed sensor (SENSOR) which could be streamed to a distance of seven kilometres; and the four missiles (ANVIL), housed in the free-flood after section of the fin, which could be fired from the control room as soon as acquisition was obtained. It contained a Combined Pulse Doppler Sensor with radio/radar wide-band receiver monitor, known as the CPDS by the scientists. Within its area the instrument could pick up most anomalies: radio/radar frequencies, audio, thermo, infra-red, air-pulse vibration and magnetic anomalies. The missile section, ANVIL, could be fired directly, on demand; or automatically, by the CPDS, if the 'fire' switch by the side of the periscope handle was made. As a precautionary measure against shooting down our Russian aircraft, this safety measure had been built in: the command had to make this switch next the periscope handle of the attack periscope to ensure that the aircraft had been identified visually or with IFF before the missiles were ejected. Once the solid-fuel rocket was clear of the surface, the missile was guided by the CPDS until within acquisition range of the target. The missile would then lock on, the final approach being automatic through its thermal-homing head. The high explosive payload did the rest.

Once again the OOW was tapping on his doorframe, a habit which irritated Boris Zragevski. Why couldn't the fellow just tell him?

'CSS completed, sir, negative.'

'Right. Recover the CSS and come up to CR depth. Oh, and Officer of the Watch...'

'Sir?'

'Don't knock on my bloody door — come in, tell me what you've got to say. I won't bite you.'

'Yes, sir.'

It was already 1052, too tight perhaps for the communication supervisor. Three minutes to take her up to the CR (the captain could feel her bow-up angle coming on) and then she would be at depth for the radio routines ... Zragevski could do with another situation report, because they had missed the last traffic routine when the carrier group passed through the area last night. The Norwegian operation should be wrapped up by now ... the High Command and the Politburo never jumped without hundred per cent certainty. The hope of a committee-ridden NATO being able to confront a determined, swift decision was fantasy...

It was 1114 when the CR was completed. He ordered the officer of the watch to return to patrol depth. Eighty metres was a good depth for this area. During the winter in these latitudes, the seas were so shaken up by the gales that few layers formed.

A pity, in one way, because the layers were a comfort if being hunted; but when 329 was herself the huntsman, these good sonar conditions rendered her attacks certainties. Her speed saw to that, plus her new sonar.

329's mission, as laid down in her sailing orders, was simple: to report and shadow any enemy movements, to prevent enemy interference with the amphibious landings. The latter had taken place successfully without any support from Zragevski — STANAVFORLANT had reacted as expected by *Minsk* and her task force. When the Norwegian resistance finally collapsed and the Red Army consolidated its hold, the Red Banner Fleet would be freed from these restricting patrols, SSN 329 could soon quit her billet in Square 15, escape through the gaps and away into the Atlantic for her primary war station. Meanwhile, he had to contain his patience and continue sweeping passively with his sonar in the hope that the enemy might pass through his billet.

'May I come in, sir?'

'Sit down. You know I'm always glad to see my signal officer.' The captain grinned. 'What've you got this morning, Skopintzoff?'

'Five operational, sir. I'm afraid we missed one of our indicator groups.'

'When's the next CR?'

'1145, sir.'

Zragevski swore with impatience. 'Tell the officer of the watch to start bringing her up at 1130.'

'Right, sir. Shall I leave these with you? There's a top classification.'

'Thanks.' He stretched out his hand for the deciphered signals.

The first message was festooned with security priorities, but was banal, the sort of thing that had been coming through daily of late. CINCKOL's staff were having a field day ... *ah-ha* ... an upping of the Rules of Engagement! About bloody well time. A Royal Navy destroyer had brought down a Backfire, had she? So all Northern Fleet units in Squares 1-28 were free of restrictions, if they considered themselves under threat of attack. *If such a situation develops,* the signal stated, *Commanding Officers are to make every endeavour to destroy the enemy totally before, repeat before, the enemy unit strikes. Detached enemy units are priority targets because no trace of the sinking is desirable.*

Bureaucratic jargon — but at least the constraints were eased and he would not be fighting half-fettered. He sifted to the next message. *Own Forces' Disposition* — so *Minsk* and her task force were back in the Barents? The infantry regiment had succeeded more completely than anyone had hoped ... the 'Iron Ring' of Victors was being maintained until further orders.

He swore beneath his breath, then continued reading.

'Enemy Forces' — A carrier ASW group (probably *Glorious)* had been reported in position one hundred miles north-west of STANAVFORLANT, the NATO hunting group. Priorities of targets were as follows:

One: the ASW carrier, *Glorious,* her support vessels, and then her escorts, in that order.

Two: STANAVFORLANT: its support ships, the Commodore's ship, *Athabaskan,* and the escorts, *Gloucester, Jesse L. Brown, Icarus* and *Goeben,* in that order.

Three: detached warships committed to defending the oil installations in the Norwegian and North Seas.

Enemy SSNs were distributed throughout Square 12, waiting presumably for outward Red Banner submarines. *But the horse has already bolted from the stable,* the message read, *so we are content to allow the enemy SSN patrols to remain there...*

There had been reports of at least two LRMPS Nimrod aircraft in his own Square 15, and one remained in his square at this moment.

Zragevski flipped over the next message, which was the sitrep on North Norway. All organised resistance was crumbling. The remnants of the enemy troops were taking to the mountains, and the European reinforcements had never got into action. The remainder of the reserves were on their way back to the Central Front.

The next signal was interesting: divers had succeeded in cutting the Fisk and Brent sea-bed pipelines to the mainland, thanks to the diversionary action of the Red Fleet. All Soviet warships were to keep clear of the area because of pollution danger to hulls and electronic equipment.

Finally there was an admonition to all submariners: CSS gear was to be used at all times now that the ASW carrier group was in the operational area. *Simple souls,* he smirked to himself, *there's no need to remind Boris Zragevski.*

'Coming to CR, sir,' the officer of the watch reported. So it was 1130 already?

'Have you trailed the CSS?'

'Yes, sir — and, sir?'

'What is it?'

'CSS is indicating acquisition, sir. The red monitor's showing.'

The captain rose briskly from his chair.

'Acquisition? Are you sure?'

'Certain, sir.'

'Bring her up to CR depth. Be careful.' He grabbed his tunic from the hook by his bunk. 'Broadcast silent routine. I'm coming into the control room.'

The intercom repeated his command throughout the boat. Fans were stopped, ventilation was shut, men moved about in soft-soled boots. As the routines were being read, the weapons officer was interpreting the CSS readings. He saluted as he approached the silent control room:

'So?'

'No doubt about it, sir. The CPDS has acquired. Identification of LRMPS frequencies is concentrated on the northern sector.'

'Close?'

'Difficult to estimate, sir. Not close, but in contact; the Nimrod's transmitting her data.'

Captain Zragevski remained standing by the all-round periscope, a rotund figure, his hands stuffed in his overall pockets. 'Shake it up with the CRS,' he snapped — but it was 1151 before the signal officer nodded from the watertight door at the after end of the control room.

'270 metres,' the captain ordered. 'Stop centre. Slow together outers. Port ten, steer 140 degrees.'

He watched the officer of the watch, noted the planesman suddenly stiffening from his slumped posture of watch-diving routine. The sailors sensed the tension as the depth-pointer swung round the gauge, slowing as she neared the 250 mark...

'270 metres, sir.' The officer of the watch looked round, a twitch of relief at the corners of his mouth. He hadn't made a balls of it.

At 1156 exactly they heard it, the unmistakable, nerve-racking sonar contact cracking throughout the boat. 'Active transmissions, sir. Surface ship. Not in contact. Bearing 210 degrees, distant.'

'Very good.' He nodded to the officer of the watch. 'Action stations,' he ordered brusquely. 'Shut all watertight doors.' The

LRMPS Nimrod must be vectoring a destroyer towards 329's position. 'Full ahead three,' he snapped. 'Bring all tubes to the ready.'

He would put in a sharp burst, directly towards his hunter. Zragevski would keep going for fifteen minutes, to clear the LRMPS's sono lay; then he'd stop, listen, review the new tactical situation...

'Plot, give me fifteen minutes.'

'Aye, aye, sir.'

The time was precisely 1202. He wondered whether it was twilight yet up top.

It was the nonchalant voice of the Nimrod's captain which made up Pascoe Trevellion's mind for him. The LRMPS aircraft, Bravo One, had been vectoring *Icarus* ever since the confirmation of the first sub contact at 1134.

At 1143, Bravo One's pilot dropped the first hint of his problem. 'Sorry, Hotel Uniform, but we're getting low on fuel. I'm trying to whip up someone to take my place. Can I have the co-ordinates, please? Over.'

'This is Hotel Uniform. Roger ... wait one.'

Julian Farge was frantically tracing the data on his underwater display. The picture was beginning to make sense, but precise range remained the problem.

'Tell the observer and pilot of *Perdix* to stand-by by a vectac,' the captain ordered. 'Report as soon as they're armed and ready.'

'Aye, aye, sir.'

Trevellion was strained to a tension he had not felt for a long time. This encounter was for real: an enemy submarine was ahead of him there, also waiting to judge what category of adversary was facing him.

'Twenty-two knots,' he ordered. In these winter conditions, the sonar was still effective at this, his maximum operational speed.

'Looks like a nuke, sir,' Fargo reported. 'Bravo One confirms Victor II signature.'

'What time are you using as datum?'

'Now, sir, 1144. Bravo One's getting out a track and speed at any moment.'

'Right.' He looked round, catching the first lieutenant's eye. Jewkes was standing unnoticed in the corner, watching developments — probably wanting to know what to do about dinner.

'Go to action stations, Number One, just in case.'

'Action stations? Aye, aye, sir.' Jewkes hurried from the ops room, and half a minute later the pipe was being made. Trevellion heard feet pounding down the passageways; he felt the bulkhead doors banging shut. He was taking no chances even though they were officially still at peace.

At 1153 the Nimrod came through again. 'This is Bravo One — Hotel Uniform.' The unconcerned voice evoked a caricature of the classic imperturbable moustachioed pilot officer from an old war film. 'Sorry to desert you fish-heads, but we'll have to leave you. I'm approaching my limits: they'll take a dim view if I have to ditch this kite because we've run out of gas. Over.'

'How long can you stick around?' Pascoe replied into the common link.

'Another ten minutes — I couldn't find another chum,' the pilot went on. 'We're a bit pushed at the moment. Over.'

'Thank you, Bravo One. Can you give me an estimated range of the contact?'

These RAF boys must be out on their hunkers: they were flying around the clock, desperately short-handed, pushed to the limit with no aircraft in reserve against the overwhelming numbers of the enemy. These Nimrods, upon whom these first days of the Second Battle of the Atlantic depended, were helpless if they ran into trouble in these latitudes: they must be priority targets for the Backfires. What use was an inflatable raft in this sea, in this cold? Better to disintegrate from a missile hit than to snuff it through exposure. The pilot was chipping in perkily again. 'Hotel Uniform, you are now 225 degrees from point zero, timed 1134. Bogey's been steering one-four-zero, speed five ... wait one.' The voice cut in, alert now. 'She's going deep.'

'Thanks again, Bravo One,' Trevellion said. 'We're going to miss you.'

'Finish the good work, Hotel Uniform. We claim half the bonus.' He was just rounding off when his voice suddenly sharpened. 'Bogey's speeding up, altering to starboard. I'll hold on another few minutes.'

There was a long wait, the tension in the ops room broken only by the murmur from the sonar room.

'Bloody good-o...!' The pilot's voice came over excitedly. 'She's doing thirty-three knots plus — really, she is. Thirty-three plus, and her heading is 210 degrees. Range to you now thirty-six miles. Time 1203. Hotel Uniform: must go now. Over.' A guest leaving after dinner could not have been more polite.

'Roger,' the captain replied. 'We have the plot. Good luck and safe return. Out.'

Trevellion jerked towards the helicopter controller who was crouched over his HCO's display.

'Fly off the Lynx,' he ordered. 'Vectac. How many minutes flying time to datum?'

'Sixteen minutes, sir, if the bogey maintains her speed.'

'Officer of the Watch, turn into the wind,' Trevellion barked into the command intercom. 'Double up the lookouts. Even in this bloody vis we might get a visual of her periscopes.'

Hob and Rollo had been itching to become airborne for the interminable half-hours that had crawled around the ops room clock. Now, with take-off drill nearing completion, Hob felt elated. The flight deck officer's batons were sweeping into the air ... all set. He swivelled *Perdix* on her wheels, gave her full boost, retracted the harpoon. Lifting her, his heart sang ... they were away, climbing to port and watching their ship merging into the black sea, invisible when she was darkened. The flight-deck lights, dimmed blue and eerie, flicked out — *Perdix* was on her own, airborne: time 1205.

'Heading zero-two-five,' Rollo ordered coolly through the intercom. He spoke so quietly that sometimes he was difficult to hear: the next minutes promised to be busy, so there must be no slip-ups through bad communication drill.

'Heading o-two-five,' Hob sang out. 'Four hundred feet, speed one-three-o.'

'Roger.' Rollo, normally a man of few words, was talkative tonight. 'I'll give you a stand-by. Fifteen minutes on this heading. We'll try our luck with the MAD bird first — the Nimrod seemed pretty positive.'

The HCO came in loud and clear from *Icarus*'s ops room. The vectac was going to plan: they had exercised it so often. 'You should be over her in two minutes,' his voice cut in. 'I still have no range — passive only.'

Rollo was tapping the glass of his watch. Hob glanced at the time: unbelievable that they had been in the air fifteen minutes. Only another ten before they ought to be landing again because of the MoD safety restriction.

'Two hundred feet,' Rollo ordered. 'Carry out MAD patterns. I'm lowering the MAD bird.'

Hob brought *Perdix* down gently, eased to cruise speed. Rollo needed a chance with his magic box. Hob brought her across the mean line, nodded when he was at the ordered height — the MAD bird would be fifty feet above the sea now.

'Bring her round to port: two-two-three.'

Hob repeated the heading, swung *Perdix* round. It was always reassuring to know that the HCO was overhearing their procedures.

'Possibly MAD contact,' Rollo shouted suddenly. 'Heading one-eight-o to port.'

'Heading two-two-three,' responded Hob, 'altering to one-eight-o.' He was astonished at the swift contact.

A stickler for detail was Rollo. Hob felt the Lynx dip as she assumed her tail-up attitude ... he'd take her along steadily at cruise speed, give the MAD bird another chance. Slowly did it, patience, the methodical approach ... the sea was very close under him, the flecks of white horses scarring the gleaming surface. Periscopes would be impossible to spot in these conditions.

Then Rollo was shouting, forgetting the racket he was making through the headset in his excitement. 'MAD confirmation!' he yelled. Seconds later, after adjusting his receivers, he passed Hob the heading. 'Two-one-nine,' he ordered. 'One more run, Hob.' Then he was reporting the contact back to mother: 'Bravo One's contact confirmed,' he said, his voice rising. 'Am localising with ASRBs. Will amplify. Time 1218. Over.'

'Roger,' the HCO replied calmly. 'Come to first degree of readiness.'

At 1213, the captain of the Red Banner nuclear fleet submarine SSN 329 reduced her speed to slow two. Remaining at 270 metres, he waited for her way to come off before ordering an all-round passive sonar sweep.

'No hydrophone effect; no active,' the chief sonar operator reported. 'All-round sweep completed, Captain.'

At least the active pinging from somewhere to the south-west had ceased — those sinister transmissions emitting from nowhere, suddenly blasting against the pressure hull, swamping them with sound waves — was always unnerving, down at these depths. But he had better play safe.

'Patrol depth,' he ordered. 'Trail the CSS.'

Those active transmissions must have been from one of STANAVFORLANT's frigates, away to the north-west ... but that was from the wrong bearing ... what was going on? They must have emanated from a frigate, for why else was the Nimrod vectoring the swine? LRMPS did not 'dunk' and there were no Sea Kings within range: the helicopter carrier was a hundred miles to the north-west. Could the transmissions originate from a detached frigate belonging to STANAVFORLANT...?

'Let's have a look at the identification tables, pilot,' he said, holding out his hand. 'Look up NATO's STANAVFORLANT escorts.' While waiting for the identification, he felt the boat levelling neatly.

'Eighty metres, sir.' It was a relief to have the first lieutenant on the trimming during action stations.

'Very good. Maintain patrol depth.'

Boris Zragevski tried to control his impatience. He'd wait for the CSS report before going on up for a quick look.

The weapons officer was on the line: 'Category 2 acquisition from CSS, sir: audio and air pulse vibration anomalies, strength three. Bearing zero-one-zero.'

Damn … Zragevski hesitated, unsure of his next move. He loathed uncertainty and liked to always know where he was going.

'Stream CSS to six kilometres,' he snapped. 'Periscope depth, First Lieutenant.' He rubbed his hands together, flexing his fingers, itching to get at the periscope handles. He would not risk giving away his position by using his radar. A quick visual look, nothing more … conditions ought to be good up top, or as good as could be expected at this time of the year. Even the dim twilight faded by 1330 on these winter days.

'Thirty metres, sir.'

'Up periscope.' The steel tube hissed as it slid upwards. Zragevski fitted his squat body into the seat, snapped open the handles, squinted through the eyepieces while waiting for the break-surface.

'Twenty-five, sir. Periscope depth.'

He twitched his thumb. The operator settled the stick and the water splashed against the periscope prism. The smear vanished, and suddenly he could see …

He caught his breath, surprised by the brightness of the flaring lights to the north. The aurora borealis was certainly putting on its best performance tonight — orange, violet and blue, carmine and deep pulsing greens — the polar horizon was exploding in a panoply of light. Zragevski slapped the handles shut. The stick slid downwards; he'd give it thirty seconds before the next look. His watch showed 1216 and twenty seconds...

'Up periscope.' The periscope engineer was used to his captain and they made a good team: most importantly, the petty officer had learnt to read his master's mind.

Zragevski stopped abruptly in the middle of his all-round sweep. Above the glistening horizon, silhouetted against the kaleidoscope, was the unmistakable outline of a helicopter — ugly and ungainly, it was hovering at no more than twenty metres above the sea. Zragevski felt the kick in his guts: he detested helos, and particularly these latest Lynx of the enemy's. The British certainly knew how to operate them, how to exploit their capabilities as an integral of a destroyer's armoury.

Zragevski snapped shut the handles. The tube slid beneath the surface. 'Anything on CSS? Radio or radar modes?'

'Negative, sir — audio, thermal and APV only.'

'Emergency change of depth, Number One. 270 metres. Don't speed up.'

The high-pitched alarm warbled through the boat; the watertight doors slammed. 329 lifted her tail as the internal trimming took charge. At 1220, she started to level off, Number One having her neatly under control.

'260 ... 275 metres, sir.'

Boris Zragevski had made up his mind. He nodded acknowledgement, then ordered:

'Course 220 degrees. Full ahead three.' He swung round on the commissar, who was watching points close behind him.

'It's all right, Dmitri,' he laughed. 'A quick dash'll get us out of this — and we'll catch the frigate bending.' But Number One wasn't smiling as the captain added, 'Remain at action stations, Number One; you can open up watertight doors.'

'Aye, aye, sir.'

'And plot?'

'Sir?'

'Let me know when fifteen minutes are up.'

'Aye, aye, sir ... Fifteen minutes at thirty-four knots.'

The captain glanced at the control room clock. When he slowed down at 1234 he would know finally whether he was in real trouble or not. He kept the information to himself: at least, he now had the authority to remedy the situation by force. The duel was developing into a personal conflict, a cat-and-mouse game between an unknown enemy frigate commander and himself. This could develop into a decisive fight in the depths of the sea, secretly, silently, without anyone the wiser. He strolled to his cabin to reflect for a few moments. The hum of the turbines, driven by superheated steam generated by the reactors bubbling a few yards from his feet, was a perpetual background to his thinking.

The ship would be safe for a few more minutes in the hands of the first lieutenant. Number One was competent and would make a sound submarine CO. When this hunt was over Zragevski would settle down to his paperwork and recommend his second-in-command for the CO's qualifying course.

The pilot of the Lynx, *Icarus* Flight, preferred to remain in manual while laying the ASRBs: in spite of the AFCS (Automatic Flight Control System) there was a lot to be said for keeping positive control in his own hands. The flecked surface of the sea swirling two hundred feet beneath the cab seemed close enough in this half-light.

'Ten degrees to starboard,' Rollo commanded. 'Steady ... hold it, Hob.'

And so it went on, Rollo working feverishly as he bent over his PPI and plot. For the first time Hob felt the excitement of this chase — a hot one this time, and for real, not just a dreary exercise with one of their own ping-running submarines.

Icarus's ops room team were good now. The HCO had vectored them smack on. Now it was just a case of tailing that invisible monster cracking along at thirty-three plus knots down in the deeps, course two-two-five ... The captain had just authorised the use of Sea Spray, the best radar Hob had used for years: sensitive, and with good presentation, it even picked up seagulls and floating beer cans. Just as well, because this Force 4 and its white horses certainly favoured the submarine.

'HCO — *Perdix*: stand by first ASRB pattern. Over.'

Rollo nodded. He needed a few minutes' warning; he was flat out even though Hob had taken over the search radar. The ASRBs were ready, but still needed dropping — and in addition to this, the fish must be checked for action, just in case. If things became hot, the Mark 46s only needed to be dropped; their homing heads would do the rest. *Icarus* would tell Rollo when to drop.

After all these years, it seemed too fantastic — how could this awful game of Russian roulette, with eternity the stakes and not merely the destruction of one of the two protagonists, really be happening?

At 1235 the HCO cut in. 'Bogey's HE decreasing. Execute vectac. Stand by first drop. Steer two-three-o, over.'

'Roger.'

Hob was concentrating on his course, his eyes jerking between the compass and radar.

'Heading two-three-o.' He was flying at a hundred feet now. The speed was good and Rollo had moved aft alongside the 196 ASRB.

'Left ten ... steady,' the HCO ordered. 'Stand by to drop.'

Hob glanced over his shoulder. Rollo was crouched over the chute, waiting.

'Drop — drop — drop!' came the tense voice of the HCO.

'One gone!'

Hob held *Perdix* level, then, when they saw the buoy bobbing in the water, brought her slowly back for Rollo to lay the remainder of the pattern. The sub must be within range of the ASRB now — the active transmissions could be receiving Rollo's attention at any second.

'I have no HE,' *Icarus* called.

Rollo was checking, checking, scribbling down the minutes in his log. MAD had done better, damn it — they had lost contact.

'Bogey range from you,' *Icarus* cut in, 'estimated four-zero-zero. Stand by visual, over.'

Hob strained his eyes peering at his instruments, glancing repeatedly at the radar.

'Okay, Hob?' Rollo was grinning inside his bone dome.

'Okay, how's yourself?'

'I'm getting a contact...' The observer had tensed and was doubled over his plot. 'Confirmed sub contact!' he shouted. 'Signature: Victor II.' Hob caught the excitement in Rollo's tense report: the time was exactly 1241.

'1234, Captain. Fifteen minutes completed at thirty-four knots — eight decimal five miles, sir.'

'Slow two,' snapped Captain Zragevski. 'Sonar all-round passive sweep.'

If he was not sensing this unease inside himself he would have been bored by now of these procedures ... *slow down, listen, patrol depth...* He'd been at it the whole morning.

'Faint HE to the south-west, sir. Sector 190-135 degrees. Steam turbine: classification, Leander frigate.'

He raised his eyebrows. So that was it? One of their ageing ships rapidly being replaced by their Broadswords?

'Helicopter ship?'

'Affirmative. Mark VII Lynx weapon systems.'

Zragevski remained silent. He'd be prudent and check again with CSS.

He nodded at his first lieutenant:

'Eighty metres.'

At 1236, levelling off at patrol depth, he streamed the CSS. His instinct had already alerted him, so he was not surprised when, at 1237, the red light was glowing on the CSS console.

'Acquisition,' the weapons officer reported briskly. 'Two-two-o ... APV bearing green three-o.'

The captain met his first lieutenant's glance. 'We're being hunted,' he said, without raising his voice.

'Aggressive bastard,' Number One murmured.

'Well, we'll have to see about it,' Zragevski said. 'Perhaps they mean business.'

'It could be them or us, sir.' The first lieutenant's face was strained and grey.

'Periscope depth, Number One.'

Zragevski had made his decision: he would not risk his boat and his crew if he was being hunted aggressively. Holding the column sensitively between his fingers, the coxswain was handling the boat superbly, swooping her upwards. Captain Zragevski was determined to survive: his family had just reached the age when life was fun. If the frigate was spoiling for a fight, he'd get his shot in first.

'Thirty metres, sir ... twenty-five ... periscope depth.'

He activated the CSS switch on the left side of the periscope, snatched at the handles.

'Up periscope!' The blurring of the lens was already clearing.

'Missile ready!' the weapons officer reported. 'Red light showing, sir.'

Zragevski worked his periscope fast. An all-round sweep and he would be happier. The northern sky was pulsating from the aurora borealis ... Ah! There was the helo...

'Lynx helicopter,' he snapped, slamming shut the handles. The tube slid down.

'She's carrying out a search, Number One. About a mile.' He glanced at the stick operator, held up his thumb. 'Put me on...'

The water cleared. There it was, that bloody chopper...

A shattering resonance boomed through the pressure hull ... no need for the sonar room to amplify.

'Active ... in contact!' called the sonar chief. 'Bearing 215 degrees, close. Time, sir, 1243.'

'Up periscope.' The drill was instinctive, smooth, after months of training. 'Bearing *that*: Lynx helicopter.'

The helo was in the turn, swooping towards his periscope.

Slung beneath her cab were two torpedoes, clearly visible, their ugly snouts gleaming in the northern lights. The Lynx was dropping out of the sky; it was flying straight towards his periscope and growing larger at every second...

The captain's hand slid up to the CSS switch. As he pressed it, he snapped: 'Emergency change of depth.' He slammed the periscope handles. 'Take her down, quick, Number One. Slow one, silent routine.'

He had felt the judder of the safety caps on the ANVIL tubes when they slammed open. The missiles were on their way. He was not sticking around, but was keeping to himself what he had sighted. To the left of the helicopter, etched against the aurora's glow, he'd seen the upper works of a frigate. She, too, was heading towards SSN 329.

'Steer 186 degrees,' he snapped. 'Bring all tubes to the ready.'

'Sixty metres, sir ... seventy...

The tube-ready lamps were flicking on, one after the other...

'All ready, sir,' the action officer called. 'Sonar has surface target. Range five, decimal four; bearing one-nine-o.'

'Stand-by to fire torpedoes.'

He turned towards the clock — 1247. He would hold on a few more seconds; the Englishman might still break away, call off his attack...

CHAPTER 25

Hob Gamble was concentrating on his heading, the Lynx in manual. The horizon was easy to pick out against the northern lights. Rollo was methodically breaking down the errors from the ASRBs. Staring through his cockpit, Hob suddenly spotted the tube, a steel sliver cutting through the waves, a white plume flicking at its base.

'Green two-o, Rollo. Periscope!' He checked on the PPI ... green 20, a definite blip ... and, four miles further out, another miniscule echo.

'I'm going in — we'll take a closer look.' He flung *Perdix* round, swooping for the tell-tale slick ... then, sighting the periscope, he watched it slowly dipping beneath the surface.

'Riser!' he called to *Icarus*. 'Riser! One thousand, five...'

He levelled her up, then took her down to fifty feet, setting her heading on the bearing. As she steadied, he spotted a strange cupola-shaped bulge on the surface of the sea ahead of them, a grey circle of foaming water.

'Log that, Rollo,' he called. '1245: dead ahead, five hundred yards, unidentified—'

Hob Gamble never finished his sentence.

His first reaction was that the tail had gone, that catastrophic tail failure which every chopper-man dreaded, the disaster he and Rollo had never mentioned since Westland's signal. There was the typical explosion; the sudden lurch to starboard as she began rotating about herself. Then there was the orange flash, a blinding light and the agony of searing heat — *Perdix* was tumbling out of the sky...

'We're being fired on!' he yelled.

The escape drill — *grab the window base.* After the shock of impact, he snatched at his harness, threshing clear with his legs as the engine shuddered to a stop; his world spun around him; and then the water burst in as she turned turtle. He felt an excruciating pain across his chest. Rollo was yelling at him, his hands clawing at Hob's overalls. He cried out with the pain, his senses fading. A red light swam before his eyes, there was a roaring about his ears, and then he knew no more.

Leading Radio Operator Osgood was searching for his chief supervisor. There was a major fault on one of the machines and, from experience, Oz was determined not to risk having his head bitten off again for not seeking advice. The chief was reputed to be with the sonar CPO.

Osgood always entered the brain cell of the ship, as most men did, with an instinctive sense of caution. Still in his anorak, he stepped gingerly through the doorway. Not only was the captain usually here, but so were most of the top brass. A certain aura of calm was essential in the ops room.

'Is my supervisor here?' he asked the plotter manning the GOP (General Operations Plot).

'In the sonar room.' The able seaman jerked his head towards the far corner. 'Wait a bit, mate. Things are warming up.'

So Osgood stood in the corner, impatient at the delay in finishing his maintenance. The clock above the plot was showing 1241 and he was already late for dinner. The ops room was dimly lit, to allow for easy interpretation of the displays. There was an unusual hum and he sensed the tension as the captain snapped his orders. The drill was smooth but whatever was going on had certainly caught the team's concentration: men crouched across the PPIs, chinagraph pencils scrawled, operators muttered into their microphones. Suddenly, loud and clear through the loudspeaker bawled Lieutenant Gamble's voice.

'Riser! ... Riser! One thousand, five...'

The tension became electric. The HCO from his display on the right was trying to vector the Lynx back on to the line. The captain glanced up at Lieutenant Commander Farge.

'Go active,' he ordered. 'Investigate contact zero-one-eight. Stream the Foxer.'

Then the measured pings began echoing throughout the ops room, against the distant sound of the doppler effect. The familiar noise enveloped the room as Osgood glanced again at the clock: 1243.

'Contact!' The leading sonar operator, who was standing behind the two operators he was directing, stood motionless, watching the PPIs.

'Go up in scale,' the chief muttered from the underwater display.

As Osgood watched, the operators stiffened where they crouched over their displays: he distinctly heard it, the firm sub contact.

Things were happening fast. It was hard to follow all the nattering, but he was startled by the yell from the bridge. It sounded like Lieutenant Neame.

'Sir! *Perdix* is ditching. She's a mass of flame ... oh, my Christ...'

'We're being fired on!' Oz heard the pilot's cry, and then the loudspeaker went dead.

'*Perdix* echo faded, sir,' the HCO reported from his display.

'Roger,' the captain said calmly. 'Mark her datum and time 1246. Bridge, hard right, steer 355 degrees. Lifeboat's crew man the boat.'

'Sub contact classified nuke, sir,' the sonar director called out.

'Pass my intentions to the Commodore,' Captain Trevellion instructed. 'I shall hold on to this contact, then recover the helicopter's crew. Ask him to send over *Jesse* if he can spare her.'

Farge peered at his display, then began speaking to COMSTANAVFORLANT:

'This is Hotel Uniform. *Hot* ... datum established four-two, nine six. Bearing zero-one-eight, range five-thousand, two. Datum error two miles: datum time 1246 — 1246.'

'Coming aft to three-four-zero,' the buffer said, adjusting the knob on his display. His operators were busy at their displays, peering, listening, jotting down the bearings across the faces of their PPIs.

'I've got it,' the operator nodded at his director. 'Cut ... three-four-eight. Two thousand, two...' The tracking was systematic, remorseless. The enemy was bloody close now.

'Good cut. Three-four-zero, two thousand, one.'

'We're hot,' Trevellion barked. Farge was adjusting his control to line up his plot with the echo.

'Steady on two thousand, one, sir,' the buffer called.

The operator continued his pinging, never taking his eyes from his screens:

'Cut — three-three-seven ... visual only. Second, no cut; no paint, PPI...' The man's back stiffened. He turned, his face amazed, all colour drained.

'HE sir. Classified torpedoes ... *torpedoes running,* confirmed, sir.'

Osgood stood transfixed. Everyone in the ops room had frozen for an instant, incapable of accepting that the impossible was happening. The captain glanced at his PWO, then crouched over his command display.

'Put a fish in the water,' he commanded. He raised his voice, calling to the bridge: 'Stream the Foxer, full ahead together! Come hard left!'

Osgood was fascinated by the scene. Here they were, a bunch of men who had been training together for months to be ready for this moment. At this second, the two adversaries were trying to blast each other to extinction. This was a private war fought to the death, out here, alone in these wastes, a sort of overture to the main concert — and neither opponent was able to halt the appalling, inevitable consequences.

'No change from sonar,' the sonar operator called. 'All round HE.'

'STWS ready, sir,' from the Chief. 'Cruising fire.'

'Fire!' the captain ordered tensely.

'STWS fired, sir. Range, one-nine,' the buffer sang out, as cool as if this was a NATO exercise. Then he was reporting through to COMSTANAVFORLANT: 'This is Hotel Uniform. Fish loose, bearing three-three-six, range one-seven. Time 1248.'

'We're on top of him, sir.' Farge said into the intercom. 'Losing him...'

'Steady on one-nine-o,' the captain was ordering the bridge. The edge of the training indicator cabinet was boring into Osgood's back as *Icarus* heeled to the turn.

Farge was talking again into his mike, his speech slow, deliberate. 'This is Hotel Uniform. *Grapeshot* ... *Grapeshot* ... *Grapeshot* ... bearing three-three-two. Time 1249. Out.'

'Any signs of *Perdix*?' the captain called to the officer of the watch.

'Yes, sir, flashing light in the water ... right astern, sir. Just visible.'

'Take her bearing.' The captain swung round to his PWO:

'Are we hot?' he asked.

'Still hot, sir,' Farge said.

Captain Trevellion nodded. 'Well done,' he said quietly. 'All of you.'

CHAPTER 26

USS Jesse L. Brown, 2 January.

Surgeon Lieutenant Joe Hennessey, USN, medical officer of the frigate, *Jesse L. Brown,* could do no more for the survivors. He had remained on the upper deck, the cold eating through him, while divers plunged into the sea to fish out the poor fellows from their rafts.

He had never seen a ship sink. The sight had proved as terrible as he had imagined: the broken back, the awful silence as the stricken ship hesitated, poised for those terrible seconds before plunging to her watery tomb. The most shattering moment of all was the realisation that suddenly nothing remained — nothing save the pathetic flotsam, some of it human, bobbing on the boiling surface.

Just bits ... human scraps from which hardened men turned their eyes. The luckiest of the frigate's crew were those who had been killed outright by the torpedo explosions, a truth which applied also to the Soviet submariners. There was little evidence left of the Soviet nuke; so far only a leather cushion, a splintered wooden bench and Russian guts.

There was hope for only eight of the eleven survivors whom *Jesse* had picked up. Miraculously, the pilot of the helicopter, though still unconscious, would be all right; but the observer, who had dragged him from the sinking cab into the self-inflating life raft, was dead from exposure. Another officer, a lieutenant commander judging by his shoulder badges, might pull through, but survival would be touch and go unless they could transfer him to *Glorious*.

Four other Britishers were still unconscious, all exposure cases. The survival of this enlisted man (his ident tally recorded the name of Osgood, Thomas) was miraculous. This sailor had remained conscious throughout, though they had to prise his arms from the inert body he was still trying to warm. This patient was suffering from acute exposure: he was the skipper of *Icarus,* who was new to the ship, apparently.

The dead were laid out abaft the after screen, a sad duty to deal with later. The doctor leant over the enlisted man who was sitting up now, sipping the coffee they held for him.

'Okay?' Joe Hennessey asked. 'Welcome aboard *Jesse L. Brown.* You're alive and well, Osgood.' The man was registering, so the doctor persevered. 'Can you tell me what happened? Yes, you're okay. We're on our way back to join the force.'

The tough, stocky Britisher nodded, then croaked, 'The skipper's dead?'

'No,' the surgeon said. 'He's just about holding his own.'

The seaman stared at the surgeon uncomprehendingly. 'Has he a chance, sir?' he whispered.

Hennessey nodded. 'How'd it all happen?' he asked kindly. 'It'll help us to know.'

Osgood shook his head.

'Can't remember much, sir,' he said. 'From where I was in the ops room, there was a thud, a sort of clang below us — then another. We'd hit the sub, so we all cheered, but the bastard had fired his fish before we did. Can't remember much after that, except that the deck sprang up at us ... a bloody great explosion. We were all hurled upwards... the skipper was groaning at our feet.

'The ship started rearing upwards, so we hauled him out to the port side ... couldn't make out what he said. It was bloody awful, sir. There weren't many of us left — most who survived the shock were trapped below or crushed between the decks and bulkheads. We were shut down for action stations...'

The surgeon lieutenant watched the man gazed around him, bewildered, as he sipped at his coffee.

'We got the raft into the water ... a few of the others were jumping, but it was no use in the cold, sir. All over in minutes ... she sank just like a lump of lead... We got the skipper into the raft. The plotter and me. I tried to warm the skipper in my anorak, but it was the plotter who went first, sir. He just rolled over the side. The cold, sir, that's what it was. I reckoned our captain was dead when you picked us up.' The sailor turned and stared straight at the surgeon. His eyes were full of pain. 'Anyone else picked up, sir? How many alive?'

'Can't say yet. Come on, sailor, you'd better get some sleep.' Hennessey nodded at the medic. 'Here, Osgood, you'll feel nothing.'

They shoved in the needle and waited for him to go limp, then enfolded him in the blankets. The surgeon checked his other survivors, then walked slowly outside to the deck. The northern lights had disappeared and darkness was closing in. He could see a blue light winking off to port, where the Commodore's ship should be. STANAVFORLANT was re-forming now that there was a gap in the screen.

It had been a cruel day. The barometer was falling and Hennessey could feel the snow in the air. It was going to be a long, long night. He shivered, pulling his coat about him. How many more nights would there be, out here, in these bitter wastes? How many more lives to be squandered before this wretched business was over? War was now inevitable, if NATO did not stand firm.

The surgeon wrenched at the steel door, and stumbled in over the coaming to the warmth and light.

A NOTE TO THE READER

Dear Reader,
If you have enjoyed the novel enough to leave a review on **Amazon** and **Goodreads**, then we would be truly grateful.

Sapere Books is an exciting new publisher of brilliant fiction and popular history.

To find out more about our latest releases and our monthly bargain books visit our website:
saperebooks.com

Printed in Great Britain
by Amazon

27577320R00155